AWAKEN THE ADVENTURE!

The Death Walkers are rising and bringing plagues of evil to the world. It's up to YOU to stop them!

1. Go to Scholastic.com/TombQuest
2. Log in to create your character and enter the tombs.
3. Have your book ready and enter the code below to play:

RM2H2TRGW4

Scholastic.com/TombQuest

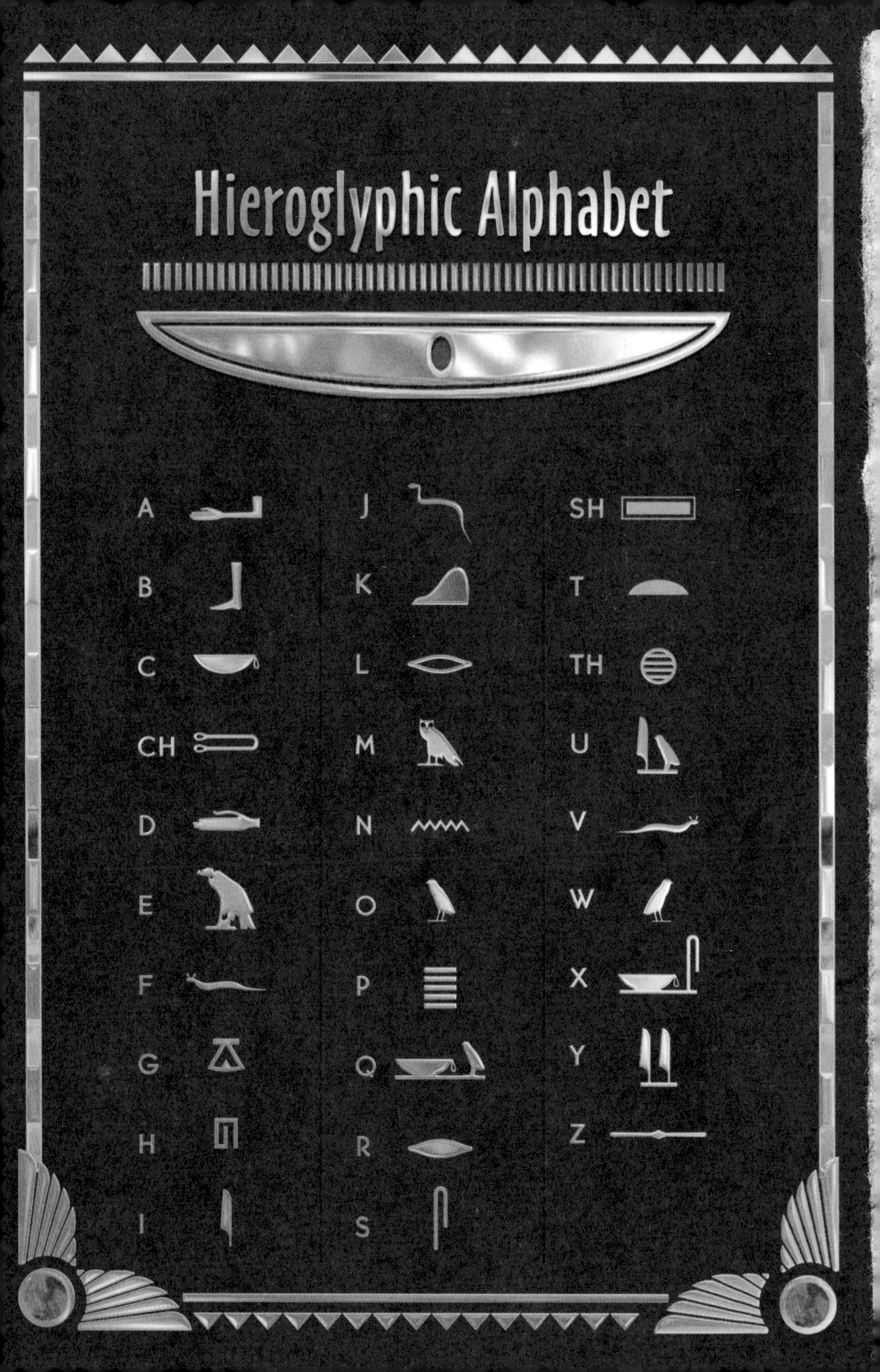
Hieroglyphic Alphabet
A
B
C
CH
D
E
F
G
H
I
J
K
L
M
N
O
P
Q
R
S
SH
T
TH
U
V
W
X
Y
Z

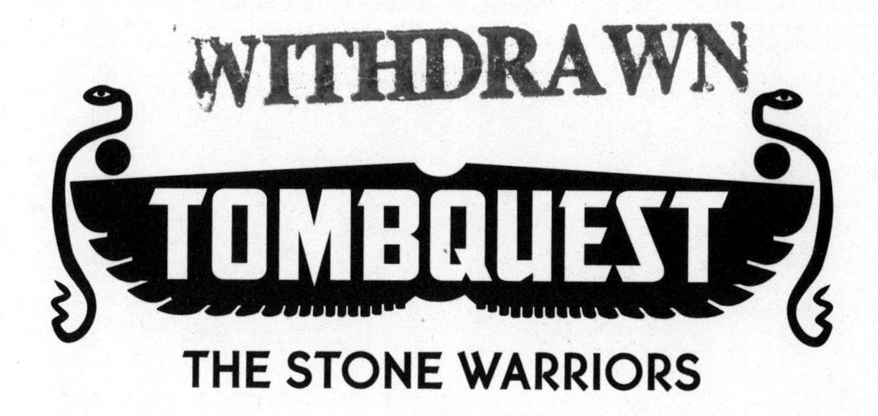
TOMBQUEST
THE STONE WARRIORS

THE STONE WARRIORS

MICHAEL NORTHROP

SCHOLASTIC INC.

Library of Congress Cataloging-in-Publication Data

Northrop, Michael, author.
The stone warriors / Michael Northrop. — First edition.
pages cm. — (TombQuest ; 4)
Summary: Twelve-year-olds Alex and Renata are on the run from the Order, which is on the brink of creating an army of indestructible stone warriors to carry out their evil schemes, and only the Lost Spells which his mother used to bring Alex back to life can stop them—and undoing the powerful magic that created the chaos that is now loose in Egypt might very well kill him.
ISBN 978-0-545-72341-1 (hardcover)
1. Book of the dead—Juvenile fiction. 2. Mothers and sons—Juvenile fiction. 3. Magic—Juvenile fiction. 4. Death—Juvenile fiction. 5. Adventure stories. 6. Egypt—Antiquities—Juvenile fiction. [1. Book of the dead—Fiction. 2. Mothers and sons—Fiction. 3. Magic—Fiction. 4. Death—Fiction. 5. Adventure and adventurers—Fiction. 6. Egypt—Antiquities—Fiction.] I. Title. II. Series: Northrop, Michael. TombQuest ; 4.
PZ7.N8185St 2016
813.6—dc23
[Fic]

2015028422

10 9 8 7 6 5 4 3 2 1 16 17 18 19 20

Printed in the U.S.A. 23
First edition, January 2016
Book design by Keirsten Geise

Scholastic US: 557 Broadway · New York, NY 10012
Scholastic Canada: 604 King Street West · Toronto, ON M5V 1E1
Scholastic New Zealand Limited: Private Bag 94407 · Greenmount, Manukau 2141
Scholastic UK Ltd.: Euston House · 24 Eversholt Street · London NW1 1DB

For Team TombQuest:
It takes many talented people to make a book, and even more to get that book to readers. When it comes to an epic adventure series like this one, the author is just the tip of the pyramid, and I am lucky to work with a team for the ages.

1

On the Run

Moving at a dead run through an unfamiliar city, Alex Sennefer risked a quick look behind him. Were the guards from the museum still after them? Had the police joined the chase? At first, all he saw was a broad street and wide sidewalks, lit at even intervals by streetlights and dotted with nighttime walkers. Then he heard a shout, sharp and clear: *"Halt!"* A guard rounded a corner and came into view, his tie flapping as his shoes slapped the sidewalk.

Is he armed? wondered Alex. *Are there half a dozen more men right behind him?* He turned to his best friend, Renata Duran, who was running beside him. "We need to get off this" — he huffed in another breath — "street" — puffed it out — "and hide!"

"Yeah!" said Ren. She was twelve years old, like Alex, but small for her age, and her short legs pumped furiously to keep up. "Which way?"

To their left was a large, dark park, a slumbering stretch of trimmed grass and thick trees, surrounded by a tall iron fence. Alex scanned the fence line for an opening but then thought better of it. A fence could protect them — but it could also trap them inside.

Across the street to the right was a long stretch of open sidewalk and closed shops.

"Go right!" Alex said.

"Okay," said Ren, "but not yet . . ."

Alex looked back — now a second guard was running just behind the first.

"Uh, are you sure?" said Alex.

"Wait!" Ren called.

"Why?" he asked. Then he noticed a vague rumbling noise.

"Just keep running!"

Alex swung his head around and saw a single, large headlight in the center of the street. Steel tracks in the road caught the growing light. It was a streetcar, heading toward them.

"Got it!" he shouted. The two friends sprinted off the sidewalk and into the street, straight toward the oncoming train.

The streetcar sounded its horn: a harsh, electric blare.

The guards were closer now and called out in German again: *"Halt! Vorsicht!"*

But Alex barely heard them as he sprinted across the deadly steel tracks right behind Ren. The horn blared, voices cried out, and the massive car rumbled forward. If he tripped, he'd be cut in half by heavy steel wheels. But with a few quick, careful strides, he and Ren cleared the tracks.

The streetcar rumbled on. Through the windows, Alex could see its few passengers gaping at the brazen duo.

By the time it passed, the two friends were gone. The street was quiet once more, and the guards were bent over, hands on knees, breathing heavily and staring into several small, dark side streets. The trespassers were headed down one of them. They just didn't know which one.

"I think we lost them," said Ren as the pair hustled down a short street called Robert Stolz Platz. The street ended in a small park, this one unfenced, and the friends skirted its dark edges.

"Great," said Alex, taking a quick look back and slowing his pace. "Then it's official: We're all lost."

They took a left onto a street bearing the improbable name Nibelungengasse and slowed to a walk. "Yeah," said Ren, breathing heavily and looking both ways down the little street. "Seriously. Where *are* we?"

He knew she didn't mean what street or even what neighborhood. She meant what city? What country? They had arrived here through a false door, a ceremonial ancient Egyptian portal that had somehow allowed them to travel from the Valley of the Kings in Egypt to another false door in the Egyptian wing of a museum here — wherever *here* was.

For weeks, Alex and Ren had been on the hunt for two things: Alex's mom and the powerful Lost Spells of the Egyptian Book of the Dead. His mom had used those Spells to revive him as he lay on life support in a New York hospital. But in doing so, she'd opened a gateway to the afterlife and the sinister ancient entities known as the Death Walkers had escaped. She and the Spells vanished after that, and Alex and Ren had traveled halfway around the world to find them.

But they weren't the only ones. The Order's deadly operatives were looking for them, too, and hounded the friends wherever they went. They knew the evil cult was working with the Death Walkers in some vast sinister conspiracy. The last Walker had spoken of *ruling* with The Order. Whatever they were up to, it was big, and if the cult found the Spells first, the Death Walkers would be unstoppable, and the whole world would suffer.

Alex shuddered slightly in the night and looked around at a scene that seemed far less grim. The buildings were lit softly by a combination of streetlights and moonlight, and the architecture was old and beautiful. "It's so pretty," said Ren.

"This whole city looks like something you'd find on top of a cake," agreed Alex. He nodded toward a nearby building. It was painted a delicate light green that did, indeed, look a bit like frosting. It reminded him of an exhibit he'd seen at The Metropolitan Museum of Art back in New York, where his mom had worked as an Egyptologist before she disappeared. "Is that, like, art deco?" he said.

Ren shook her head in disapproval. "Don't be ignorant," she said. "It's art nouveau."

"Oh, *obviously*," he said sarcastically, but he didn't doubt her. He was aware that she knew a lot more about it than he did. Her dad was a senior engineer back at the Met, his mom's most trusted coworker, and Ren had inherited his love of elegant angles and solid construction.

"What was that?" Ren gasped, interrupting his thoughts.

"What was what?"

"I thought I saw something slip between those buildings," said Ren, pointing. "Just, like, a shadow."

Alex followed her finger but didn't see anything. "It's the middle of the night," he said. "There are shadows everywhere."

New voices echoed down the little street. A small white dog turned the corner and then two people appeared behind it. "Let's ask them where we are," said Alex.

"Can we trust them?" said Ren.

Alex understood her cautiousness. They had already been betrayed once that night. He could still picture his cousin Luke standing up in the moonlit desert and shouting, *Over here*, giving away their position to the brutal death cult. He was still stunned that his own cousin was working for The Order . . . but another glance at the middle-aged couple put his mind at ease. "They've got a shih tzu," he said. "Not exactly an attack dog."

He waved as the couple approached: a man and a woman, wearing casual clothes but fancy shoes. The signs — and shouts — had all been in German so far, but that was the only clue they had about their location. Fortunately, his mom's family was from Germany.

"Hallo!" he called. He knew that part. *"Wo,* um, *sind wir?" Where are we? Maybe?* He was less sure of that, and longed for the smooth, fluid German his mom had always used on the phone with his grandmother.

The man holding the leash smiled and responded with a barrage of rapid-fire German that baffled Alex.

"Ich spreche nur ein bisschen Deutsch," said Alex with an apologetic shrug. *I speak only a little German.*

The woman answered this time, wearing a patient smile and speaking precise English. "You are American, yes? You are on Nibelungengasse."

Ren spoke up. "Not what street," she said. "We'd like to know what city this is."

The dog walkers exchanged quick, confused smiles. Even the dog seemed to regard them with tongue-lolling pity.

"You are in Wien, of course," said the man. "Vienna. Is there something you need help with? Are you . . . lost?"

"No, we're fine," said Alex. "But thanks."

The dog walkers went on their way, but the strangest thing happened as Alex turned to give one last embarrassed wave. He thought he saw a shadow, too, a thin slice of night slipping from one side of the streetlight's glow to the other.

"Wow, Vienna," said Ren, looking around with fresh eyes.

"That's got to be two thousand miles from where we were," said Alex. "And it felt like it took a minute." He remembered their desperate sprint through a strange and murky landscape . . . *Had they really traveled through the afterlife?*

His mind was full of big questions and confusing new realities, but right now he had a more immediate concern. As his eyes scanned the dark edges of the street, he felt the ancient scarab amulet at his neck growing warm against his skin. A warning: Death was lurking nearby.

"Maybe we should, uh, find someplace to stay," he said.

He suddenly wanted to be anywhere other than the dark streets of an unfamiliar city. He reached into the pocket of his jeans, but all he pulled out was a handful of Egyptian bills. Useless. What good was Egyptian capital in the capital of Austria?

"Maybe we can find somewhere to change those when the stores open tomorrow," said Ren.

"Maybe tomorrow," Alex repeated absently. His eyes were fixed on a dark corner that seemed, somehow, to be darker than the rest.

It was tonight he was worried about.

II

Shadow of a Doubt

A little while later, they found themselves hiding in a secluded park. Around them, as night settled in, the city's lights blinked out one by one.

"I wish we had our tents," said Alex, trying to find a way to sit that didn't involve getting stabbed by tree roots. The park was nice and clean and leafy — as everything in Vienna seemed to be — but it was still a dark and open space. And Alex had other concerns. Shadows shifted all around them, with every gust of wind through the trees.

"Well, the tents are back in Egypt," said Ren matter-of-factly. "All we have is this." She swung her small backpack onto the thick grass and began pawing through it. She pulled out her flashlight and clicked it on and off quickly. "Still works!"

Alex unzipped his backpack, too. He pushed his hand inside and felt around for his flashlight. He felt the burned shirt he'd changed out of, the smooth cover of his passport, and then a little pool of sand that had settled at the bottom of the pack. "Can you believe we were just in the desert?" he said as his hand finally closed around his flashlight.

"I kind of can't believe any of it," said Ren. "We basically ran through a fake door painted on solid stone in Egypt and straight out another one in Austria. And I know the only thing that makes sense is that we traveled through the afterlife — I mean, I saw it. But I still can't believe it. It creeps me out."

Alex was listening, but also looking out into the night. As he did, he saw it again. The darkness seemed to coalesce into a slice of deeper black. Alex pointed his flashlight and clicked it on. But the light cut straight through and hit the trunk of one of the two thick trees they were camped between.

"What are you doing?" said Ren.

"Nothing. I guess I'm just freaked out, too."

Ren looked at him carefully. Her face was a gray oval in the night. "Do you think we're okay?" she said. "I mean, if we traveled through the afterlife . . . were we — are we — um, dead?"

Alex shook his head. "I don't think so. I think we were just, like, passing through? It must be the amulets that let us do that." He glanced over at her Egyptian ibis amulet, the image of a pale white bird, glowing faintly in the moonlight. He felt the weight of the scarab hanging from his neck.

"Well, I guess you would know," said Ren, before quickly adding: "I mean because you've had your amulet for longer. Not because . . ."

Alex nodded. He knew what she meant: Not because he'd been dead before.

Not because his mom had accidentally unleashed death so that he could live.

His mom.

The thought hit him like an avalanche: a cold and massive weight. They'd picked up her trail in the Valley of the Kings. They'd been so close to her — and now, just hours later, they were a continent away. It felt frustrating and unfair. He didn't know why she was running. She had always looked after him, always known what to do, so why abandon him now? He couldn't figure it out. But he knew he needed to find her. And not just to put his growing doubts to rest, but also because the Spells she had with her were the only things powerful enough to end the evil spreading across the globe.

A memory flashed through his mind: his mom's handwriting in a government logbook in the Valley of the Kings. She'd signed a fake name, but a familiar one: Angela Felini, one of his old babysitters. But there was no one looking after him now, not his mom and not Angela, who'd moved to Alexandria, Virginia, years ago. Now he felt like he alone was responsible — for himself, and for all the trouble he'd caused.

Ren interrupted his thoughts. "We should call Todtman."

Dr. Ernst Todtman was the leader of their unlikely group, and the last time they'd seen him was in Cairo. They hadn't heard from the mysterious German scholar since they'd split up to cover more ground.

"Yeah, definitely," said Alex. He dug into his pocket for his disposable cell phone — what Ren called his "spy phone." He clicked it on and checked the screen. He'd had calls from his own phone forwarded to it — just in case his mom tried to reach him — but he had no missed calls at all. And now the battery was almost dead.

"Do you think our phones will work here?"

"Maybe. They worked in London and Egypt. Todtman must have gotten, like, the international plan when he bought the phones."

Alex dialed, but once again the call went straight to voice mail. He left a quick message.

"It's me. We're in Vienna. Austria. I'll try to explain when you call us. A lot has happened. Don't trust Luke. Please call!"

Ren ruined some of the urgency of Alex's message by letting out a mighty yawn. "Sorry," she said. "Really tired."

"Me too," said Alex. "I guess we should get some sleep and try Todtman again in the morning."

"What if they find us?"

They. Alex knew she didn't mean the guards from the museum. She meant The Order. "We left them in the dust back in Egypt," he said, hoping it was true. "Or the sand, anyway. There's no way they could know we ended up here."

"Okay," Ren said sleepily. She put her backpack behind her head and lay down on the soft grass. "Maybe one of us should stay awake and keep watch."

"I'll take the first watch," said Alex. He was really tired but felt like he owed it to her. He was the reason she was here in the first place.

Ren fell asleep immediately, leaving Alex alone with his thoughts. He leaned against his backpack and gazed into the dark summer night. The air was warm and the faintest strains of classical music floated out from some open window far away. He scanned the shadows, measured the darkness. He told himself there was nothing there — but he didn't quite believe it. He needed to know for sure.

He reached up and slipped the ancient scarab amulet from under his shirt. It was plain and chunky as Egyptian artifacts went, just polished stone and refined copper. But the scarab beetle was a powerful symbol of resurrection in ancient Egypt, and the amulet had tremendous power. It could activate the Book of the Dead and banish the Death Walkers; it could move objects and summon powerful winds; and lastly, it could detect the undead.

Alex closed his hand around it. Even as his pulse revved with ancient energy, he sought to calm his mind. To open up and stretch out with his senses . . . For a second, he thought he felt something: a slight presence no more substantial than the last soap bubble in the sink. But then it slipped away. It was such a weak signal that he wasn't entirely sure he had felt it at all.

He released the amulet and chastised himself. He had too much real trouble to go inventing more. A Death Walker would light up his amulet like a battleship on a radar screen. Why drive himself crazy with a weak, slippery signal that might not exist at all?

It had been a long day with lots of running. Alex's grimy nylon backpack wasn't much of a pillow, but he was sure he could lie back and relax a little and still stay awake. But a moment later, his eyes fluttered closed, and he fell fast asleep.

The shadow had followed them from the afterlife. It liked this new boy who was shadowed by death, too. How was it possible to bear the marks of death and still be so full of life? The shadow didn't know, but it wondered if it could take that energy for itself. If it could gorge on this boy's life and become full. Maybe it would even remember who it had been, once upon a time, so long ago.

It leaned over Alex as he slept, and pinched his nose shut.

Alex immediately began to squirm. It was a soft movement at first, as if rolling to get more comfortable. But as the oxygen ceased to flow, he twisted with a bit more urgency.

The shadow concentrated. At first it was all it could do to hold the nostrils of the squirming boy closed. It was still a weak presence in this world, and this was the outer limit of its influence here.

Alex opened his mouth and gasped. That was what the shadow had been waiting for. The strange creature breathed deeply, sucking the warm air leaving Alex's lungs straight into its own dark form. And as it did, it grew stronger. Its hand grew more defined. What had been little more than a cold, dark paw now resolved itself into individual fingers, a wrist.

The shadow pressed its new hand down over Alex's nose. He thrashed beneath the increasing force and, finally, his eyes snapped open.

What he saw made no sense to him, just an impenetrable darkness hanging over him. And then he saw its milky gray eyes.

It was a sheut, the shadowy vessel that the ancient Egyptians believed contained a person's spirit and self, their ka and ba. Alex had seen the pooled blackness at the feet of the living in the ancient art at the Met. But the body of this one was long dead, and the ka and ba had fled. Something had gone wrong, and they hadn't been reunited in the afterlife. All that was left was this thing of darkness: a shadow of its former self.

Alex watched in horror as a stream of soft white fog rose from his own open mouth and disappeared into the sheut. He rolled and thrashed, but the hand pressed down hard. *How can a shadow hold me?* Alex wondered desperately. But hold him it did. Stronger with each breath it stole, it pinned his head hard against the ground. *It is taking my strength*, Alex suddenly realized. *It is taking my life force as its own!*

Alex reached up to wrestle the thing away, but his hands passed straight through the apparition's arms. It could affect him, but he couldn't affect it.

His amulet!

Alex's lungs cried out for oxygen even as they gave it up. He felt his vision narrowing. He was on the verge of passing out. He reached desperately for his amulet and found only its silver chain. The heavy scarab had swung around behind him as he slept and was now pinned between the back of his neck and the ground.

As its gray eyes turned milky white, the sheut lowered them toward Alex. *How isss it you arrre alllliiiive?* it asked, the words taking shape not on the air but inside Alex's mind. He had no breath left to answer. And it didn't seem to matter: He wouldn't be alive for long.

III

The Moon in Her Hand

Under the stars and between the trees a few feet away, Ren was sound asleep and dreaming of home. Since this mission had started, she'd traveled around the world to battle Death Walkers and search for the Lost Spells and Alex's mom. And along the way, her homesickness had progressed to something like home flu. Sleep was her only chance to visit.

Her mom and dad were at the table in the small kitchen of their New York City apartment. Ren could tell immediately that it was a workday. Her mom was dressed in a sharp jacket and pencil skirt combo, set for another day of high-powered public relations work. She didn't yet know which of the company's clients had said or done something stupid, but she was prepared for anything. Her dad was in one of his familiar button-down shirts, the sleeves already rolled, the mechanical pencil in the chest pocket. Ready to solve problems of a more precise variety.

They talked softly over the last of their coffee, slipping into Spanish now and then as they sometimes did. Ren understood every word this time. That wasn't always the case at home, but she was dreaming these words, after all. As she slept, a tear slipped through the corner of one closed eye. They were talking about her.

They were wondering how she was doing in London. They were proud of her internship at the British Museum. They missed her.

I miss you, too, Ren wanted to say. The rest of it she wouldn't mention, because she was a long way from London now — a long way from a fake internship. But it didn't matter. She had no voice in this dream.

The phone began to ring. Her father stood up. But something was wrong. He walked over to the sink and dumped out the dregs of his coffee, ignoring the phone entirely. And that ring — or tone, rather — flat and electronic. Generic, like . . .

A disposable cell phone.

Ren's eyes drifted open.

She reached up to wipe the tear away with one hand and reached down for her phone with the other. But her phone was quiet and still. "Alex," she said, turning toward her friend. "Your phone."

And that's when she saw it. Alex was flopping limply, like a fish too long on the dock, and a dark shape was looming over him. A human shape. Weak light filtered into the park from the streetlamps at its margins and the moon above, and it all ended at the edges of this entity. Its hand was clamped down over Alex's face, and a thin vaporous line ran from his open mouth to the creature's. Right away, Ren knew it was killing him.

"Stop it!" she screamed.

The sheut turned and regarded her with softly glowing eyes. It was strong now, unthreatened.

Ren balled up her fists. She was small for her age, but brave for anyone's. This thing was terrifying and she felt her own chest tighten with fear, but she was not going to let it take her friend. She. Was. Not. She needed to knock it loose, to allow him to breathe. She took a deep breath — and leapt at it!

She passed straight through, feeling nothing but a profound chill, and crashed to the ground on the other side. She looked back, baffled and desperate. The line of vapor was almost gone now. She got up and swung at it with her fists.

Nothing. It felt like dipping them in cold milk but had no effect at all.

Think, she told herself. *Be smart.*

My amulet.

She reached up. The ibis was a symbol of Thoth, the ancient Egyptian god of wisdom, writing, and moonlight, and its main power was to show her images and provide information. She'd grown a little more comfortable with it lately, but she still distrusted the magic behind it. It just felt weird having it in her head like that — like letting a wild horse into a quiet study hall. But now she needed that power. She needed that wild horse — for once, she didn't even care if she could rein it in.

Her hand closed around the ibis. This time she asked it not for answers, but for justice. Thoth was the one who wrote down the verdict at the weighing of the heart ceremony, the test to determine whether a soul gained entrance into the afterlife. He was the divine scribe, the one who made sure everything was in the right place, written in the right column. Ren liked things in their right place, too, and she knew for a fact that this deathly presence did not belong here.

She squeezed the ibis tight, feeling its edges dig into her palm.

"Go!" she shouted. And as she did, a burst of blinding white light flashed outward, like the full moon pressed down to the size of one small, fierce fist and then released again.

The sheut hissed against the light and was torn to shreds, like a cheap black suit caught up in a hurricane.

When the light faded, it was gone.

Alex gasped for breath.

His phone beeped once. Voice mail.

The sheut had popped like a black balloon in the moonlight. Now, a few last wisps of Alex's breath hung over him like a pale white cloud in the warm night. *So that's it*, he thought, looking up at the slowly scattering vapor. *That's what all this is about.* It was more than breath, he knew; it was life.

How can this little cloud of breath be worth so much trouble? he wondered as the last gasp dissolved. *How can* I *be worth so much trouble? Ren saved me this time, but how many others have died because I lived? How many more will die before we can find the Spells and end all of this? If we even can. The doorway to the afterlife seems to open wider every day. All because of me . . .*

Ren knelt down by his side. “How do you feel?” she asked.

Alex forced a smile. “Awful,” he said. It was a familiar feeling and one he’d hoped he’d never feel again. There were painful pinpricks in his arms and legs, fingers and toes, as if he’d just come in from too long in the cold. He felt tired and nauseous. He’d felt this way nearly his whole life, before the Spells had transformed him. He looked up at Ren. “I feel like before.”

“Oh no,” she said. Apart from his mom, Ren was the one person who knew just how bad “before” had been. She shook off her concerned expression and forced a smile of her own. “You just need to recover your strength.”

Alex nodded and sat there breathing and rubbing his arms. The more he breathed, the better he felt. Finally, Alex reached for his phone to check the missed call. Now he smiled for real.

“Todtman?” said Ren hopefully.

Alex gave her a big thumbs-up and put the phone on speaker so Ren could hear the message, too.

“Hello, Alex. I got your message. I am sorry for the . . . delay. I am glad to hear from you.” Alex leaned closer to the phone. He was glad to hear the crisp consonants of Todtman's familiar German accent again, but his voice was obscured by a faint buzzing. "Things have gotten worse in Cairo. The voices of the dead are everywhere now; the city is in chaos. I had to leave. I can be in Vienna by tomorrow, mid-morning. There is a small restaurant on Linke Wienzeile, near the Naschmarkt." As he rattled off the address, Alex heard Ren rustling around for her ever-present pen. "I will meet you there at ten thirty. Stay safe."

They played the message again with the last of the battery power, just to make sure they had the address right.

"I am going to eat *so* much at that restaurant," said Ren.

But Alex didn't want to talk about Wiener schnitzel. He pictured the terrible darkness that had loomed over him just minutes earlier. "Thanks," he said. "You saved my life."

"Saved your life *again*. But," Ren added, "I have no idea how."

"You banished it," Alex said, "with the light from your amulet."

Ren considered that. "I just knew that thing didn't belong here," she said. "And you're welcome."

Alex didn't get much sleep for the rest of the night. Instead, he kept watch. He was sure the sheut had followed them from the afterlife. *What if something else had?*

And there was another shadow that wasn't so easy to dismiss. This one wasn't looming over him, but lurking inside. Ren's words played on a loop in his head: *That thing didn't belong here*, she'd said. And she was right. It had returned from the afterlife, after all.

But then, hadn't Alex done the same thing when his mom brought him back?

He watched the new day dawn in softly glowing purples and pinks and wondered: *Do I have any more right to this sunrise than that desperate spirit did?*

11

Boxed In

They arrived at the restaurant a few minutes early. "Schnitzel Box," said Ren, reading the sign. "Promising."

Alex heard his stomach rumble in agreement. He'd recovered his health, and with it, his appetite.

"How do you say *large* in German?" asked Ren.

"Gross," said Alex.

"Seriously?"

He nodded.

"Well, I am going to have the grossest schnitzel they've got," said Ren. "Let's go on in and wait for Todtman inside. They won't mind."

"We don't have enough money for a place like this," said Alex.

"We can just drink a bunch of water until Todtman gets here," said Ren. "And use the bathroom."

They pushed through the door into the restaurant's dimly lit, dark wood interior. The place was dead.

"Welcome," said the lone waiter, a tall man in a white shirt and black vest. "Sit anywhere you would like. We have just opened."

Alex was surprised to hear the man greet them in English. Was it that obvious they were Americans? *"Danke!"* he said. "Thanks."

He headed straight for the restrooms, looked for the picture with pants, and went in that door. After taking care of some pressing business, he headed to the sink. He felt like a mess after a night in the park and another near-death experience, and let the water run until it was nice and hot.

After scrubbing his hands, he swished some water around in his mouth. His own dirt-smudged face stared back at him from the mirror as he ran one wet hand through his mussed-up black hair. His fingers caught halfway and he winced. He'd need to get some shampoo in there one of these days. There'd be time for that later. He felt a buzz of anticipation. Soon they'd see Todtman, have a big meal, and resume their search for his mom and the Spells.

Finally, he bent down and splashed hot water on his face. He dipped his hands in the sink again as he straightened up and checked the mirror to see if he'd gotten at least some of the dirt. But he barely saw his face at all, because the face behind it was so much more terrifying.

Looking straight at him was a man with the head of a giant housefly. On either side were large eyes the size of half grapefruits and made up of thousands of individual lenses. Alex's body froze from fear, but his mind raced. A mask in the shape of an animal head told him this man was an operative of The Order.

They'd found him.

He whirled around, splashing hot water on the tile floor as his hand reached desperately for the scarab. The thousand-eyed gaze followed him, the eyes of the mask shifting and moving as if alive. Painful experience had taught him that the masks were as ancient and powerful as his own amulet.

A strong hand grabbed Alex's left wrist before he could reach the chain at his neck. He reached up with his right, only to have that pinned, too. He struggled, trying to free his wrists, water still dripping from his hands. The fly head leaned in and regarded him with its bulbous eyes, and an overwhelming stink of garbage made Alex gag. A crashing sound reached his ears as furniture was overturned and silverware clattered to the floor out in the restaurant.

Ren. He'd led her into trouble — again.

Desperate, he struggled harder. It was useless. The fly man held him tight with hairy gnarled hands and regarded Alex with the eight thousand shifting lenses of his composite eyes. Then the fly man spoke: "Hello, Alex. I got your message. I am sorry for the . . . delay."

His voice was a perfect imitation of Todtman's, though it was true, there was a slight buzz to it. The phone call, the meeting — it had all been a trap! Alex needed to act now to have any chance of escape. There was another crash from the restaurant and a high-pitched yelp. *Was Ren hurt?*

Alex kicked out hard. The toe of his boot sank into the thick folds of the fly's grimy robe and clipped the knobby leg underneath. His attacker flinched slightly, but instead of releasing him, his grip grew tighter. Alex kicked again. He was wearing good boots, designed for the desert, and this time, he caught the fly flush on the shin. The fly doubled over, releasing his grip and coughing out a cloud of disgusting brownish green gas.

Alex held his breath — and grabbed his amulet with his left hand. Wet palm against cold stone, he formed the now-familiar words in his mind: *The wind that comes before the rain.* The scarab was a symbol of rebirth in Egypt, and this was among its most powerful manifestations. His right hand shot forward and with it an invisible lance of rushing wind.

The fly-headed operative took the blast directly in the gut. The wind was strong — and the floor was wet. His sandaled feet skated straight back.

WAMMP! He hit the wall hard.

Alex bolted out the door. In the dining room, Alex was relieved not to see a squad of Order gunmen. Instead, he saw the waiter holding a large carving knife and chasing Ren around an overturned table.

"Hey!" shouted Alex.

The waiter turned toward Alex. He might as well have stepped into a wind tunnel. He tumbled over the upturned table and landed amid crashes and clinks on the other side. *"Autsch, eine Gabel!"* he cried. *Ow, a fork!*

The door to the men's room flew open and a fetid stink seeped into the chase-wrecked room, but as it did, the front door flew open as well. The two friends rushed out into daylight — and fresh air.

The friends took twenty blocks' worth of twists and turns at a dead run, stopping only when they were sure — well, pretty sure — that they'd given the world's largest fly and rudest waiter the slip. At the end of it, they'd found a public bench and another voice mail from Todtman, this one on Ren's phone.

"How do we know it's really him this time?" she huffed.

"Look at the time: 10:28 a.m.," said Alex, pointing down at the screen of Ren's phone. "It has to be Todtman. That's when the fly guy was busy attacking me. Remember? We got there a little early."

Alex took another look at the screen, this time eyeing the little sliver of remaining battery life. "Play the message again," he said.

She did. And then, looking both ways and huddling close together on the little bench, they called the new number he'd given them. Todtman answered immediately. Ren put it on speaker and Alex listened carefully to his voice, but this time there was no buzziness as they got down to business.

They gave Todtman a quick recap, including Luke's betrayal and their current location, so that he could send someone to pick up the two remaining friends. Alex knew that Todtman was well-connected and never seemed to be short of cash. Still, he was surprised when a snow-white limo pulled up to the curb in front of them half an hour later. Somewhat skeptically, he asked the driver for the password.

The man was wearing a black suit and a Bluetooth earpiece. "Tutankhamun," he said flatly as he walked around the car to open the back door for them.

Ren nodded — she had chosen it — and they both climbed in and headed to the airport, where their plane tickets back to Egypt were waiting.

"No offense," she said as the long car snaked through midday traffic, "but was this, like, the last car left?"

The driver gave her a half look over his shoulder. "Not at all," he said. "Your uncle requested this one in particular."

Alex and Ren exchanged looks, and Ren silently mouthed two words: *Our uncle?*

Alex had heard worse cover stories. "Why?" he said.

The driver shrugged. "Because the airports are being watched, and no one will expect you to pull up in a white limousine." He glanced in the mirror and must have caught the surprised expressions of his passengers, because he added: "I am a professional. Now relax and enjoy the trip."

"But what if —" began Ren.

Alex cut her off: "Don't mind my *little* sister," he called up to the driver. And then, more softly: "You probably can't see her over the seat, anyway."

Ren gave him a good-natured punch in the arm. Good-natured — but not exactly soft.

In an hour and a half, they were on a small plane. Three and a half hours and fourteen tiny bags of free pretzels later, they touched down at a small, regional airport thirty-five miles outside of Cairo. Todtman met them as they were headed for customs, which was, of course, against all the rules.

"How did you get past security?" said Alex. He tried to keep his tone as businesslike as Todtman's, but he couldn't help smiling at the sight of the old German alive and well, with his froglike bulging eyes and trademark black suit. "Did you bribe them or hypnotize them with your amulet?" He glanced at the jewel-eyed falcon at Todtman's neck.

"Why can't it be both?" Todtman whispered with a sly smile of his own.

The customs official waved them through, not even pretending to look at their passports. The trio exited into the brightly lit expanse of the terminal.

"We must hurry," said Todtman, the rubber tip of his jet-black walking stick plunking the tile and his eyes sweeping the terminal. "We are not safe here."

"In this airport?" said Ren, looking around warily.

"In Egypt," said Todtman.

Reading the Signs

Driving a large, beat-up rental car, Todtman took off from the airport with only slightly less velocity than the jets roaring by above. Stuck in the backseat, Alex fastened his seat belt tightly. Ren had called shotgun before it had even occurred to him, claiming the front seat with a triumphant chirp: "Revenge of the 'little sister.'"

Todtman shifted to coax more power out of the big engine, but the gears caught and the car lurched alarmingly. "Sorry," he said. "There were no German cars available."

A turn came up, and Todtman took it. Another one appeared, and he took that one, too. Soon, there was more traffic, and the low smudge of a small city appeared on the horizon. Todtman downshifted, slowed. Alex relaxed. They'd slipped free from the airport into the teeming mix of a country of nearly ninety million.

They skirted around the little city, avoiding narrow streets and slow traffic, and stuck to a wide road surrounded by surprisingly green country. A battered old tractor appeared up ahead, and Todtman switched lanes and left it in the dust.

"Why'd you pick us up out here in the boondocks?" asked Ren.

"Cairo is too dangerous," said Todtman. "The spirits have driven too many to madness; the authorities are overwhelmed — and The Order does as it pleases."

Alex peered out the back window, remembering the chaos he'd witnessed in Cairo: the shouts and sirens, the people haunted by voices in their heads, the woman who ran headlong through a shop window, the police huddled together for their own protection, The Order thugs carrying their guns openly . . . "So it's even worse now?" he said, trying to imagine it.

"Much worse," said Todtman. He caught Alex's eyes in the rearview mirror. "I barely escaped with my life — or my soul." He fell silent for a few moments, as if fighting back a painful memory.

Alex broke eye contact. He felt like he was riding in the back of a police car: *guilty*. Cairo was lost, all of Egypt was unsafe, the madness spread farther every day . . . and he was the cause of it all.

"So it's more important than ever that we find my mom and the Lost Spells," he said, trying to keep things on track. "Have you found out any more about where she might be?"

Todtman shook his head. "Nothing."

"So which way are we headed, then?" Alex demanded. He looked out the tinted window and saw a green field. Two skinny black cows stood grazing on ankle-high grass, while acres of deeper green leaves stretched out behind them.

They were in the Nile delta, north of Cairo, a land of dark, fertile soil.

"That is what we must determine," Todtman answered. "Our next destination, the next step."

"We know Alex's mom was in the Valley of the Kings," offered Ren. "But that was more than a week ago."

"And now The Order will know she was there, too," said Alex glumly. "Because Luke was spying for them the whole time."

Alex had been betrayed by his cousin and abandoned by his mom. It was a powerful one-two punch, and once again he felt the impact. He shook his head hard, trying to refocus. "Yeah, she'll be far away from the Valley by now," he concluded.

Todtman nodded and then added: "The thing that makes finding your mother so hard is . . ." He paused. Alex leaned forward in anticipation of some difficult admission, some new truth about his mom. But when it came, the truth was more about Todtman. "She is smarter than I am. She always was — just a little."

Despite the clouds hanging over his thoughts, a small smile slipped onto Alex's face.

"That's okay," said Ren. "She's smarter than Alex, too."

The smile slipped right back off.

They zoomed by more fields, the stalks of golden wheat on one small farm giving way to a grove of short, squat banana trees on the next. Shallow irrigation ditches divided the landscape. Todtman downshifted as they slipped onto a side road, kicking up a dusty plume behind them. "We will need to think carefully, to figure out what Maggie is trying to do," he said. "We must think back over everything we've found — see if there are any clues we missed."

Alex hesitated, but there was one thing he'd kept circling back to. "I don't know if it means anything," he began, "but the name my mom signed in the logbook when she left the Valley of the Kings, Angela Felini . . ."

Ren leaned across the front seat toward Todtman. "Angie was his old babysitter," she said, in that teacher's pet way she sometimes fell into.

"Yeah," said Alex. "It's just . . . after she stopped working for us she moved to Alexandria. I mean, Alexandria, Virginia, but still. Do you think that my mom signed that name as, like, a message? To me? To us? Because I know there's an Alexandria, *Egypt*, too."

"Hmmmm," said Todtman. "It seems possible. If she anticipated us following her . . ."

"Well, she is smarter than us," said Alex. He wanted desperately to believe it: that even if his mom had deserted him, she hadn't forgotten him. If she'd left him a clue, it could mean that she was still looking out for him. That she wasn't completely abandoning him.

"She talked about Alexandria sometimes," he added hopefully.

"Yeah, because she went to school there," said Ren.

Had she really? Alex tried to remember. When he thought of his mom in school, he thought of Columbia, in New York

City. That was the sweatshirt she wore, the campus they visited for alumni events sometimes. He knew she'd gotten her PhD in Egypt, though. He tried to remember exactly where, but Ren was still one step ahead of him.

"There's a degree on the wall of your place," she said. "By the bookshelf."

"Oh yeah," said Alex. He had a vague memory of a framed sheet of old vellum on the wall of the little apartment where he'd grown up. He'd seen it so many times that he'd almost stopped seeing it. He tried to remember the big words at the top. It was a degree, had to be, the writing in Arabic and English. He closed his eyes . . . *Alexandria University.*

"You're right," he said, looking up toward the front seat, but the little grin on Ren's face told him she already knew that. *Leave it to Ren to notice all the degrees on the wall*, he thought. Still, it was a little awkward for his best friend to remember something about his mom that he hadn't. "You're not *really* my sister, you know," he added.

Ren opened her mouth to reply, but Todtman cut in.

"Yes, that's right," he said, his froggy face bending upward in a smile of his own. "I knew she finished her dissertation in Egypt. But I assumed it was in Cairo. Alexandria University is an old school, and a good one."

"That's why she still talks about Alexandria," said Alex. "It was the first place she lived in Egypt."

"Yes," said Todtman, "her roots in this country are in Alexandria. And if I'm not mistaken, yours, too, Alex."

"What do you mean?" he said. She definitely hadn't told him that.

"What is your name?"

"It's Alex — oh!" He slumped down in his seat, his head reeling from the implications. *Alex . . . Alexandria.* "Wasn't Alexandria named after Alexander the Great?" he said.

Todtman nodded, and Ren snorted, clearly unconvinced of her best friend's Greatness. Alex didn't notice. He was staring down at his own legs. His own Egyptian legs.

"That university is her oldest and deepest connection to this country," said Todtman, taking the next left with the car, pointing them back toward the main road. "So that is where the trail points us."

A buzzing line of fast-moving cars appeared up ahead. A highway. Alex scanned a tall blue sign near the entrance. Various destinations were listed in Arabic and English in reflective white paint. His eyes ran to the third line:

ALEXANDRIA 153 KILOMETERS

"Look, Alex," said Ren, turning around in her seat to face him. "You're going home!"

Ren glanced to her side and saw Todtman's eyes staring straight at the road ahead, his hands precisely at ten and two o'clock on the steering wheel. She looked into the mirror and saw Alex lost in thought in the backseat.

They had their destination, but the clue leading them there felt like a long shot. She wanted to know if they were headed in the right direction — or off on another Egyptian goose chase. Slowly, silently, she peeled her hand from the cool vinyl of the car seat and reached up for her amulet.

She'd never done this before. She'd never asked the ibis for answers without being forced to — without a Death Walker looming or Todtman insisting. But maybe she could try now, she thought. Maybe if she just kept it to herself, she wouldn't feel the same pressure to get it exactly right.

Ren took a deep, nervous breath. She exhaled softly and whispered two words: "Extra credit." They were powerful words for the girl known as "Plus Ten Ren" back in school. She had always had a bad habit of putting too much pressure on herself on tests and assignments, and sometimes it cost her. But she gobbled up every bit of available extra credit, work that could only help, never hurt. And back in the Valley of the Kings, that approach — viewing her amulet's mysterious offerings as a bonus — had helped her get a handle on its magic, as well.

As her hand closed around it, she once again asked for a little extra. She felt the smooth stone against her palm and, a split second later, a sudden jolt of energy. Her eyes closed and her mind filled with images:

A baby with fat, tan cheeks and wide brown eyes, staring out at a massive container ship gliding slowly across smooth, dark water . . .

A young woman's hand, reaching down to pick up a stack of thick books, a rubber band around her wrist — a rubber band just like Alex's mom used to wear sometimes . . .

Her eyes opened.

"What did you see?" said Todtman.

She looked over at him, blinking twice to refocus her eyes back in the here and now. "Is Alexandria on the coast?" she asked.

"Yes, the Mediterranean," said Todtman. "It has been Egypt's main port for centuries."

"What are you two talking about?" chirped Alex from the backseat.

"Nothing," said Ren, catching his eyes in the mirror. His cheeks weren't quite so chubby anymore, but she was pretty sure his was the face she'd seen. And that must have been his mom's arms, picking up her schoolbooks. And if all that was true, then that seaside city was Alexandria.

"Is there something we should know?" said Todtman, eyeing her ibis.

Ren shook her head. "No, we're good," she said. "Just keep driving."

Their destination no longer felt like such a long shot to her, but there were still a lot of *ifs* and *maybes* in those images. And the only thing she hated more than being unsure was being wrong. She'd used her amulet voluntarily, and it hadn't been so bad. But it had tricked her before — and she knew there were much tougher tests ahead.

Alexandria

They drove through the evening and approached Alexandria in the dead of night. Alex felt a little spike of hope as he saw the modest skyline take murky shape in the moonlight. Maybe his mom's past really was the key to her present. It made sense. *In a vast, foreign country, wouldn't she stick to the places she knew?* He hoped they'd find another clue — or better yet, his mom herself.

But Alex was worried, too. The closer they got, the more the questions dogged him: *Why was she running? Why didn't she contact him?* A scary thought popped into his head, fully formed: *She's given me life twice now — is she angry about what it has cost?* He shook his head hard to clear it. He felt frustrated and guilty and lost as his thoughts slid by darkly, like the view outside the car windows. *I need to make this right. It's up to me.* This time his head stayed as still as stone.

Alexandria was a city of millions, and the houses on the outskirts quickly gave way to bigger buildings: apartments, offices, stores. But most of them were dark now, lumbering shadows slipping silently by. Only streetlights and sparse headlights lit their way.

"I have an old colleague that we can stay with," said Todtman. "We'll be safe there while we follow your mom's trail."

Alex leaned forward to assess their surroundings. The neighborhood had changed again. The big blocky buildings had given way to smaller, sleeker ones. Shiny metal edges and wide glass windows caught the headlights as they passed, the subtle flourishes of expensive modern architecture. "Uh, these are really fancy houses," said Alex.

"This is like the Upper East Side of Alexandria," said Ren, and Alex laughed despite himself.

"How do you say *Park Avenue* in Arabic?" he said.

Ren chortled. "Is this guy rich?" she asked Todtman, leaning forward for a better look.

"This *woman*," said Todtman. "And very."

Todtman pulled into a driveway and stopped at a metal gate. He lowered his window and said something into a speaker in rapid, hushed Arabic. A few moments later, the gate slid back with a smooth mechanical hum.

There was a conspicuously expensive car in the driveway in front of them, and the gate slid shut behind them with a firm, precise *SHUUNK*. Alex looked up at the ultramodern cube of a house. A ring of outside lights had come on, and a few of the inside ones were now visible behind large squares of blue-tinted glass on the second floor. "What does this lady do, exactly?" he said.

"She is" — Todtman pursed his lips, considering his word choice — "a collector . . . Yes, a bit of a scholar, certainly, but only in a private capacity. Mostly she . . . collects."

Alex didn't like all those pauses one bit. He knew that private collections of Egyptian artifacts were put together on the black market as often as at the auction house. "And how do you know her, again?"

Todtman flashed him half a smile, but in the dim light of the car's interior, Alex couldn't tell if it meant "trust me" or "you don't want to know." He looked up at the house again and saw a shadow glide silently across one window.

The door clicked open as they approached it, and Alex gawped at the little fish-eyed camera lens as they passed. They entered the hushed, half-lit entryway and were met by a large, imposing man — who imposed himself immediately.

"Wait here," he said gruffly, but his expression changed when he saw Todtman's face. "Oh, hey, Doc. Just a minute."

Alex sized up the man — extra-large — and guessed he was a live-in security guard.

"It's all right, Bubbi," called a woman's voice from somewhere in the shadowy house. "I'm in the study, Doctor!"

The big man stepped aside, and Alex wondered if his bodyguard buddies knew he was called Bubbi. Todtman led the way up a flight of stairs and into a broad and brightly lit room. A woman approached them dressed in business attire despite the hour: tapered tan slacks and a crisp white blouse. She was about his mom's age, he figured, and carried herself in a similarly professional manner.

She greeted Todtman warmly and then turned to Alex and Ren.

"My name is Safa," she said. "You are welcome in my home."

Alex felt tense. He didn't know anything about this woman, and here they were boxing themselves up inside a walled compound with her. He'd planned to say something polite but measured, like "Hello" or "Thanks for letting us crash." Instead, he found himself gawking wordlessly at the room around him. Ancient stone relief carvings lined the walls; a life-sized statue stood in a lit alcove.

"Are these all Hatshepsut?" he blurted finally.

Safa's measured expression broke into a warm smile. "Yes, the world's finest private collection," she said, the pride unmistakable in her voice.

Alex took another quick look at the array of ancient artwork, all showing Egypt's first female pharaoh. "Wow. Wasn't most of her stuff destroyed?" he said. The Met had an entire room of carvings of Hatshepsut, but those pieces had been reconstructed.

"I see the apple doesn't fall far from the tree," said Safa. "But look closer."

Alex took a few steps toward the statue, and now he saw it. The same light lines in the stone that the ones at the Met had, the subtle scars of expert reconstruction. And what he had initially thought was a heavy shadow on one side of the face was, in fact, all that was left of the face. One side had been chipped away, and there was a patch of rough gray stone where the left eye and cheek should have been. Her chin ended not in the symbolic beard of a pharaoh, but in chisel marks.

"This one is all in one piece," said Ren, pointing to an elegant relief along the wall that showed the sleek, regal figure of Hatshepsut standing on one side of a bearded pharaoh as the falcon-headed sun god, Amun-Re, stood on the other.

"Good eye, child," said Safa, turning. "Images of Hatshepsut as queen were left untouched. It was only the ones that showed her as ruler in her own right that were destroyed. The next pharaoh wanted to make sure it was his descendants and not hers who would take the throne."

"So unfair," said Ren.

"The world has always been a difficult place for powerful women," said Safa with a somewhat weary smile. "I keep these here as both a tribute and a reminder."

As she began walking out of the room, Alex remembered what he'd meant to say in the first place. "Thank you for letting us stay here," he said. "It helps a lot."

"And I am happy to help," said Safa, still walking. For a moment, it seemed like that would be all, but a few steps later, she stopped and turned to face him.

"You know, it was your mother who first led me to Hatshepsut. I knew her in school."

Alex leaned in, listening carefully. Despite everything, he found himself trusting this woman. He took a deep breath, filling his lungs for the questions he wanted to ask her about his mom, but Safa cut him short.

"Your mother had been offered a grant to study Hatshepsut—very prestigious," she said. "But she'd just had you, you see, and she declined."

"She had to give up her grant?" said Alex.

"You were quite sick at the time," said Safa.

"Yeah," said Alex, looking down at his feet. "That sounds like me." *Sick . . . and already causing her trouble.*

Safa smiled sympathetically. "The grant did not go to waste," she said. "I'd planned to do my postdoc work on Ramses VI. Do you know what she told me?"

Alex shook his head, still not looking up.

"She said that the world needs another paper on Ramses like Giza needs another tourist. And then she recommended me to the grant administrator, Dr. Alshuff."

"Mahmoud Alshuff?" asked Todtman.

Safa nodded. "Alshuff had been Maggie's doctoral adviser, as well. He trusted her recommendation. And so I found myself studying a woman who took power without apology. A woman whose legacy was too big to be erased by men. Studying Hatshepsut changed what I thought about my country, my history, myself. So, yes, Alex Sennefer, you are welcome to stay here. You and the doctor and" — she looked over at Ren — "your better half."

Then she turned and continued out of the room. "Now, if you'll excuse me, I must go. Bubbi will show you to your rooms once you're done in here. I have a videoconference to get back to."

"But it's the middle of the night," said Alex.

"Not in Tokyo," she said, giving them a small over-the-shoulder wave and closing the door behind her.

"I like her!" said Ren.

"She is an interesting woman," said Todtman, his voice betraying his admiration.

"How do you know her?" said Ren.

"I have advised her for years on her purchases," said Todtman, pulling up a chair as Alex and Ren collapsed on either side of a sleek modern couch. "Whether the pieces are real, how much to pay, how likely she is to get arrested for having them . . . It is a relationship based on trust."

Alex leaned back into the soft black leather as he listened. A relationship based on trust — and on an opportunity he'd cost his mom. Her first sacrifice for him. He pictured a little web of connections — Todtman, Safa, the university — with his own mom at the center.

"So what next?" said Ren.

"Tomorrow we go to the university," said Todtman. "And talk to her old adviser."

"Dr. Alshuff," said Alex. He was in the web, too.

Todtman nodded. "I know Mahmoud. In fact, I believe I owe him money."

An hour later, they were all sound asleep. It had been an intense day, both physically and mentally.

Around the house, Bubbi and another man watched carefully, peering out windows and into monitors. They knew these guests brought danger with them. But neither man saw the tall regal woman in the front garden, her feet leaving no prints in the soft soil.

She was not seen for the simple reason that she did not want to be, and she left no prints for the simple reason that she was not actually touching the ground.

Instead, she hovered there among the fragrant herbs, staring up at the second floor with half a face.

Schooled

Their hostess was nowhere in sight the next morning, but a traditional Egyptian breakfast was waiting on the kitchen counter downstairs: three plates of fava beans — some whole, some mashed, all cold — with thick pita bread tucked along the sides. "What is this?" asked Ren, grabbing the nearest plate and shoveling some of the beany mix into a pita.

"It is called *fuul*," said Todtman, doing the same.

"Fuel?" said Ren.

"Close enough," said Todtman.

Alex looked around for doughnuts or Pop-Tarts before reluctantly picking up the third plate. He watched the others devour their food without injury and took a bite. Earthy and bitter, the *fuul* tasted like a combination of hummus, lemon, and something grittier. He took another bite. Then another. It wasn't so bad, actually. Alex wolfed down his second overstuffed pita and burped. Ren gave him a disapproving look, but Todtman ignored it and said, "Let's go. The university will be open by now."

As soon as they stepped out the door, they saw Safa and Bubbi standing next to the rental car in the driveway, their eyes on a small electronic sensor in Bubbi's hands. Finally, he looked up and shook his head: *No.* Safa walked straight toward them and met them halfway down the walkway.

"No tracking devices," she said. "At least none that we could detect."

"Oh!" said Todtman, an involuntary exclamation that told them all that the possibility hadn't occurred to him.

Safa gave him a sympathetic look. "Sometimes I think you actually live in the ancient world, Doctor."

"Sometimes I wish I did," he said with a slightly abashed smile.

The well-traveled old rental car started on the second try. The gleaming security gate seemed to kick the sputtering clunker out with some disdain, hissing open and then shutting with a loud thunk.

"Who'd want to track this hunk of junk?" said Ren from the backseat.

Alex smiled, but his eyes were alert. They were out in broad daylight in a major Egyptian city. The Order's influence was everywhere in Egypt, and this particular hunk of junk held three very wanted individuals. He felt better in fast-moving traffic. It would be hard to see his face at that speed, and apart from that, he didn't really stand out from the crowd around them. He'd inherited a lot of his father's Egyptian features, even if he'd never known the man.

He looked around the car. Ren's eyes barely topped the rear windows, but Todtman couldn't have stood out more if he was wearing bright green lederhosen.

They'd arrived in Alexandria at night, and now he sized it up by daylight. History revealed itself in layers from block to block. Some stretches were distinctly Egyptian, with mosque minarets needling upward. Other areas were almost European, like a faded, peeling version of the pastel beauty he'd seen in Vienna. And now and then, in between buildings and avenues, he caught sun-sparkling glimpses of the massive blue Mediterranean beyond.

A chorus of car horns erupted all around them as the traffic on the street came to a halt. As Alex looked around for the problem, the horns were drowned out by the sound of an approaching siren. He swung back around in time to see a fire engine roar into view in front of them.

"Where's the fire?" said Ren, ducking her head between the front seats.

The crowd began to scatter on the sidewalk up ahead, and Alex heard shouts in Arabic and a few screams. As the last pedestrians ducked into nearby doors or rushed out into the stopped traffic, he finally saw the cause of the commotion: a ragged mummy, stumbling down the center of the sidewalk!

Three firefighters appeared behind it, running fast despite their heavy coats. As the first of them approached the ancient corpse from behind, he began pumping feverishly on the sort of small metal canister used to spray chemicals on lawns.

"Are they going to, um, fertilize it?" said Ren, retreating slightly into the backseat.

The creature began weaving unevenly between the side-walk and the edge of the road. The screams coming from within the cars were more muted now, as any open windows were rapidly raised. The mummy was just a few car-lengths away, and Alex could see its dry wrappings flapping loosely in the morning breeze and one skeletal foot bent nearly back-ward. The fireman gave the canister one more pump and then pointed the little nozzle. Clear liquid sprayed forth, dousing the mummy's back.

"BROAN!" it cried hoarsely. "STAHK!"

It turned around and faced its pursuers. The eyes of the man with the spray can turned into wide white-rimmed circles, and he began mumbling prayers, but still he pointed the noz-zle. He doused the mummy's front, then tucked the nozzle and ran as the thing stumbled toward him, arms out, bony fingers reaching for living flesh. The second firefighter turned and ran, too. The third prepared to bolt, but before he did, he tossed a small glowing object toward the lumbering corpse.

FOOOF!

The mummy went up in flames. It roared angrily and took a few more steps before collapsing facedown in the street.

The firefighters rushed back, not with gas this time but with a long hose from the truck. They waited until the dried-out corpse was little more than ash before turning the hose on. Ash and steam and scraps of aged linen rose up into the morning sun.

The pedestrians reappeared from the doors and walked almost casually around the remains as the firefighters coiled their hose. The honking resumed. "It appears that they have seen this before," said Todtman as the fire truck pulled away and the traffic began moving again.

Alex had never seen firefighters *start* a fire before — much less by lighting a desiccated corpse — but the world was changing. He remembered the angry, haunted streets of Cairo. The dead there had been only whispers, voices. Now they were part of the morning rush hour.

<—+—+—+—>

As the car picked up speed, they lowered the windows again. The warm, slightly salty breeze felt good as they rolled through the city, their eyes peeled for mummies or Order operatives. From her perch in the backseat, Ren saw Alex's head swiveling from side to side, like an electric fan. Scanning the sidewalk, always on the lookout.

She knew he'd been joking about the "little sister" thing, but he really did treat her like one sometimes. He was so determined that he sometimes took on more responsibility than he should. *Don't say you have first watch if you can't stay awake*, she thought, staring at the back of his head. What if that thing had attacked her? She was pretty sure he would've slept through the whole thing. And it definitely wasn't the first time he'd bitten off more than he could chew and gotten them into trouble. Yeah, he knew a lot about ancient Egypt. Yeah, he was good with his scarab.

But he wasn't the only one who knew things, who could *do* things. She glanced down at her ibis. It had allowed her to zap that shadow, and it had shown her this city. *Was she really getting better with it?*

Ren didn't believe in luck; she believed in probability. When she used the amulet, it still felt like rolling the dice. It had failed her before. Still, it was nice to have a few wins under her belt. For now, she reached up and tucked the ancient artifact under her shirt, careful not to hold it too tightly and invite more images in.

As for Alex . . . She glanced toward the front seat. He had his entire head out the window now, like a wind-drunk dog. She smiled. It was hard to stay mad at him. *But if he messes up again*, she thought, *it will get a lot easier.*

They reached the university, found a parking spot in the visitors' lot, and walked toward the main building, a massive redbrick structure. Even in the middle of the summer, students and professors were walking by, carrying books and having intense conversations. And not just in Arabic. Ren caught snatches of English and French and other languages she didn't know. Not yet, anyway.

As a girl who'd been browsing college websites since fourth grade, she felt, if not at home, then at least more at ease. She remembered her dad's words: *Negativity accomplishes nothing, unless you're an ion.* She wasn't a subatomic particle, and they had work to do. They pushed through the big double doors of the administration building.

"We're going to stop them," she said with a sudden rush of optimism. The mid-morning heat faded inside the cool, hushed hallway.

Todtman, who seemed to know these hallways, looked over at her. "Oh yes?" he said, his expression somewhat bemused.

"Yes," she said firmly, spreading her arms to take in their scholarly surroundings. "Because we're smarter."

Alex agreed immediately. "Those are some ignorant individuals," he said. He looked over at Ren and added, "My mom went here." His eyes were wide with wonder. He pointed emphatically down at the marble-tiled hallway. "She probably walked *right here*!"

Todtman brought the group to a halt in front of a heavy wooden door. A little plaque beside it read ROOM III-B, DR. ALSHUFF. "This is it," he said.

He knocked three times with the rubber tip of his cane.

Puhnk! Puhnk! Puhnk!

"*Willkommen!*" a voice called through the door.

Clearly, they were expected.

What Ren had no way of knowing as they walked into the sunny, book-lined office was that the old professor within wasn't the only one expecting them.

IIII
IIII

A Fly on the Wall

Dr. Alshuff had had it rough.

The old academic stood and greeted them with a forced smile and a black eye. "It is good to see you again, my old friend," Alshuff said to Todtman, but he sounded more nervous than happy.

Alex stared at the ugly purple bruise on the loose skin around the old man's left eye. "And you!" said the doctor, turning and catching him looking. "You look just like —" Alex's ears perked up. He knew he didn't look much like his mom, and he had never seen so much as a picture of his father — but had this man? "Um, just like I imagined," Alshuff added after an awkward pause.

Alshuff extended his hand and Alex shook it. He'd trusted Safa immediately, almost despite himself, but trust was still in short supply in Alex's world. And he didn't trust this nervous, shifty-eyed guy at all. "What happened to your eye?" he said bluntly.

Alshuff immediately launched into an elaborate story involving a heavy book, a top shelf, and some dust. Alex couldn't help thinking about his cousin. During the time they'd spent together in London and Egypt, Luke had fooled Alex completely. Alex had fallen for his act, thinking they were allies — even friends — all while Luke was spying on him and Ren. But he wasn't so naive anymore. Alex's expression hardened. He was more alert now, more wary — and he was sure Alshuff's story was a lie.

Meanwhile, Alshuff had turned toward Ren. "And who is this?" he said.

"I'm Renata Duran," she said. "Is this school hard to get in to?"

The old professor released a dry, clucking laugh. "Not for an Amulet Keeper," he said, eyeing her ibis. Ren nodded, making a mental note.

Alshuff took a seat behind his big wooden desk and the others pulled out the three chairs arrayed in front of it. "So," he said. "How can I help you today?"

A smile formed above Todtman's sloping chin as he considered the man. Alex could tell he'd picked up their host's phony vibe, too, and he was glad. "As I mentioned on the phone," said Todtman, "we are looking for information about Maggie."

Alshuff shooed a fly away from his face with a wave of one sweaty palm. "Of course," he said. "And what is it you would like to know about her?"

"Ah," said Todtman. "That is the question. We are looking for anything that might help us understand where she is now, where she would go. We believe she's in Egypt, and we know she has history in Alexandria. Beyond that . . ." Todtman let his words trail off, but Alshuff was quick to offer his own.

"You are trying to find her," he offered. "And she does not want to be found."

"Exactly," said Todtman.

Alex looked from one man to the other. There was something going on between them, something extra being communicated in their looks. Alshuff swatted at the fly again, harder this time. Todtman watched him closely.

"Well," said Alshuff, leaning back in his chair, "as you know, Maggie was primarily interested in the Ptolemaic period, when the Greeks ruled Egypt."

He raised his voice as he said this, and Alex got the annoying impression that it was for his benefit. *He knew what the Ptolemaic period was!* It was funny, though: He didn't really remember his mom being particularly interested in it. She rarely even ventured over to the Greek section at the Met.

"You might want to take a closer look at some of the major Ptolemaic sites," Alshuff continued. "The Temple of Philae, perhaps. She would be quite at home in that area, I think."

Alshuff's voice was loud but shaky, dotted with little pauses as if making it up as he went along. His eyes were on the ceiling, his desk — anywhere but on the people he was talking to. Alex had heard enough of his lies. "But my mom never —" he began.

Alshuff cut him off immediately. "Well!" said the old professor, filling his voice with false confidence. "I wish I had more time to talk, but it is a busy day here, and we have a departmental meeting in a few minutes." He pushed his chair back and stood up. "One of our mummies was apparently burned to ashes downtown, and they will want to remind us again to lock our doors."

Todtman pushed back his own chair and stood. Alex and Ren followed suit. Alshuff came around the desk and put his hand on Alex's shoulder. Alex flinched. The gesture seemed friendly enough, but he was also gently but firmly guiding him toward the door. Alex looked up and saw Alshuff looking down at the scarab beneath his collar.

"It has been a very long time since I have seen the Returner," he said, his voice suddenly quite steady. *This*, thought Alex, *is what the man really sounds like*. "Your mother's most significant discovery. Until recently, of course."

Alex looked up at him. "You mean the Lost Spells?"

Alshuff gave him a look he couldn't interpret: Sad? Patient?

A buzzing grew in Alex's right ear, and he reached up and swatted at the fly. Missed it. They were almost to the door now.

"Oh, one more thing," said Alshuff, his voice soft and casual. "You might take a look at her dissertation. I doubt it will offer any more than I have already told you, but you might find it interesting. It should be in the main library, along with her notes. Tell them I sent you."

He took one last look at the scarab as the three guests filed out of the office. "With such an impressive pedigree," he said quietly to Alex, forcing a smile, "I wouldn't be surprised if you found a space already set aside for you in there." Then he turned to Todtman. *"Danke, Doktor."*

And with that, Alshuff swung the door shut.

Todtman stopped it with his good foot. "One more question," he said. "Do you still host the department's poker night?"

Alshuff gave a quick grin, this one somehow more genuine than the others. "Every Friday," he said. Todtman nodded and removed his foot, and Alshuff slammed the door for good.

The friends headed down the hallway toward the nearest exit. The fly, Alex couldn't help but notice, came with them.

"That dude was lying through his teeth," said Alex once they'd put some distance between themselves and Alshuff's office.

"Definitely shady," agreed Ren.

"And what was all that Ptolemaic stuff?" said Alex. "My mom was always going on about the Middle Kingdom, the Early Kingdom — the *Egypt* part of ancient Egypt. I mean, I seriously doubt the Lost Spells were written in Greek!"

Alex looked up to see if Todtman would weigh in on his "old friend," but the German seemed lost in thought. So

Alex pushed open the big exit door and squinted into the bright sunlight.

"And he was just so bad at it," continued Ren as they headed across a wide courtyard. "He was practically sweating bullets, wouldn't make eye contact. That guy is a horrible liar."

"But that's the thing," said Todtman, his cane thumping softly beside him as he walked. "He is a terrific liar."

"Uh, are we talking about the same guy?" said Alex.

"Yes," said Todtman. "I have lost many games of poker to that man. He is notorious. You can never tell what he is thinking. His expression never betrays him. He is well known for it in . . . certain circles."

"Wait," said Ren. "Is he a member of your, what do you call it, book club?"

"That is what *you* call it," Todtman pointed out. "We consider ourselves more of an international association of scholars."

Alex tried to wrap his brain around that. *How could that shifty old dude be a member of the same secret group as Todtman?*

His mom had been a member, too, but now she seemed to be playing a dangerous game all her own. He didn't know what the objective of that game was, but he knew that, just like in poker, deception was key.

"So, should we check out that temple he mentioned, or what?" said Alex, trying to figure out if this whole thing had been a waste of time.

"No," said Todtman. "You are right, he was lying about that. Maggie was never very interested in the Ptolemaic Dynasty — she doesn't even speak Greek."

"Do most Egyptologists speak Greek?" said Ren.

"The ones who are interested in that period do," said Todtman. "As they say in Athens, *Mía glóssa then íne poté arketí.*"

"Uh, sure," said Ren. "So, he was lying and, what? He wanted us to *know* he was lying? Why?"

"I don't think he was speaking entirely for our benefit," said Todtman.

Alex remembered the black eye. "Maybe The Order has already been here," he said. He remembered Alshuff's raised voice, practically shouting "Temple of Philae." "Maybe they still are. Maybe he thought they were listening in somehow."

Alex swung his head all around as they reached the edge of a large courtyard. *No one behind them.* Todtman led them down a narrow walk between two old redbrick buildings. "This way," he said.

"Where are we going?" said Alex.

"I think perhaps it was the other place he mentioned that we are meant to go," said Todtman.

"The one he mentioned *quietly*," added Ren.

Now Alex got it, too: "The one he said wasn't very important."

Todtman nodded: "Her old dissertation, in the library."

"Gah!" blurted Ren, slapping down hard on her neck. "This fly is driving me crazy!"

That thing is persistent, thought Alex. They turned the corner and he saw a large, six-story building rising into view. This place had *library* written all over it.

"Let's see what she was really studying — and, more importantly, where," said Todtman, eyeing the impressive structure. "Whatever is in these files represents her roots in this country — a paper trail of her first years here. But keep your eyes open and your amulets ready." And on that note, they entered the cool, hushed world of the central library. The swirl of air as the doors opened caused the persistent little fly to tumble end over end, and the doors closed before it could recover. It landed on the glass and peered in with its many-sectioned eyes. Then, finally, it buzzed off.

Shelf-ish Behavior

"Whoa, this place is huge," said Alex. "There are *miles* of books."

"It's so beautiful," said Ren.

Alex looked over and thought, not unkindly, *Nerd.*

A guard near the entrance looked at them skeptically and asked to see their university IDs.

"Dr. Alshuff sent us!" proclaimed Ren, standing on tiptoes so that more than her head was visible above the top of the man's tall desk.

But the guard's interest in their credentials had already vanished — the moment Todtman had wrapped his hand around his amulet. "We are visiting scholars," he said. That seemed true enough to Alex. He and Ren, for example, were in middle school. "And we are expected." That seemed true enough, too: Alex just hoped it wasn't by The Order.

"Of course," said the man, as if talking in his sleep.

They headed toward the information desk.

"I am a professor from Berlin," Todtman said to the young lady behind the desk. He left his amulet out of it this time, but made his normally faint accent almost comically thick. "I need to see the dissertation and notes of one of my colleagues."

The graduate student looked up at Todtman and then down at Alex and Ren. "Yes," she said. "Professor Alshuff told me to expect you. You are looking for an older file, I believe. Those files are in the archives now. Please follow me." She stood up. "My name is Hasnaa, by the way."

Hasnaa led them to the elevator bank and pressed DOWN. She moved with calm confidence, completely at home here. Like so many things, it reminded Alex of his mom. He wondered if she'd also worked in the library when she was studying here.

Everyone else was going up, so they were the only ones who got in when the door dinged open with the down arrow lit up above it. Hasnaa pulled out a key chain and flipped it around until she was holding a very small key. Alex had one just like it for the elevators at the Met. She put the key in its slot at the bottom of the panel, turned it, and then pressed the button that read BASEMENT ARCHIVES: STAFF ONLY.

It lit up in red and they began to descend.

"Uh, are there any other exits?" said Alex, not sure how much of the sinking feeling in his gut was coming from the elevator. "In case of, like" — *an Order ambush* — "a fire?"

Hasnaa gave him a curious look. "There are stairs, of course," she said. The elevator bumped to a stop and the doors slid open. Hasnaa stayed inside as the others got out.

"Here you are," she said. "But please, no fires."

⟻+++⟼

"It's not here," said Ren.

"Are you sure?" said Alex, leaning in to look over her shoulder.

"Now you're in my light," she protested. "But yes, I'm sure."

She'd been given the job of checking not because she was diligent and detail-oriented, although she was both, but because her small stature and nimble fingers were perfect for searching the overstuffed bottom shelf. She flipped through the files one more time to be sure: BATTAR, BATTEN . . . And then straight to BAVALAQUA.

"No *Bauer*," she confirmed. "But there is something odd . . ."

"What?" said Alex, leaning in and casting everything into shadow again.

Ren sighed deeply.

"Oh, right," said Alex, stepping back.

Ren eyed the little gap in the files. It seemed strange, considering how jammed the rest of these shelves were. Old, yellowing paper and dry manila folders spilled out like overgrown plants. She touched the gap with her finger. No dust. Then she reached in with both hands and pushed Batten's file away from Bavalaqua's. She peered into the space beyond. It was dark back there, so she raised her amulet, not to ask it questions or offer more inscrutable images but just for . . .

A flash of brilliant white light lit the space — and told Ren what she needed to know. Boxes of additional material were stacked behind the archaeology department dissertations. Notes, fieldwork, maybe the occasional bone fragment or piece of pottery . . . She wasn't sure, exactly, but she could see the spot where a large box had been plucked out like a bad tooth.

"The file's gone," she said. "Someone took it."

She stood up and brushed her dusty hands on her shorts. "I guess Alshuff told The Order first," said Ren. "And now they have it."

She looked over at Alex and Todtman. They both looked like they'd just been slapped. "I never thought Alshuff would betray us," muttered Todtman. "Even fearing for his life . . ."

"Betrayed," mumbled Alex. "But I thought . . ." He let his voice trail off, and then Ren saw him shake his head hard, like he did sometimes. "There's got to be something else. It really seemed like he was trying to tell us something."

"Yeah," said Ren. "He was telling us to go to the library — but the file is gone."

Alex looked down at the floor, "We must be missing something . . ."

Ren decided to ignore him this time. It was a dead end, and they needed to let it go. Determination without information just got them into trouble. But his hangdog expression bothered her — and now that she thought about it, Alshuff had said something else. She remembered, because the comment had made her slightly jealous.

"Well," she said, sighing, "he did say that weird thing about you having a spot down here someday."

Todtman stared at her.

"What?" she said.

"Not someday," he said. "*Now.*"

Ren searched her memory banks for the exact words: "He said, *I wouldn't be surprised if you found a space already set aside for you.*"

"Yeah," said Alex. "A spot set aside for me. That's what he wanted us to find. I knew it!"

Ren looked at him, goggle-eyed. "*You* knew it?"

Alex shrugged. "Okay, *you* knew it — but I suspected!"

A spot set aside for Alex Sennefer . . . Ren headed straight for the shelf that held the *S*'s. Unfortunately for her, it was the top shelf this time. *Maybe if I stand on my tiptoes* . . . Todtman brushed past. "I think perhaps I should handle this one," he said.

"Fine." She sighed. Everyone told her she was due for a growth spurt, and all she had to say to that was *WHEN?* She was getting pretty sick of coming up short.

She squinted up at the faded labels.

"I see a *B*!" whooped Todtman. "Yes, here it is!"

He reached in to pull out several thick folders.

"Hold this," he said, shoving them behind him.

Alex grabby-handed them away from Ren. "Let me see," he said.

Ren leaned in for a look of her own.

"You're in my light!" he chirped.

Meanwhile, Todtman was staring up at the top of the bookcase. The boxes of notes and supporting materials for the files on the upper shelves were piled on top of the case. Ren began to scan the names on the boxes: old black marker on old brown cardboard. "There!" she said, pointing.

And there it was, the name of the woman everyone was looking for, hidden in plain sight behind a simple veil of alphabetical misdirection.

"Prima!" exclaimed Todtman. *Awesome.*

A moment later, his hand closed around his falcon amulet, and the chunky old box floated free and drifted feather-like to the floor.

Pictures from the Past

They got to work immediately, hauling the box and files over to a little cluster of desks in the middle of the room. The lights hummed overhead and even the tall shelves seemed to lean in for a closer look as Alex carefully peeled back the dry old tape holding the top of the box shut. It came off with only the faintest whisper of protest.

Next to him, Todtman and Ren split the files containing the hefty dissertation and finished papers in half. That seemed like a good place to start for the two more academically minded members of the group. Alex was happy to do the dirty work.

He peered inside the old box and pawed through the top layer with his hands. In jumbled piles and half-spilled files, in ziplock baggies and Tupperware tubs lay his mother's fieldwork. There were notes and photos and bits of carved stone and pottery pulled from the Egyptian ground.

Alex wished he knew what he was looking for. Could she have come here? Snuck a note for him into the box? Or would he have to be on the lookout for something less obvious? He began pulling stuff out and arranging it on top of the nearest desk, trying to make some sense of the jumbled mess.

Unlike the neatly typed pages Todtman and Ren were poring over, the papers Alex found were often handwritten: notes and dates and circles and underlines. "BIG DISCOVERY!" was written in fat, dull pencil at the top of one page. The rest of the page was taken up with numbers — coordinates, maybe, or measurements? Alex wasn't sure, but he set that one aside, anyway.

He picked up the largest of the Tupperware containers and peered through the opaque plastic at the ancient pottery shards inside.

Alex's head swam as he went through the old material. He tried to focus and be rational instead of emotional. More than once he asked himself: *What would Ren do?* She was sitting just a few feet away, of course, but was far too absorbed power-skimming the old dissertation to talk.

He glanced over and saw the title page, set carefully aside on the top corner of Ren's desk: BURIED SECRETS: THE LOST — AND FORBIDDEN — ASPECTS OF MIDDLE KINGDOM FUNERARY RITES. *Now* that *sounded like his mom.*

But his attempts at an even-keeled approach capsized among the messy piles. Going through the materials in the box felt too personal for that. Even in grad school, his mom's distinctive handwriting had already taken shape. The precise, sharp-edged capital *A*'s Alex knew so well shared the page with little loop-de-loop *e*'s and the guesswork mystery of her nearly identical *g*'s and *q*'s.

Sometimes, it was thrilling. *Could this note on hotel stationery be a clue to his mom's current location? Or this unsent postcard from the temples at Abu Simbel?*

And all of it — all of it — felt dangerous. Pushing through these old papers and baggies of little clay statuettes and unlabeled, unexplained stone fragments felt risky, as if somewhere in all of it was a single poisoned pin . . . Because if they did find something that led them through the decades and straight to her, what then?

He'd had these thoughts before, but they felt closer now, more possible: His mom had always looked out for him, always done what was best — and necessary. If he needed to go to the doctor again, she took him. It didn't matter if he'd just gotten back or if he begged her to wait. She made the tough calls, and she'd always been right. *So what about now?*

You are trying to find her, Alshuff had said. *And she does not want to be found.* He was telling the truth then, too. It was hard to keep ignoring that fact while they were pawing through her old work. Still, as he zipped a plastic bag closed, he wished he could seal those thoughts up with it.

We need to find her, he told himself for the one-hundredth time. *We need to find the Spells.* The entire world depended on it — *She just doesn't realize how high the stakes are.* That had to be it.

Or maybe she knows exactly . . . He shook his head hard to dislodge the thought. This one was so sharp that it caused the contents of the folder he'd just picked up to spill out. Old photos went everywhere, some on his desk and some on the floor. The others looked over.

"Ooooh," said Ren. "Pictures."

Clearly tired of reading, she stood up and headed over. *How long had they been at this?* Alex wondered. He'd been so wrapped up in the process that he wasn't exactly sure. He looked down at the scattered snapshots along the desk's edge. And there she was, looking up at him, the woman who would become his mom. She looked so much younger: her cheeks fuller and her skin red from the sun, but it was unmistakably her.

It was like looking at pictures from a family vacation he hadn't been invited to. And then he saw a shot of her leaning over to inspect a hole in the ground. Even wearing a loose, untucked shirt, the bulge in her belly was clearly visible. *He'd been there after all.*

Ren reached over and grabbed the photo, along with a handful of others. "The dates are written on the back," she said. "We should put them back in order. Because *somebody* dropped them."

Time slipped by unnoticed down in the sunless, shadow-cornered archive. Once the box was empty, Alex stared down at the piles he'd made on the table. He'd hoped he'd see something that would jog his memory, some secret clue that only he would know. But there'd been no lightning bolts of recognition, no revelations. He'd ended up sorting the carefully labeled pages and pictures and pieces by place. He'd made big stacks for Alexandria, Cairo, Luxor, and the Valley of the Kings — places they had already been — and another pile for Abu Simbel to the south. Then there were smaller stacks: Edfu, Minyahur, Aswan.

Was his mom in one of these places? He'd heard her mention many of them — but then, she was an Egyptologist. Cairo came up all the time at work. She'd once brought him a King Tut T-shirt from the Valley of the Kings. Was that a clue, or just a T-shirt?

He looked down at the less-familiar piles. Aswan sounded familiar, and he was pretty sure he'd heard his mom mention Minyahur. He chased the memory but it sped away like an NYC taxi.

Todtman and Ren came over to see his work.

"Find anything?" said Ren.

"I'm not sure," he admitted, unable to keep the disappointment out of his voice.

"Ren," Todtman said. "Perhaps if you used the ibis? With all this information in front of us, it could carry us the last step."

Alex watched Ren's expression carefully, but she had a pretty good poker face herself. He hoped she could help, but he knew her amulet was tricky. It flashed fast-forwarded images into her mind. Sometimes they were clues, and sometimes they were warnings — and sometimes she couldn't tell the difference. Still, what choice did they have now?

"Okay," she said.

She took one last look at the piles. Then she took a deep breath, reached up for her amulet, and closed her eyes. A moment later, she gasped and opened them.

"What did you see?" Alex said.

She turned to him, blinking to refocus on the world around her. "Nothing," she said.

Alex frowned, annoyed. He knew Ren didn't like to be wrong, but if she wasn't sure, they could help her puzzle out the images. "Come on," he said. "You can tell us."

She looked him in the eyes. "No, really, there was nothing. I asked it which of these piles was right, and I just got, like, a *blank*."

"Has that ever happened before?" said Todtman.

Ren shook her head. "Never. Sometimes I don't understand what it shows me, but it has always shown me *something*."

Todtman nodded. "Maggie's location could be masked somehow, protected." He sized up the stacks of papers and pictures. "Okay," he said. "There will be no shortcuts. We need to go through everything again. We must ask ourselves: Where would she go, when everyone was looking for her? Where would she feel safest? Let's forget about the places we have already been for now and concentrate on what is new."

He leaned forward and pushed the large piles for Cairo, Alexandria, Luxor, and the Valley of the Kings farther back.

Alex looked at the remaining piles: Abu Simbel, Edfu, Minyahur, Aswan. He'd heard of the famous tombs at Abu Simbel and knew his mom had mentioned Edfu and Minyahur. A memory flashed by, yellow and gray, but he still couldn't pin it down. And why did Aswan sound so familiar? He reached for that stack, but Ren got it first. He sat down by the Minyahur pile instead, and began going through the pictures.

He picked up a photo of his mom sitting in the sand in front of a campfire with a big metal cup in her hand. It was early evening and a teakettle was set up above the fire. He looked at her face. She was relaxing after a long day. He lingered over it a little too long and Todtman leaned over to see what he'd found.

"It's nothing," said Alex, slightly embarrassed, "just a shot from camp."

Todtman looked more closely. "It's funny, I never saw your mother drink tea."

"Mostly she drank coffee," Alex said. "For the caffeine. She was so busy all the time. But every once in a while, she drank tea. There's this one old brand she likes. I forget the name, but it has a purple flower on the label. Sometimes . . . at home . . . she . . ."

He could barely get the words out. He was chasing that elusive memory: yellow and gray . . .

He was sick that day, and her arms were full . . .

Of what? When? Why?

He heard Ren rummaging through the papers, but he didn't dare look over. *He was so close . . .*

"Alex?" said Todtman.

"Sometimes she would drink it to relax at home." And as soon as Alex said "home," he remembered. *They'd been heading home.* He could see it clearly.

"I remember now," he said, and the others leaned in a little closer.

"Remember what?" said Todtman.

"It was a rainy day." His voice was far away, lost in the memory. "Mom left work early to take me to the doctor — again — and she'd brought a big stack of work home with her. We were waiting to cross Third Ave., and a taxi went by too close to the curb."

"Did you get splashed?" said Ren. "I hate that."

"Yeah, exactly," said Alex. "We got blasted with a big puddle of garbage-water, like the kind where you can see the oil floating on the surface."

"Nasty," said Ren.

"So nasty," said Alex. "And Mom got the worst of it. I remember looking over and seeing her just hugging the soaked files to her raincoat with a look on her face like *I give up.*"

"It sounds like a very bad day," said Todtman. "But I'm afraid I'm not following."

"Yeah," agreed Ren. "What's your point?"

"It's what she said next. It was kind of under her breath but I was listening so carefully that I heard it. She looked down at her stained coat and soaked files and said: 'Time to go to Minyahur.' Then we went home and she had a big mug of hot tea."

"Wait!" said Ren. "I saw something in the pictures."

She began pawing her way backward through the Minyahur pile, and then: "Here it is." She held up another snapshot of his mom. "Look at the label," she said triumphantly.

Alex looked at the picture. It was the same campsite, even the same teakettle, but his mom was standing now, holding up a small alabaster bowl. It must have been the team's prize discovery that day. But Alex wasn't looking at the bowl. He was staring at a small metal container by his mom's boots. It was a tin of loose tea, with a purple flower on its label.

"Let me see the photo," he said.

They all crowded around as he looked at it closely. He liked it because she was smiling. She was holding the bowl high, raised toward whoever was taking the picture.

"She looks happy," said Ren.

"She looks completely comfortable," said Alex. "Like she did at home sometimes."

Todtman eyed the empty expanse of desert behind the campsite. "It's a good location," he said. "Remote and hidden, but familiar to her."

Alex thought about it. When life in the city had gotten to her, when just for a moment it had all been too much, the place she wanted to go was a little desert village named Minyahur. It was her place to get away from it all. And was there any better phrase for what she was doing now, pursued by both enemies and friends?

Getting away from it all, thought Alex.

But not anymore.

A crazy mix of emotions bubbled and swirled inside Alex: excitement and anxiety and loyalty and loss. But the one that bubbled highest was love. "I think this is where we need to go," he said.

Ren turned to Todtman: "You said we were looking for the place she'd feel safest." She pointed to the photo. "This fits the description to a *tea*."

Todtman ignored the pun. "Yes," he said briskly. "Let's pack this up, and we can leave immediately."

Alex slipped the photo into his back pocket, and they began stuffing the material back into the box. Ren picked up the stack she'd been going through. "Aswan," she said. "Isn't that where the Temple of Dendur is from?"

"Oh yeah," said Alex. The huge, glass-walled room housing the old stone temple was his favorite place in the whole Metropolitan Museum of Art. "That's why that sounded so familiar." He allowed himself a quick smile. For just a fleeting moment, things seemed to make sense. But his smile faded as quickly as it had appeared.

"What is that *smell*?" said Ren. "I think a rat died down here or something."

She reached up and pinched her nostrils, then looked over at Alex for confirmation. His expression wasn't one of disgust, though. It was one of *fear*.

"That's no rat," he said. "I know that smell."

The same words echoed through the maze of shelves behind them. "That's no rat. I know that smell." The voice was an exact match for Alex's, save for a slight buzzing.

The friends wheeled around and saw a nightmare striding toward them. It wasn't the first fly that had followed them that day.

But it was the largest by a good six feet.

∩|

Pretty Fly for a Bad Guy

"I knew you were in this building somewhere." The fly spoke in his own voice this time. It was not an improvement. Scratchy and uneven, it made Alex's skin crawl. Actually, everything about the fly bugged him: the way his filthy robes clung heavily to his frame, as if greased; the way the small, strange mouth of his mask puckered and smacked, as if alive.

"Yeah, 'cause that old man told you!" called Ren, doing her best to disguise the fear in her voice. She quickly turned to Todtman and mouthed: *Not you.* But his attention was divided between the approaching enemy and the piled evidence.

The fly tilted his mask and considered Ren with its bulbous composite eyes. "The old man told me nothing but lies," said the fly, his jagged voice betraying a certain amusement. "A little birdy told me you were here."

He raised his right hand and extended his long, gnarled index finger. But it wasn't a little birdy that landed there; it was a buzzing black dot. The fly perched briefly on the hairy digit before buzzing off.

"That fly . . ." Ren began.

"Was a spy," finished Alex, his eyes beginning to water from the stink.

"You should never trust old men," added the fly, directing the comment toward Todtman.

The elder Amulet Keeper finally tore his attention from the piled papers and focused fully on the fly. Alex's stomach lurched as he realized the reason for Todtman's divided attention: If the fly went through those piles, he'd see they were sorted by place. They were all searching for the same person, and unlike the friends, The Order had the manpower to search all of those places at once. Alex glared at the masked operative. Not only was The Order standing in the way of where they needed to go, they were also a threat to get there first!

"It is not like you to dispense life lessons, Aff Neb," said Todtman, giving this horror a name. "Death is more your style."

Aff Neb's many eyes shimmered like water as they shifted focus. "True," he rasped. "Death tastes better . . . Let me show you."

Aff Neb's mouth puckered and smacked one more time — and then released a thick stream of greenish-brown vapor. The putrid plume billowed forth, filling the little clearing among the shelves.

"Don't breathe it in!" shouted Alex before slapping his hand over his mouth and nose.

"No kidding!" called Ren, her own eyes bugging out from the approaching grossness.

Just a few feet away now, it smelled more like a thousand sweaty feet. Alex held his breath and shifted his grip, dropping one hand to his amulet and pushing the other out in front of him.

The mystic wind rose up with merciful swiftness, ruffling books and papers all around — and pushing the stink cloud back where it came from.

"Guhh!" Alex gasped. He released the sour breath he'd been holding and gulped a fresh lungful that smelled like approaching rain.

Aff Neb seemed entirely at home in his own stink. "I see you have been hard at work down here," he said, eyeing the half-full box and remaining stacks of paper. "Tell me, what have you found?"

Alex tried to step between the thousand-eyed gaze and the table, but there were better ways to obstruct the view.

"Hey, fly guy!" called Ren.

Aff Neb's eyes shimmered as they shifted toward her. They had thousands of lenses — but no lids. Ren squeezed her ibis tightly.

FOOOP! A bright-white flash lit the dim basement.

"Grehh!" called the fly, his hands reaching up too late to cover his creepy peepers.

Alex caught some of the flash, too, but before the swirling spots even faded from his vision he was already at the table, dumping the remaining stacks into the old box with both hands. "Got it!" he said, slapping the top closed.

"Let's go!" called Todtman, and the three Amulet Keepers turned to run.

But as they did, Alex caught a glimpse of movement in the gaps in the bookshelves. In the narrow space between the tops of the old books and files and the shelves above them he saw cloth, arms, legs, a quick flash of metal — *guns!* "Uh, guys," he said as they rushed away from Aff Neb and into the nearest row of shelves.

"I see them," said Todtman.

"What are we going to do?" said Alex. Aff Neb had recovered and was in hot pursuit, and an ambush of Order gunmen awaited them among the rows.

"Get in the clear," said Todtman.

His words came out in a sad, almost wistful sigh, and suddenly Alex knew what he was planning. "Oh no," said Ren, figuring it out, too — and sharing Todtman's academic reservations.

The old scholar wasn't happy about it, but he didn't hesitate. He squeezed down hard on the falcon and grunted slightly with the effort. By the time they reached the narrow gap at the end of the first row, the heavy metal bookcases had already begun falling like dominoes.

Thousands of pounds of bound books and thick files tipped and toppled, and twice as much weight in metal shelves and stacked boxes came down, too.

"GAAARARB!" shrieked Aff Neb as the heavy case they'd just rushed past fell over on him, pinning him against the next case as it fell, too. On either side, Order thugs were squashed like Order bugs. Somewhere in the stacks, a pistol went off, the bang muffled as the bullet buried itself in some old book or other.

Standing in their tiny clearing amid a veritable paper apocalypse, Todtman and Ren cast horrified looks all around. Even Alex was stunned by how fast decades of neatly filed scholarship had been reduced to toppled chaos.

"That is going to take *forever* to re-alphabetize," moaned Ren.

But even as they surveyed the wreckage, their pursuers began to push free. An arm punched through a stack of books to the left, the sound of shifting, tearing paper was heard to the right, and then: *FOOM!* A stack of books was blown clear up to the ceiling by the telekinetic might of the fly mask.

"There!" said Todtman, pointing to a door along the wall. "The staircase."

Alex and Ren began picking their way over the fallen books and files and shelves. Ren made decent time hopping from one flat spot among the books and boxes to the next, but Alex was carrying a crumpled box of his own and couldn't quite manage the jumps. He hunted for level surfaces to place his feet.

"Hurry, hurry!" called Ren. "I see a gun!"

Alex turned to look. Sure enough, a hand pushed a black pistol through the piled paperwork. Alex used the scarab to send the weapon flipping end over end across the room, but he knew there would be more. They needed to get to the stairs fast, and if this shifting terrain was tough for him, how would Todtman ever manage on one good leg?

"Watch out!" Todtman called as he zoomed past.

Alex stumbled out of the way, then did a double take. Todtman had his hand on his amulet and a book under each foot. Alex couldn't believe it: He was using his amulet to ride the old books like skates, the flat surface of each one hovering a few inches above the scattered debris. He zipped toward the door like a bug skimming across the surface of a pond.

Alex spotted some big books in front of him and looked down at his own amulet. *No way*, he thought. Todtman had had decades to practice with his amulet. If Alex tried, it would be 3, 2, 1: face-plant! Instead, he and Ren hopped and stumbled and hustled across the last half shelf.

Todtman reached the heavy fire door to the stairwell first, and as soon as the other two arrived, he flung it open.

Alex's breath caught in his throat as he stared into the stairwell — and at the wall of guns directly inside.

A row of three tightly packed men stood in the doorway, and there were three more a few steps up, all pointing semiautomatic pistols directly at them. With two barrels pointed at his face, Alex knew that any move toward his amulet would mean death. Or maybe they would just shoot them all, anyway.

"What?" came a jagged voice behind them. "You didn't think we would cover the exits?"

Alex and the others slowly turned to face Aff Neb, the guns that had been pointed at their faces now jabbing into their exposed backs.

"I will take that box now," the fly said. His greasy robes were torn, and it seemed as if all eight thousand lenses in his eyes were brimming with annoyance. Other gunmen were rising from the scattered debris and filling in alongside their leader. Their bodies were battered, their guns were pointed, and they all seemed pretty eager to pull the trigger.

Alex knew better than to anger them now, and yet . . .

He glanced down at the box. It was because of him that the Death Walkers had been released, because of him that The Order's plans had been set in motion. Now he was being asked to hand over the keys to victory, as well.

"Here you go," he said, pulling the heavy cardboard cube out from under his arm and extending it forward.

"Alex!" hissed Ren.

"You mustn't," said Todtman.

He wouldn't. No matter the cost.

As Aff Neb took a step forward, Alex continued the motion, using all his strength to toss the box up toward the ceiling.

"Catch it!" cried Aff Neb.

But as all eyes followed the modest flight of the box, Alex quickly grasped his amulet, thrust out his free hand, and absolutely obliterated the thing with a concentrated spear of whipping wind. The old cardboard was torn to shreds, and the last thing Alex saw was a shower of paper and pictures and pottery scattering through the air and drifting down toward the waiting chaos all around. Toward a floor full of books and paper and pictures and pottery from all the *other* fallen files and boxes.

That ought to keep 'em busy, he thought.

Then the butt of a pistol smashed down on the back of his head and his whole world went dark.

∩II

Into the Pit

Alex woke slowly. There was a dull pain on the back of his head and the feel of stone beneath him and something gritty on his face and neck. He reached around to touch the sore spot. As soon as his finger pressed into the tender, swollen bump, he remembered how he'd gotten it.

His eyes opened wide, only to be flooded by harsh light. He forced himself to sit up, and scanned the space above him for Aff Neb or his gunmen. But all he saw were the gently curved walls of a deep round pit and, far above that, a clear blue desert sky.

Where was he? Why —

"Good morning, Alex," he heard. "Or should I say, good afternoon."

Todtman. As Alex turned toward his voice, he was surprised to feel the scarab shift against his chest. *Aff Neb hadn't taken it?*

Todtman was sitting up against the sheer wall of the pit, looking a little worse for wear, his familiar suit jacket and cane nowhere in sight. Ren was seated next to him. Alex felt his tensed muscles relax ever so slightly. He let out a long breath and pulled another back in. "I'm glad you're both okay," he said.

"Are we?" said Ren. "I doubt it. I'm glad you're awake or conscious, or whatever — but it's not like we can go anywhere." She gestured up at the pit.

Alex took a quick look around. The pit had to be forty feet deep and at least as far across, the walls ranging from light tan to bone white. *Limestone*, he thought. *Just like in the Valley of the Kings.* The air was warm, and he reached up and brushed a sprinkling of sweat-stuck sand from his face and neck.

"We're in the desert," he said.

"Yes," said Todtman, wincing as he rose to his feet. "Somewhere in the central desert, if I had to guess. It wasn't an especially long flight."

Flight? thought Alex. He must have been *really* out of it.

"Did they . . . hurt you?" he asked. It was a dumb question. He could already see a cut above Todtman's left eye and a swollen bump under his right. He'd been roughed up. He quickly glanced over at Ren, relieved to see no visible injuries.

"I may have resisted a little," admitted Todtman, taking a few short steps. Without his walking stick, he limped noticeably on the leg that had been crippled by a scorpion sting during their pursuit of the first Death Walker. He began to slowly move across the pit. Ren popped up beside him. Her ibis and Todtman's falcon were in plain view at their necks. Alex groaned as he climbed to his feet to join them.

"Why didn't they just finish us off back in Alexandria?" he said. They were approaching a new stretch of the pit's gently curved wall, following Todtman's slow progress. Alex had no idea where they were headed. There was no visible means of entrance or exit, no doorway or ladder or rope.

"Yes, that does seem odd," admitted Todtman, coming to a stop. "They may be curious about what we know."

An ice-cold wave washed through Alex. *Minyahur.* "We can't say anything!" he said urgently.

"We may not have a choice," said Todtman, and the ice-cold wave doubled back. Torture. Magic. What lengths would The Order go to? He resolved then and there that they could do what they wanted to him. As much suffering as he had caused, the least he could do was endure some. Besides, he had a lifetime of practice with pain. But it wasn't himself he was worried about. He looked over at Ren.

"But it may not come to that," continued Todtman. He lifted his sloping froglike chin toward a scattering of symbols cut into the wall. The shallow marks were nearly invisible in the light stone.

"Why aren't those cut deeper?" said Alex.

"They were," said Todtman. "But they've worn down through the ages. These symbols are very old — even by Egyptian standards."

"Old Kingdom?" said Alex.

"Indeed," said Todtman. "Close to five thousand years old, if I had to guess."

Instinctively, Alex and Ren closed their hands around their amulets. Only a moment later, they released them.

"That's weird," said Ren. "Normally, the ibis lets me read hieroglyphs."

Todtman nodded. "As I said, they are very old. Precursors to the hieroglyphs we know today. But I think I can puzzle out a few. Here" — he pointed to the stacked symbols before them and then to another cluster a few yards away — "and there."

"What do they say?" said Ren.

Todtman ran a finger along the shallow groove of the nearest symbol, pursing his lips and taking one last look before delivering his verdict.

"It seems fairly clear to me," he said, "that they brought us here to be . . ." He pointed at the last symbol in the bottom row. "Do you see that one? Very similar to a common hieroglyph found in nearly every Middle Kingdom tomb."

"Death?" guessed Alex. "Burial?"

"Close," said Todtman. "A sacrifice, an offering."

Alex stared grimly at the symbol, his head reeling with the realization. He felt, for a moment, like he might black out again. It might have spared him some suffering if he had, because he now understood why they'd been left with their amulets. In ancient Egypt, all sort of things were sacrificed to appease the spirits and please the gods: Everything from animals as large as oxen to treasures of incalculable value.

He looked down at his scarab. The amulets were the priceless treasure.

Then he looked up at his friends, the small, huddled group of three.

And they were the animals.

∩ III

Their Vile Host

"We must get out of here," said Todtman, peering up at the sky above. "And if we can, they have already taken us almost halfway to our destination."

Alex looked around, trying to calm his racing pulse. They were in deep trouble — literally — but Todtman's presence gave him some extra confidence. They needed to concentrate on escape. But they needed to be smart about it. He remembered the spying fly at the university, and knew that this pit could be bugged in other ways, as well. "So *that place* is close?" he said.

Todtman nodded. "It is in the southern desert."

"Yeah, *if* we can get out," said Ren. "And if we can't, we're toast. Sacrificial toast."

Alex scanned the walls. "There must be a way out somewhere."

"There is an opening," said Todtman. "Three meters up, behind us."

"Yeah," confirmed Ren. "They dropped us out of, like, a door. We had to *catch* you. But I can't find it now."

Alex eyed the stone nine feet up. "I don't see one, either," he said.

"You are not meant to," said Todtman. Where he stood, the shadow from the pit's edge fell across him so that his chest and head were sunlit and everything below that bathed in gray. As Alex watched, the line of shade shifted and grew. There was something moving along the pit's edge!

Alex spun around.

"Mmuh-rack?" The strangely familiar sound echoed clearly through the pit below.

Alex exhaled. It was Ren's undead BFF, the mysterious mummy cat she'd freed from a shattered museum case in London. They'd last seen her in the Valley of the Kings, which, Alex suddenly realized, probably wasn't too far from here.

"Pai!" called Ren, and immediately regretted it. Even forty feet below, they could see the mummy cat gather her haunches underneath herself and prepare to jump. "Don't! Pai! No!" called Ren, but it was too late. The formerly frisky feline had already taken the leap. She whistled down the open air of the pit, legs slightly spread, ancient wrappings rustling.

Ren started forward, like an outfielder approaching a fly ball, but she didn't get there in time. She winced as Pai hit the ground in front of her.

FFLONNK!

Pai flattened out, spread-eagle, on impact. But by the time Ren reached her, the ex-cat was standing in the middle of the small cloud of sand and dust she'd kicked up, licking one bony front paw. "Mmm-rack!" she said as Ren scooped her up.

Alex leaned over to Todtman. "I guess cats really do land on their feet — even undead ones."

Five feet away, Ren took one of Pai's raggedly wrapped front legs in her hand and waved it back at them. "Pai says hi," she said, her fear making her goofy.

The mummy cat immediately leapt from her arms. Pai-en-Inmar, sacred servant of the cat-headed goddess Bastet, had her pride.

Todtman watched the little exchange grimly. "Tell me," he said. "Have you seen this cat out in the daylight before?"

Alex thought about it. "Not usually," he said. "We saw her at, like, sunset once, though. With King Tut."

Todtman's eyebrows lifted at the mention of the boy king. Alex saw it and added: "He was a pretty cool guy. Tough, too — wish he was here to help us now."

"I don't like it," said Todtman.

"Don't like what?" said Ren, who had followed Pai back into their general vicinity.

"Any of it," said Todtman. "A simple mummy was one thing, and the ghostly voices in Cairo had no form. But Pai is a powerful and sacred creature. She used to visit this world only in the dead of night; now she walks in broad daylight. The two of you traveled into the afterlife, and something followed you *out*. Each Death Walker we encounter is more powerful than the last. And Tutankhamun, a pharaoh, a living god, was among us . . ."

"Okay, but what does that —" Ren began.

"The Final Kingdom," said Todtman in a hushed tone.

Alex, who had been scanning the pit wall for the hidden door or any other sign of weakness, choked on his own breath. He'd heard the same words on the sun-parched lips of the last Death Walker.

"Wait, what?" said Ren. "Seriously, what?"

Alex explained. He knew his friend hated not being in the know. "It's, like, when the world of the living and the world of the dead join, when the barriers between them open, and . . ." He turned to Todtman. It had been years since his mom had told him the story. "What's the rest?"

Todtman looked down at the mummy cat, sunlight lighting her back. "And life and death wash together like the waters of the Nile."

"So, wait, that's what this is all about?" said Ren, a quick study. "The Spells and The Order and the Death Walkers — and Pai?"

"Mmm-rackk?"

"I think so," said Todtman. The old German's tone remained distant and flat as he spoke, a retreat from his own fear into rationality. "The Spells opened a doorway between the world of the living and the world of the dead. It was a breach, a jailbreak. The Death Walkers were waiting, and they escaped. But now the walls are crumbling, too. The borders are opening. If they do, the worlds will merge and the living and the dead will exist side by side. One kingdom, and one in which The Order and their Walker allies would be unstoppable."

Alex stared down at the hard, sand-dusted floor. His growing guilt dug in with sharp fingers. He kept his eyes down in case the others were looking at him. *That breach had been caused for him, to let him back through . . .* He felt the sudden overwhelming urge to do something — anything! — to try to repair the damage. *If we could just get to Minyahur,* he thought. "Okay, I am not going to die in this pit," he said, desperate for forward motion. "Maybe we can open the hidden door with our amulets . . . Maybe if I stood on your shoulders . . ."

Todtman nodded. "Possibly. It is what is behind the door that worries me, but . . ."

But above them, the doorway was already opening.

The friends turned toward the grating sound of stone sliding along stone. The doorway swung inward, finally revealing its carefully hidden edges. Disliking the sound, Pai crept away into the shadow cast by the near wall. Alex, on the other hand, eyed the dark opening hungrily. A moment later it was filled by a looming figure.

The man stepped forward, so tall and broad-shouldered that his thick black robes seemed to fill the entire frame. He regarded them through the eyes of a golden mask.

"Another operative," whispered Alex, his eyes transfixed by the pockmarked realism of the mask's golden skin and the iron beak that curved down into a brutal point.

"No," whispered Todtman. "That is their leader."

Alex finally placed the image on the mask. It was an Egyptian vulture, a species that was both fearsome predator and opportunistic scavenger. This man was the leader of the ancient death cult that had hounded them across three continents. And now, he spoke.

"You have come a long way," he said. "You have troubled me more than you know. Weighed on my thoughts."

The vulture mask had two small eyeholes, and Alex caught a subtle glimmer in the darkness behind them, a flash of white and reflected light. The man's words could apply to any of them, but his eyes were fixed on Alex.

"I should have killed you already, but even now, I am tempted to offer you a deal. Tell me what you know in exchange for your little lives . . ." Alex still felt as if this man was talking directly to him, but a beat later his gaze shifted to take in the others. Looking for takers, he found none — and then he withdrew the offer. "But you would lie to me. I would torture you and stare into your souls — but still you would lie. You Keepers, you act like such heroes, and yet you lie so well . . . It makes me wonder how different we really are."

But he didn't wonder for long. He turned back toward Alex and continued: "I am sorry. But it is over. Soon, we will piece together what you found in that library." Alex glared angrily up at the man. "Your part is done, your struggle is over, but die knowing two things. First, you serve a noble purpose. Your sacrifice will win us the favor, and more control, of a powerful ally. And second, death, as I am sure you understand by now, is only the start of your journey."

Alex caught a glimpse of heavy leather boots, just visible beneath the hem of the leader's robes. His feet were mere inches from the edge of the doorway. Alex's amulet had thrown a man across a room before. How hard would one good tug be? But as he began slowly sliding his hand up toward the scarab, his fingers began to twitch and spasm. He had lost control of his own hand, and a moment later it jerked back down to his side in one convulsive movement.

"Ah, Alex — Alex Sennefer — I do appreciate the fight. I do. But I assure you, I am in control here." The leader's gaze shifted between Alex and Todtman. Alex's eyes followed, and he saw that Todtman's hands were also twitching slightly at his sides.

The German tried reason instead. "It is a dangerous game you play," he said. "In your rush for power, you are unleashing forces that you can't possibly —"

"Oh, but it is not a game at all," said the leader. "It is deadly serious. And you should know better than to underestimate me." He paused, though Alex couldn't say if it was to savor the moment or mourn it. Either way, the leader ended with a flourish: "Enjoy the other side."

He took one last look at Alex and spun around. The hems of his robes whirled. Alex and Todtman reached for their amulets, but it was too late. Two quick steps had carried the leader back into darkness, and he was gone. Stone ground against stone as the door began to slide closed.

"Stop it!" called Todtman. "Keep it open!"

Alex grasped his scarab hard with his left hand and pushed his right palm straight out at the closing door, directing all the amulet's force against it. Todtman did the same. The door slowed briefly and then . . .

KHHRUUNNK!

It slammed shut.

"No," gasped Ren as the noise echoed through the pit.

"He is not staying to watch, to take credit," said Todtman, his tone shaken and uneasy. "Whatever is coming scares even him." He turned toward Ren. "You must use the ibis. We must know what we are facing."

Alex was ready to jump in if she needed more convincing, but Ren just nodded. Alex watched her carefully as she took hold of the pale white bird. She'd drawn a blank last time — literally. Would this time be any different? Her eyes closed briefly, and when they opened again, Alex could see the fear in them.

"What is it?" said Todtman.

Alex had a pretty good idea what she was going to say, but he held his breath, hoping he was wrong.

"Death Walker," she breathed.

"Oh no," said Alex. They all understood the danger. The Walkers were powerful ancient entities. Knowing they would fail the weighing of the heart ceremony to gain entrance into the afterlife, they had clung to its edges by sheer force of will, waiting for their opportunity to escape. The only way to defeat one was by using the scarab's power and the right spell from the Book of the Dead — the spell that connected with what the Walker had been in life. But none of that mattered now. They didn't have a copy of the Book of the Dead, not even a single spell, much less all two hundred.

"Did you see anything we can use against it?" whispered Todtman. "Any way to escape?"

Ren shook her head. "It's too late," she whispered. "It's coming." She pointed at the limestone wall to her left, taking a trembling step back as she did.

Alex peered at the pale stone. There was nothing there, and for once, he hoped his best friend was wrong.

She wasn't.

The wall itself — the ancient, weathered stone — began to shift, to push outward.

A shape began to emerge.

Stone Meeting Bone

Ren watched in horror as the flat stone of the wall began to bulge outward into a bubble of pale stone about six feet up. She didn't realize it was a face until the sunken eyeholes took shape and the neck began to push outward underneath it. Then came the shoulders, then the chest.

The head pulled free of the wall with a wet tearing noise that sounded more like meat than stone. The rest of the body dragged itself free of the wall, leaving no indentation, no indication whatsoever that a section of stone the size and shape of a ragged human body had been removed.

Its steps were stiff and uneven. Chunks of stone flaked off and fell to the ground with each bend and flex. The creature stopped, crossed its stony arms in front of it, and pointed its featureless visage toward the sky above.

There was a soft cracking sound.

"Turn away!" called Todtman, covering his face with his hands and turning his back on the macabre spectacle. As he turned, his bad leg gave out and he crumpled to the ground.

Ren rushed over to help, but as she did, there was a muffled crash — like thunder heard from under a blanket — and rock exploded outward from the Walker. Limestone dust turned the entire pit white, and here and there Ren felt the sting of larger chunks against her skin.

She heard Alex cry out but could see nothing. Her eyes stung from the powdered stone, and when she tried to call Alex's name, thick white dust filled her mouth. She convulsed into hacking coughs and covered her face.

As the heavy dust settled to the ground, she risked a peek back. The Walker's true form was revealed. It looked like death itself: a ragged mummy — or most of it, anyway. The wrapping was mostly torn away, and some pieces of the body were missing. A few of the fingers were just gone, but the larger gaps had been filled in with clay and pale stone. Half its skull was clay, much of its torso was stone, and none of it quite fit or matched. For eyes, it had two white stones.

And yet it moved. And yet, somehow, it lived. It took a step forward and drew in a long, rasping breath. In the warm desert air of the pit, Ren went cold to the tips of her toes. As the Walker's chest expanded, a few remaining sections of rib rose beneath the shabby wrapping. Even the limestone that made up the rest of its chest seemed to flex and breathe.

Ren, on the other hand, felt as if a horse was sitting on her chest. Fear constricted her breathing. The other Walkers had looked scary, sure, but they'd also looked alive. They'd come back, and they had the skin and clothing to prove it — even if that skin was sometimes burned or swollen.

Todtman spoke softly, his voice colored by both awe and fear: "This Death Walker is older than the others, beyond ancient. Made when the mummification process was still crude. And whatever he was buried in must have given out. This one's been in the ground. Its body has calcified."

Ren eyed the vein of living limestone in its chest — stone meeting bone — and felt the same sense of unreality she always did when confronted with the brazen illogic of magic. It felt like floating free from the world she knew, with nothing to grab on to, nothing to stop her from floating away so far that she'd never find her way back.

And as the creature took another step forward and Ren took another step back, she realized that it might be true this time. She might never get back to the world she knew: *home.*

Here, at the end, the homesickness that had grown inside her since she left New York became a razor-sharp ache. She'd never sit in the Met again, staring at her beloved Rembrandts and knowing her dad was somewhere nearby. Knowing that she could go ask him for ice cream money or just hang out and watch him work. She realized she'd never have another "girls' day" with her mom, going to Serendipity and getting "drippity" sundaes.

"Marr fesst dol!" croaked the Walker, snapping Ren back to the overheated reality of the pit. Like the others, Ren already had her hand around her amulet. Normally, that allowed them to understand the ancient Egyptian of their adversaries. Not now.

"Can you understand it?" she asked.

"A lost tongue," said Todtman.

Ren peered into the creature's open mouth as it spat out more inscrutable syllables and saw that its real tongue was lost, too, replaced by a thick slab of clay. The thing flicked and curled with the liveliness of a fat brown toad. Ren wanted to vomit.

The Walker took another step forward; the friends took another step back — only to find their backs were nearly to the wall. Soon they would find out what terrible, deadly power this Walker possessed. Unless . . . Her mind flashed back to midnight in Vienna. If that shadow creature had been out of place in this world, well, then this earthenware weirdo definitely was.

"Stand back!" she said to her friends. "Cover your eyes!"

She squeezed the ibis tight in her left hand and called on its power once more. She thrust out her right hand. There was a quick white flash and then . . . nothing. What had seemed so mighty at night amounted to little more than a camera flash in the daylight flooding the pit. The Walker flinched slightly.

And then it attacked.

The Walker rushed forward, its stone-patched legs moving with surprising fluidity. "Split up!" called Ren.

Alex turned to run — and couldn't! He stared down, incredulous. The floor of the pit was solid stone, but he felt his feet sinking down into it as if it were mud. He watched in terror as the stone reached the laces of his boots. He could hear the creature's footsteps heading toward him, and he tried desperately to lift first one leg and then the other. Nothing. He could only squirm as his feet sank farther.

He saw Ren struggling, too. Her head and shoulders turned to rush along the wall, but her lower half refused to follow.

Only Todtman had managed to stay a step ahead. A vine of stone rose up and grabbed the heel of one of his black dress shoes, but with one hand on his amulet, he swept the other downward, shattering the stone shackle.

Alex followed his example, squeezing the scarab hard and then forming his other hand into a fist and smashing it down directly over each foot in a quick one-two. He felt like he'd just dropped a bowling ball on each foot, but he heard two muffled cracks and quickly pulled his feet up through the powdered stone.

He turned and saw that the Walker was just a few yards from Ren now, already stretching out one bony three-fingered hand. Stuck in the floor, all she could do was stare at the approaching horror with eyes gone round with fear.

"No," Alex breathed. He felt a sudden, achingly sharp sense of responsibility for his friend's safety. She had followed him halfway around the world, through one peril after another, and he could not let anything happen to her now. He rushed toward both of them.

"Hey, stone-face," he shouted desperately at the creature. It turned and regarded this new threat with pale eyes. Alex battled back his fear and squeezed his amulet hard, but before he could use it, a slab of stone shot out from the back wall of the pit, like a dresser drawer opening outward. It cracked Alex hard in the side and slammed him to the ground.

He landed with a loud "Ooouff!"

He rolled over and scrambled to his feet. The stone grabbed at him the whole time, but by moving fast, he was able to stay out of its rough grip —

The Walker's shadow fell over him.

Alex stumbled back and to the side to create some space. Left hand on his amulet, Alex pointed the fingers of his right hand into a spear and lashed out at the Walker with a whipping, whistling column of super-charged wind. *If this creature is really of the earth*, thought Alex, *let's see how it handles some erosion!*

Bits of clay and chunks of stone chipped and slipped off. Another finger sheared off the Walker's right hand and went flying end over end out of sight. The ancient menace roared into the unrelenting gale and stumbled backward a few steps. Alex narrowed his eyes, tightened his fingers, and stretched his arm out farther. His head pounding, his body aching from the force channeled through it, he willed the wind to increase.

He stared directly into the two white stones pressed into the clay-patched front of the Walker's skull and saw the evil there. What he did not see, until it was too late, was the creature raising a now two-fingered hand, palm down, and slamming it hard toward the ground.

The pit floor pulsed like the skin of a bongo drum. The force was so strong Alex could feel it in his teeth, and he found himself tossed two feet into the air. He crashed down on his back and smacked the tender bump on the back of his head. Looking up, he saw stars spiraling in the blue sky above.

A moment later, his head cleared.

It was a moment too long. He desperately tried to sit up, to take hold of his amulet again — but he was pulling against stone. The pit floor had already encircled him with its tendrils, and now he felt himself sinking back into it. Legs, arms, pinned.

He was helpless.

Todtman, however, was still free and using his amulet to fight back. A lance of invisible force carved into the creature, blowing a clean, round hole in its torso. Alex's hopes rose, even as his body sank. He heard Ren let out a triumphant "Yes!"

But the Walker didn't so much as look down, and as its next step touched the pit floor, Alex saw limestone flowing like liquid up the creature — from foot to leg to body — filling in the hole. "Oh no," whispered Alex, his arms and legs now fully encased in stone and only his chest, neck, and head still above it.

Todtman steeled himself for another attack, his eyes wide, seeking out the next threat. Would it come from below? Behind?

Above.

A chunk of stone no bigger than a baseball broke off the top edge of the pit. There was a faint whistling sound, Todtman looked up, and . . .

KLONK!

The stone hit him smack in the forehead, and he hit the ground like a sack of potatoes. The pit floor immediately encircled and immobilized him.

Alex's heart sank. He had failed both his friends, and he knew what came next. Death Walkers fed on the souls of the living — and they were messy eaters. The earthen entity surveyed its three trapped foes. It watched them struggle uselessly against the pit's stony grip, like a finicky diner perusing a menu, deciding what to eat first.

A flash of white light made up its mind. "No, Ren!" called Alex, but it was too late. The Walker headed directly for her, closing the distance in long, hungry strides. She released another blast of white light. It was weaker this time, and had even less effect. But then —

"Mmmm-rack?"

Pai stepped into view, brushing past Ren's sunken legs and sitting down directly between Ren and the Walker.

Alex had forgotten all about Pai. It was easy to do with an enchanted feline who had a habit of vanishing abruptly. But at the moment, Pai wasn't going anywhere.

"Mmm-RACK!" she repeated, not as a question this time.

The mummy cat's vocabulary might not stretch much past one word, but her meaning seemed clear enough: *Over my long-dead body.*

The Walker looked down and opened its mouth. It took Alex a few moments to recognize the hoarse rasp that came out as a laugh.

"No, Pai," Ren said softly. "Go."

Alex saw the tears in his best friend's eyes and felt guilt stab into him again. Others had died on this quest, but he didn't think he could take it if she did. She was only here to help him, and now . . . He struggled as hard as he could against the stone all around him, jerking one way and then the other. The stone didn't even hint at budging.

"Get out of there, Ren!" called Todtman from his own confinement. "Try to free one foot at a time!"

But the stone was up past Ren's ankles now and neither foot would budge. Her last line of defense was an undead temple cat — which the Walker now casually flicked aside. He waved his hand and a two-foot-tall wave rose in the stone floor, heading straight for Pai, moving fast.

The mummy cat hissed and raised one bony paw, but the stony wave overwhelmed her. Her small body was carried off and — *SSPLACKK!* — smashed hard into the back wall of the pit. As the stone sank back into the ground, Pai wobbled upright, but she barely had time to look up before the next strike. A ten-foot-tall stone column crashed down on her with enough power to crush a car. As it receded, her little body lay motionless along the wall, bent in ways it should not have been.

"Noooo!" cried Ren.

And then everything changed.

In the middle of a cloudless day, a strange darkness fell over the pit.

Violence Itself

The darkness lifted a moment later, revealing a woman with the head of a cat. She stood in the center of the pit, considering her surroundings. Everything was quiet and still. The Walker stood perplexed, its crude mouth hanging open. Even the light wind that had played on the warm air of the pit had stopped. The world itself seemed to be holding its breath.

"Shhhhh!" hissed Todtman, before adding in a rushed and barely audible whisper: "Do not move, do not provoke her."

Not moving, Alex could manage. Still lying on his back, sunk up to his neck in stone, he really didn't have a choice. But he could not take his eyes off this . . . this *what?* She had the body of a woman, clothed in a long, sleek gown, but her head was that of a giant cat — the shape of a Siamese but the size of a lioness. The soft fur rippled as the wind picked up again. She began to walk, and as she did, the colors of her clothing shifted, red bleeding seamlessly to blue flowing easily to green. A new color for each graceful step. Alex held his breath as she passed close by. Her floor-length gown brushed the ground with a soft, velvety swoosh.

He craned his head as far as his stone-stuck neck would let him. She was heading toward Pai's motionless body. And just like that, he knew.

Bastet.

The cat-headed goddess had been Alex's mom's favorite. He ran through everything he knew about her: a powerful goddess, revered by the ancient Egyptians as a protector of both the pharaoh and the people.

And he remembered the little information plaque they'd salvaged from Pai's wrecked case in London: PAI-EN-INMAR . . . FROM THE TEMPLE OF BASTET . . . Cats were considered sacred in ancient Egypt because of their association with Bastet. And temple cats like Pai were the most sacred of all.

Bastet glided ever closer to her fallen servant.

To harm any cat was considered bad luck, thought Alex.

The goddess stood over Pai's twisted frame.

To harm a temple cat, well, that was just dumb . . .

Bastet bent down.

The Walker moved. Perhaps he had seen enough or perhaps he considered the cat's remains to be his now, part of his sacrificial offering. Perhaps he simply wanted a closer look. Whatever the reason, he took a step directly toward Pai — toward Bastet.

And it's never a good idea to challenge a goddess.

Her head turned and the slits of her cat eyes narrowed.

And she *changed*.

What had once been elegant and beautiful became fearsome. Her cat head was consumed by flames — red, then orange, then blue. Under the flames, Alex saw the shadow of her face, not a cat's now but a lioness's. Alex held his breath. Bastet was revered in ancient Egypt, but feared, too, and this was why. This was her other half. In her anger, she had taken on her predatory aspect. Standing before them now was her sister goddess . . .

Sekhmet.

The Destroyer.

Violence itself.

"Look away from her!" called Todtman.

Alex did as he was told. He looked instead toward the doomed Walker, who began to burn. The flames started at the edge of his ragged frame, and he writhed as they rushed inward, consuming him. Suddenly, his flaming body flew backward across the pit. He hit the far wall at incredible speed, like a missile.

FWOOOOM!

Alex felt the impact through the stone surrounding him and closed his eyes against the advancing wall of pulverized stone.

Quiet moments passed and the dust settled.

"She is gone," breathed Todtman at last.

Alex opened his eyes and turned to look, surprised to find his neck no longer encased in stone but rather surrounded by powder. Slowly, he leaned forward and sat up. The powdered stone fell away, and he stood up, his limbs stiff but free. Todtman did the same, though the process was a bit harder on his old bones. Ren merely pulled her two feet free as if stepping out of a pair of stony slippers.

They all looked to the spot where Pai had been. The mummy cat was gone, and so was the one she served.

"Pai was just protecting me," said Ren, her voice both sad and unsure. "Do you think she's . . . dead?"

"She always was," said Todtman with characteristic bluntness.

Ren glared at Todtman, and then did a quick double take in that direction. "A way out!"

Alex followed her eyes. Now that the dust had settled, he saw a huge hole blown into the far wall. Behind it was a dark hollow space. "Sekhmet blasted the Death Walker right through the wall," said Alex, shaking his head. "That dude seriously picked the wrong cat to pick on."

"Pai saved us," said Ren.

Alex felt another quick stab of guilt: *Pai had saved them when he had failed, and it had cost her everything.* He felt the new burden settle atop all the others, and all he managed to say was a halfhearted "Yeah."

"No!" said Ren, insisting on it. "She. Saved. Us."

"Yes," said Todtman. "She sacrificed herself. She was noble — now let's get out of here!"

Todtman took four steps forward, two of them limps, but by his fifth step, Ren was under one arm, supporting him. By the sixth, Alex was under the other. They hurried through the gaping hole in the pit wall. There was no sign of the Walker, not so much as a rib or pale stone eye.

"You remember how you said that without the Lost Spells the Walkers might be able to come back again?" said Alex.

"Yes," said Todtman.

Alex took one more look around as they stepped through the smashed wall. "Well, I don't think this one is coming back."

Todtman smiled, but only briefly. As they stepped into the shadows, the finished floor and right angles told them this was not just a hole blasted into the rock. This was a room, and that meant this whole place was an underground stronghold.

"We must find a way out quickly," said Todtman. "The leader is here and possibly others — a small army of men and guns, at the least. This is not a fight we want right now."

Alex's mind flashed to the rogues' gallery of masked Order operatives they'd faced so far. But as they rushed across the room, it turned out it was the men and guns they had to deal with first. There were two of them, wearing the unmarked khaki uniforms The Order favored.

As the guards saw them, their eyes widened and their hands went to the pistols at their belts. But Alex's hand was already on his scarab, and Todtman's on his falcon. A wicked wind shear shot from Alex's right hand. And his target was no ancient evil this time — this dude was maybe twenty-four. The wind slammed him backward into the wall, and he slowly slid down it, stunned and gasping.

Todtman took a different approach. The jeweled eyes of the falcon glowed softly, and the eyes of the second guard glazed over. The Watcher exerted a powerful hold over weak minds, minds used to taking orders. The man slid his pistol back into its holster. Todtman pulled himself free from Alex and Ren and approached him.

"What is this place?" Todtman asked.

"It is a secure facility. The Death Walker protects it."

Alex nudged Ren. "Not anymore."

"Protects what?" said Todtman. "What is here?"

The guard's subjugated brain seemed to search for the right English words. "The . . . stone warriors," he said at last. "And the prisoners."

Alex's eyes opened wide. *Had they caught his mom?*

Todtman was clearly thinking the same thing. "Americans?"

"One," said the guard.

Alex's heart stuttered. The first guard shifted on the floor and reached for his head, but Alex couldn't react. He needed to hear this.

Todtman pressed him. "A woman?"

The man looked confused for a moment and then shook his head. "Boy," he said.

Not his mom. Alex exhaled. Then something else occurred to him: *An American boy . . . Could it be Luke?* But the next moment he was chastising himself for being so stupid. He knew all too well that his super-jock cousin was working with The Order — probably getting ready to buy an NBA team with the money they must have paid him to betray them.

Alex saw movement out of the corner of his eye and turned just in time to see the first guard recover his bearings and reach for his gun. Alex spun around too late — but not Ren. She kicked the man hard in one bent shin.

The guard grabbed his shin and swore, giving Alex enough time to unleash a second blast of wind. The guard's head smacked back into the wall with a hollow coconut *BONK*, and he was knocked out cold. But no sooner had one threat ended than a larger one loomed. Voices echoed through the room, coming from somewhere out in the pit.

"We need to get out of here," said Ren.

Todtman nodded but didn't budge. "Where are these stone warriors?"

The guard resisted. Todtman clutched the falcon harder, leaned in, and repeated himself in a hoarse, angry whisper: "WHERE?"

The guard raised his hand despite himself, pointing to a doorway along the half-shattered side wall. "One . . . flight . . . up . . . to . . . right," the man spat out, fighting himself on every word.

"One last thing," said Todtman, leaning back.

"We have to go," hissed Ren, the echoing voices louder now.

Alex gave her what he hoped was a reassuring look. "I'm sure it's important," he whispered.

"Do you have a broom?" asked Todtman. "It must get sandy in here . . ."

The guard looked confused but pointed to one shadowy corner. *"Vielen Dank,"* said Todtman. *Thank you very much.* "Now sleep."

The guard crumpled to the floor as Todtman hobbled to the corner.

"Let's go," he said as he used the falcon's power to shear off the head of the broom.

They rushed through the side door and up the stairs, one step ahead of the approaching voices. The only sounds were the soft, wooden thuds of Todtman's new walking stick.

Rock Stars and Fast Cars

The staircase led up and away from the shattered wall, and by the first landing, the electric lights were working again. "One flight up and to the right," Todtman repeated softly. "Here it is." He gestured toward a large, vaultlike door.

Alex was less interested in these "stone warriors," whatever that meant, and more interested in escape. "Why don't we keep going up the stairs?" he said as Ren nodded emphatically in agreement.

Todtman turned the large door handle. Locked. He reached for his amulet. "We still know too little about The Order's plans," he said. "I must know what they are capable of, what tools they have. I saw something in Cairo, and it . . . troubled me."

Alex knew he had a point: The cult was up to something massive, and they needed to know more — not just what they planned to accomplish, but how. He took one last longing look up the stairwell and then turned his attention toward the door. Hand on amulet, Todtman's eyes slid closed and his augmented senses probed the inner workings of the lock, finding its weak point.

KLICKICK!

The lock opened, but still he searched.

CRECK!

The sound of a second, larger lock opening . . . *There's something important in there*, thought Alex. Todtman pushed the door open and stepped inside, Alex and Ren following a step behind.

The room was dark and Alex was on edge. He jumped when Todtman swung the heavy door shut behind them. Then he heard a third click, much softer this time, as the old scholar found the light switch.

Alex's breath caught and his heart nearly stopped. His hand flew up to his amulet and he took a quick step back, nearly shouldering Ren into the wall. "Hey!" she said.

And then she saw it, too, and gasped sharply. Facing them were five massive, menacing figures. Menacing — and familiar.

They were in the shape of the five Order operatives who already haunted their nightmares. There was the treacherous, jackal-masked Al-Dab'u, their first adversary in New York; the cruel, crocodile-headed Ta-mesah from London; Peshwar, the sinister, lioness-skull-wearing huntress who'd pursued them halfway across Egypt; the vulture-veiled leader; and the grotesque Aff Neb.

But these were carved from blocks of rugged stone: ten feet tall and powerfully built, like Hulked-out versions of the sinister originals.

"The stone warriors are . . . statues?" said Ren. "That's so *vain*!"

"No," said Todtman, his voice grave and fearful. "Not vain — terrifying. I was afraid of this. They hadn't taken shape yet in Cairo. I only saw a glimpse. But now . . ." He looked from Alex to Ren. "We must destroy these!"

"Why?" said Ren, but there was no time for explanation, much less destruction. Behind them, the locks of the door were beginning to turn. The Order had caught up with them.

"We're trapped in here!" said Alex, surveying the featureless room.

"No," said Ren. "There has to be a back door."

"How do you know?" said Alex.

She rolled her eyes. "Because these things are too big to fit through the front one!"

The first lock had already clicked open and the larger second lock was beginning to turn. The friends rushed across the bare, echoing chamber, slaloming between the looming statues. They gave Alex a serious case of the creeps, a mix of bad memories and foreboding. *What are these things for — and why do they scare Todtman so much?*

They passed the last statue — the graven image of the cult leader — just as the door swung open and the man himself strode into the room. They reached the back wall. In its center was the sort of large, rolling door you'd find on a loading dock.

"Phew!" said Ren.

"You two open it," said Todtman, turning back toward their pursuers. "I'll hold them off."

Alex looked at him like he was crazy. *How could he hold off the leader and the steady stream of armed men pouring in the door behind him?* But there was no time for second thoughts.

"I'll unlock it," said Ren. "You push!"

Alex gave her a skeptical look, too. She had the least experience using an amulet — and this looked like a big lock. But she looked confident, and for the first time he realized that she had more faith in the ibis than he did.

He was plenty confident with his own amulet, though. He grasped the scarab, and once again the ancient energy coursed through him, quickening his pulse, sharpening his senses. He extended his right hand, palm up, and slowly raised it.

As he began to push, he saw a pop of white light and heard a muffled *klink*. Ren had done it! The big door began to move.

Behind them, Todtman's delay tactic was a masterstroke. Rather than attempt a direct attack on The Order forces, he threatened what they held dear. As the door rose to waist height, Alex risked a quick look back. The first of the statues, Al-Dab'u's, was wobbling and . . . falling! The Order forces shouted in confusion and concern. "Stop it!" barked the leader. "Do not let it fall!"

Todtman's froggy face was red, his eyes protruding even more than usual from the effort of tipping the massive statue. But now gravity was on his side. The leader extended his own hand, pushing back, as half a dozen men rushed to prop the thing up. Behind them, Alex saw the pale skull of a lioness enter the room.

"Peshwar's here," he gasped.

"Let's go!" yelped Ren.

Todtman wheeled around, releasing the amulet with an exhausted gasp.

The three friends quickly ducked under the half-open gate as the room lit up red and one of Peshwar's energy daggers rocketed toward them. The deadly dagger slammed into the edge of the door as they straightened up on the other side.

"Glad I didn't have time to open it all the way!" said Alex.

Another advantage of the half-opened door: Closing it was much faster.

"Lock it!" said Todtman, already beginning to hobble across the broad concrete floor in front of them. "And break the lock!"

The same augmented senses and subtle manipulations that made it possible for Alex to open a lock with the scarab made it surprisingly easy to break off one of the small pieces inside.

He rushed to catch up with the others as a dozen hands began pounding on the stubbornly stuck metal behind them. The friends were in a large, bare room, its walls mostly lost in shadows. Up ahead, he could see a ramp sloping upward. It looked like an empty loading dock — but it wasn't empty.

"Hey, guys?" Alex heard. Just two words, but the voice was so familiar that he recognized it immediately. He wheeled around, reaching for his amulet once again. But the person he saw posed no threat this time. Pressed between thick iron bars along the far wall, a face floated like a ghost in the shadows.

"Luke?" The word flopped weakly out of Alex's mouth as he tried to come to terms with what he was seeing. He took a step forward and saw that there were three large doors along the far wall, each with a barred window in the center. Luke was in the middle cell. *But why?* His cousin was working with The Order — wasn't he? Then why was he in a sunless cell in their desert citadel?

"You traitor!" shouted Ren. He'd betrayed her, too, but her tone softened as she stepped forward and got a better look at his pale, grime-streaked face. "You . . . snake?"

Luke managed a weak smile. "Okay, I had that coming," he said. "But you gotta understand, I didn't want to do it. I mean, at first, yeah. The money was good, but then —"

Pa-KRACK! Ba-DOOOM!

Two quick, explosive sounds came through the door behind them, and two large bumps appeared on its metal surface.

Todtman peered into the gloom. "They are coming through. That door will not hold them much longer."

But Alex couldn't bring himself to leave just yet. Todtman had interacted with Luke only briefly, but Alex's cousin had been a big part of the team in London and the Valley of the Kings. His athletic ability and knack for saying the obvious had saved them more than once — even if he had been passing on information to The Order the whole time. Alex needed to hear this. "Why did you betray us?" he said.

Thin hands appeared on the bars of the other two cells, but the faces stayed hidden inside. For the first time, Alex caught a whiff of the stink coming from the cells. These people were being held in darkness and filth, and barely fed, by the looks of it.

"When I realized how bad these people really are," said Luke, "I couldn't do it anymore."

"But you did!" yelled Ren. "You gave us away! We could have died!"

As if to punctuate her angry point, a third explosion rocked the door behind them. The metal began to give. Crimson light flickered through a long crack.

"I know," breathed Luke. "I feel terrible, but . . ."

"WE HAVE TO GO!" shouted Todtman.

Alex looked at his cousin closely. He *had* betrayed them. They'd survived it out in the desert, but if he kept them here any longer this time, he'd deliver them into the hands of The Order agents — whether he meant to or not.

"I'm sorry, man," he said, and turned to run. Sympathy and old loyalty tugged at him, but he pulled away. They didn't have time to listen to Luke's excuses.

Ren followed half a step behind. They'd already reached the ramp and started up it when Luke called out his last words. "They were going to kill my parents! I'm sorry, cuz!"

Alex wheeled around and stared back down into the darkness. An image formed in his head, one perfectly suited to this shadowy place. Once again, he pictured that complex spiderweb. Back in Alexandria, he'd imagined his mom was the center, but really he was the spider. This was all his fault, and not just on some big, abstract level, but right down to each person involved.

Luke had gotten pulled into that web because of Alex. He never would've betrayed them in a million years if it weren't for the lure of money and the worst threat imaginable. Luke's drained face watched him through the gloom, a glimmer of hope shining through now.

Hardly believing his own words, Alex heard himself say, "I have to save him."

He turned and took a step back down the ramp, once again heading toward danger, but quick footsteps came up behind him.

"No, Ren, don't —" he began, just as a burst of crimson light blew a massive hole in the metal gate. *Fa-THOOOM!*

In the quiet following the explosion, Ren made it crystal clear that she had no intention of following his suicide mission. She reached up and slapped the swollen lump on the back of his head. Alex winced as if he'd just bitten down on a lemon, and sucked air through his teeth. "OW!"

"Listen to me!" she said. "I don't know what this cowboy craziness is all about, but if you don't turn around right now, we are *all* going to end up in that cell — or worse."

"But it's all my —" Alex began, but Ren cut him short.

"It is not!"

Alex heard the metal gate begin to roll upward and the angry voices massing behind it. He was paralyzed. He felt responsible for all of them, but saving one meant putting the others in danger.

It was Luke himself who broke the deadlock: "Go, man!" he shouted. "Just go!"

Alex released a wordless shout of frustration and anger — but he went. He took one last look back at Luke's face and then rushed toward Todtman, who was using his amulet to try to slow the rising gate.

Ren added a blinding flash to the delay tactics, and then they all turned and rushed up the ramp toward freedom. By the time the battered gate rattled fully open behind them, Todtman was already opening the next gate with his amulet. They hurried through, the slap of footsteps and crackle of energy close behind. Sunlight and dry desert air met them on the other side.

As Todtman and Ren closed the gate and broke the lock, two gunshots pushed little cones into the metal from the other side. Alex stared at them, understanding that if he'd hesitated even a few seconds longer, those bullets might be lodged in his back — or his friend's.

"Our getaway!" called Ren, pointing.

A small fleet of expensive new cars sat in a square lot, all in identical gunmetal gray. Even with sun-stung eyes Alex could make out the familiar logo. Mercedes-Benzes.

"Ausgezeichnet!" shouted Todtman. *Excellent!*

They hustled toward the nearest one. "Can you start it?" asked Ren as Todtman slid into the driver's seat.

"Of course!" Todtman said, grabbing his amulet. "These cars make perfect sense — they're German!"

The powerful engine roared to life, and they burned rubber leaving the lot.

Alex took one last look behind them as the car hit the long ribbon of hot asphalt that would lead them to safety. He stared at The Order's subterranean stronghold . . . Sand-colored canvas had already been drawn over the top of the shattered pit. The pit where they had lost Pai, and nearly each other, before encountering a goddess. The gate they'd come through was just beginning to slide open again. And somewhere behind them, his cousin, held captive and caught in the crossfire of all this, his life or death dependent on the whims of maniacs.

Finally, he allowed himself to look at the road ahead, but he didn't really see it. What he saw instead was a spiderweb. He looked down at himself, turned his hand over and considered it. He was the spider. And he was *poisonous.*

As the luxury sedan's air conditioning kicked in, he took his first deep breath of cool air in what felt like ages. He filled his lungs with air and his mind with one single word, the only thing that could make this all worth it. The only thing that could tear the web apart and release everyone who'd been caught up in it.

Minyahur.

To Minyahur

Todtman punched their destination into the navigation system, shifted the powerful sedan into gear, and pressed the gas pedal to the floor. Alex settled into the backseat, not noticing the fat black fly crawling slowly along the edge of the door.

The Mercedes sped south as the sun began to set in the west. Todtman took them through a few small towns and made a series of seemingly random turns, in case they were being followed. But Alex saw no suspicious cars tailing them, and the sleek vehicle seemed like a safe haven: a little bubble of tinted glass and air conditioning.

For a while, nobody said very much. They were too tired and all working through what had just happened in their own ways. Alex couldn't see Ren's small frame on the other side of the big front seat, but he heard her sniffle a few times and knew it was about Pai.

But eventually they recovered, like boxers picking themselves up off the mat, and the need to make sense of what they'd seen was too strong for silence.

Ren had been trying to puzzle something out herself for about thirty miles, and now she was just going to ask Todtman. "What was the big deal about those statues?" she said. "Why were you so — I mean, no offense, but why were you so freaked out about them?"

"They are powerful and dangerous weapons. I dearly wish we'd had time to destroy them."

"Dangerous?" said Ren. "What's The Order going to do, hit people with them? They can't even move."

"Not yet," said Todtman. At first, she thought he was joking, but the grim look on his face didn't crack, just deepened. "You already know that the ancient Egyptians believed they could make a statue of themselves in life and inhabit that form in the afterlife . . ."

"Right," said Ren, remembering. "Like in London, the second Death Walker, Willoughby . . . He looked just like the statue in his crypt."

"And King Tut looked just like his famous mask," added Alex.

Ren was happy to recall the sight of Tutankhamun in the Valley of the Kings, looking less like a boy king and more like a member of a boy band. "Yeah," she confirmed. "He was supercute."

"I will take your word for it," said Todtman. "But these statues were not made for their looks. They were made to be warriors."

"So wait," said Alex, "The Order guys want to 'inhabit' those forms? They want to be ten feet tall and made of stone?"

"They want to be invulnerable to harm," said Todtman. "Unstoppable."

"But wouldn't they need to be dead first? Like Tut and Willoughby?"

Todtman took his eyes off the road and turned back toward Alex in a way that made Ren fear for her own life. "And you don't think they would do that?" he said sharply. "The Order —"

"Is a death cult," she said. "We know. Could you please keep your eyes on the road?" But then she finally understood the full implication of what he was saying. "So wait, they plan to sacrifice themselves? They plan to turn *themselves* into Death Walkers?"

Alex groaned. "Into supersized, indestructible Death Walkers."

HONK!

An approaching truck finally caught Todtman's attention — with its horn rather than its grille, thankfully. He veered back into his lane. "And I suspect their powers would be just as large as their bodies," he said. "The Lost Spells unleashed the Death Walkers into this world, and the Lost Spells would allow these new ones to cross over, as well. And with the protection of those Spells . . ."

"They would be impossible to banish, brought back for good," said Alex. Ren turned and saw him looking down at his scarab. "The Book of the Dead, the scarab, nothing could stop them."

Ren tried to imagine it. Supersized Death Walkers with supersized powers. "Can you imagine how powerful Peshwar would be?" she said. "Those energy daggers could take down a building! Or their leader? Oh wow . . ."

"He could control presidents, nations," said Todtman. "And nothing could stop them — or even harm them."

"No wonder they're working with the Death Walkers," said Alex. "They are planning to *become* Death Walkers."

Todtman nodded solemnly. "The world of the dead is already bleeding into the world of the living, already taking hold. The Order and the Death Walkers plan to use that opening to rule — to live forever and rule a world shadowed by death."

Ren sat back, trying to imagine a world ruled by The Order and the Death Walkers. It was not a world she wanted any part of. "It's a good thing we're on our way to find the Spells right now," she said. "We need to slam those doorways shut and put everything back the way it was!"

She looked at the other two. Todtman was nodding, but Alex . . . Alex looked like she'd just punched him. She didn't understand his reaction at all, at first. And then she did. "Oh," she said. "Oh no."

Todtman kept his eyes fixed on the road. "Yes," he said. "We have no way of knowing what will happen if the doorways close for good, but the risk was always clear — the risk to Alex."

Always clear? she thought. *Clear to who?* She hadn't signed up for this.

"Was it clear to you?" she said, staring back between the seats at Alex and not entirely succeeding in keeping the pity out of her voice.

"I was kind of trying not to think about it," he admitted. "But if we use the Spells and everything goes back to the way it was before, well . . ."

He couldn't bring himself to say it, and she didn't blame him.

Because he was sick before — sick, at best.

At worst, he was dead.

That night, with the sun gone red again and just kissing the horizon, they arrived in Minyahur.

A Land of Sand and Secrets

Alex climbed out of the car into what felt like a different world, one where stone monsters were waiting to be born and where winning the battle against them might mean losing his life. He looked around as the others stood and stretched beside him. The little village was locked up as tight as a bank vault. It wasn't even nine o'clock yet, but the half dozen buildings that made up the center of town slumbered like huddled animals. The doors were locked and the windows were dark and shuttered. The only light came from the rising moon and one lone streetlight.

This was Minyahur, the place his mom thought of as a sanctuary, a quiet shelter in a mad world. The place he hoped to find her now.

"Well, at least they have electricity," Ren said, stretching her legs and gazing up at the flickering bulb.

There wasn't much for the faint light to reveal: A sandy landscape stretched out into the darkness. Lopsided mud-brick huts slumped together in modest bunches, with squared-off redbrick structures scattered among them like dropped Monopoly houses. Even the most run-down buildings seemed to have heavy doors and thick wooden shutters on the windows. *Are there lights burning behind those shutters?* he wondered. *Is the town asleep, or is everyone gone?*

"Not very welcoming," said Ren, looking around skeptically.

Alex removed his scarab from under his shirt. It felt hot in his hand. Whatever the fate of the villagers, he now knew this: *The dead are walking here.*

"Why don't you two start looking around?" said Todtman. "I will try to find us somewhere to stay."

Ren looked at the dark, quiet buildings, each one as silent and still as a gravestone. "What if something has happened to them all?"

"Exactly," said Todtman. "We need to make sure that everything is all right here, that we will be safe for the night. But don't go far."

Alex and Ren watched him turn and head toward the street, his broomstick cane making soft stabbing sounds as it punched into the sandy ground.

"Come on," said Alex. "There are some more buildings over this way."

They started out along the road, but it felt too exposed and without a word they veered off into the soft sand alongside. Wearing the boots he'd broken in in the Valley of the

Kings, he felt at home in the sand. Boots just like his mom had always worn on her work expeditions.

For the first time in what felt like forever, it seemed not just possible but likely that she was nearby. The familiar anticipation stirred inside him. He looked around at the desolate village: It looked like she had run to the very ends of the earth to escape them. To escape *him*. And this time, he didn't really blame her. *Who wouldn't run from a spider?*

They headed deeper into the village's sandy outskirts. One direction, Alex knew, led to the Nile — the source and anchor of all life in Egypt, rolling slowly north somewhere just beyond his sight. The other led farther into the vast Sahara desert. He looked out at it. The sand glowed like endless snow in the moonlight. It was beautiful, but he needed more than his eyes could give him now. He reached up and wrapped his hand around his amulet. His pulse quickened and his breath caught as he felt the exhilarating rush of ancient energy crackle through his system.

Suddenly, the world around him began to shimmer ever so slightly. He'd hoped he could use the scarab to pinpoint a single strong signal. Instead, the living dead — or the death magic that brought them back — seemed to be all around them.

"Not good," he said, letting the scarab go. Using it for too long gave him a headache, anyway.

They were approaching a little hut made of mud bricks, and Alex wasn't sure if they should avoid it or check for signs of life. Up close, he could see that it was painted a mustard yellow that seemed oddly cheerful. As he eyed it, he saw a ragged figure pull itself from the dark side of the house and out into the open. "Ren!" he said, but she'd already seen it.

They both reached for their amulets with gunfighter speed.

The figure stepped clear of the house and out into the moonlight. It was a raggedly dressed old man. Ren let out a deep breath and Alex felt his shoulders relax. But neither of them let go of their amulets as the old beggar began to speak.

"Ah, children, strange children," he said.

Alex looked at the man. His skin was leathery and his hair was a matted and windblown mess. His frame was extremely thin and covered in an old brown robe. Alex hadn't expected khakis or anything, but a ratty robe? They really were in the middle of nowhere now.

Alex took a deep breath and plastered on a smile. "We're looking for someone," he said.

"Oh yes? And who might that be?"

"A woman," he said. "A foreigner."

"I think I might know something about that," said the old man enigmatically.

"Alex!" hissed Ren, taking a step back.

But Alex ignored her, taking a step forward. *Does this old man really know something about my mom?*

"I'll tell you," the man said. "For a coin."

Alex reached into his pocket.

"Alex!" said Ren, louder this time.

He shot her a look: *Not now!* With his hand still on his amulet, he felt safe. He pulled a handful of Egyptian coins out of his pocket. The man extended his hand, long nails pointing out, his palm creased with dirt. But as Alex dropped the coins into the man's hand, something occurred to him. *How can I understand this man? What are the odds that a beggar on the fringes of Arabic-speaking Egypt speaks perfect English?* As the change began to fall, he looked down at his amulet — the one that allowed him to speak ancient Egyptian when he held it. *Uh-oh.*

The change hit the man's greasy palm — and fell right through it. The coins thunked softly into the sand below.

The old man — or his spirit, anyway — looked down at the fallen coins and then looked up at Alex with a sheepish grin. "I never was very good with money," he said. And as he did, he began to change. His mouth widened, his eyes went black in the moonlight . . .

Alex scrambled back and felt his foot catch on a stone. He windmilled his arms for balance but it was too late. He hit the ground hard enough to feel a sharp pain shoot up his tailbone into his spine. He looked up and saw a ring of sharp teeth with a pure blackness at its center. His hand had come off his amulet in the fall, and he fumbled for it desperately.

FWOOOP!

A blinding white flash lit his vision, leaving him seeing stars and nothing else. He rolled away blindly, the gritty sand rubbing against his skin and slipping into his clothing.

When his vision cleared, he looked up to see the teeth replaced by . . . Ren.

"If I am going to keep saving your butt," she said, "the least you can do is stop falling on it."

"Yeah, ha-ha," said Alex, extending his hand and attempting to salvage at least a little of his dignity. "If you're going to keep blinding me with that thing, the least you could do is help me up."

Ren reached down and took his outstretched hand. "I think we should probably head back now," she said, giving him a tug.

"Yeah, good idea," said Alex, eyeing a desert that suddenly looked less beautiful than eerie.

They walked back wordlessly. Alone with his thoughts, Alex finally allowed himself to really think about what Todtman had said: *"The risk was always clear."* A risk . . . Not a certainty.

And what exactly was the risk? He could deal with being sick again, though he would dearly miss this new health. He stood up straight and breathed in the clear desert air. He felt his system working smoothly and efficiently: extracting oxygen, pumping blood. There was no needles-and-pins stinging in his limbs, no bowling-ball queasiness in his gut, no lead-heavy exhaustion. He'd gotten so used to this, almost took it for granted now. Yeah, he'd miss it. But it was the other possibility that he needed to face: *Will this mission cost me my life? Or is there some way we could end The Order's plans without ending* me, *too?*

The truth was, he didn't know, and that's what he needed to make peace with. He listened to the muffled crunch of his best friend's footsteps and stared up at a moon as pale as bone. He'd caused so much trouble to so many people already. Maybe this was the way it had to be. Ren had been risking her own safety for him this whole time. Maybe it was time for him to take the biggest risk of all, for her — and everyone else.

He glanced over at his friend, her small frame dwarfed by a barren desert that stretched to the horizon. He felt as if he had dragged her to the end of the earth, too, put her through so much. *Am I willing to die to end all this?* he wondered.

He kicked the ground and walked on.

I should be dead already.

𓎆𓏻𓏻

Called Out

Todtman had found them a place to stay, all right — right back in the Benz. "There are people here," he had said. "But they are afraid. I think, perhaps, it is best not to impose on them right now — or to trust them."

An hour later, Ren was lying in the backseat, since she was short enough to fit. The other two had the front seats reclined as far as they would go. She looked out the wide rear window at the sky above. It was so dense with stars that it seemed to shimmer and pulse. It didn't press down on her vision as much as lift it up. They were still parked behind the same little cluster of buildings. *Are we safe here?* she wondered.

A car, when it came right down to it, didn't offer much shelter. And yet, she didn't feel afraid. Part of that was her company. Todtman was formidable with his falcon — even if he was snoring a little too loudly at present. And sometimes it seemed like Alex could move mountains with that scarab. *Amazing for a kid who couldn't even get through gym class a year ago* . . . But part of it had nothing to do with the others. She looked down to see the ibis glowing softly in the starlight.

She considered it again with fresh eyes. She could do so much more with it now. She could pick locks and zap spirits and blind the occasional giant fly. And as for the images, maybe she had just been thinking about them the wrong way. She'd always thought that it was giving her answers and she was failing to understand them half the time. But what if it was just giving her information, guidance? *What if it isn't the answer key? What if it is the studying?*

Alone in the backseat, she smiled. More than anyone else she knew, she liked studying.

A moment later, she was snoring, too.

The next morning dawned sunny, despite it all.

Alex woke up first, seat-sore and hungry. His body felt creaky, but inside he was buzzing. If this was the day they finally found his mom, it could be the best day of his life. It could also be the last. It felt like Christmas morning, with maybe a little too much Halloween thrown in. He tried to imagine seeing her again, after so long. *Would I run up and hug her?* he wondered. *Would she let me?*

He twisted his stiff neck toward the backseat. "Hey, Ren," he said over the sound of Todtman's precise, measured snoring. "You awake?"

"I am now," she groaned.

The exchange woke Todtman. *"Guten Morgen,"* he croaked.

Alex and Ren responded with grunts.

Donk! Donk! Donk!

All three heads whipped around. There was a man outside the car, knocking on Todtman's window. Todtman straightened his seat and lowered the window. There was a quick conversation in Arabic, a few bills handed over, and the man vanished.

"That is the owner of the store we are parked behind," said Todtman. "There is a fee for parking here. I suspect it has been in effect for exactly as long as we have been here. Also, he wanted to know if we want breakfast."

"Definitely," said Alex. His feelings were a confusing swirl, but his stomach was making itself very clear by rumbling loudly.

The three climbed out of Hotel Mercedes and into the bright Egyptian daylight. They walked around the buildings and onto the main road, doing their best to stretch and smash down their Benz-head hair as they went.

Alex was surprised by the number of people on the street. Minyahur had been a ghost town the night before — literally — but now it was alive with activity. He checked the time on his phone. Apparently, the village that shuts down early wakes up early, too. Looking at the heavy wooden shutters, flung open now, he thought he understood. Ren had saved him from a terrifying fate with her ibis last night, but these people didn't have amulets. They had only solid walls to hide behind.

He heard footsteps and stepped aside as a group of women walked past on the cracked concrete sidewalk. They were wearing traditional Muslim garb, covered head-to-toe in long black abayas and veils that left only their eyes visible.

"Aren't they hot?" whispered Ren as they passed, looking down at her own sporty, short-sleeved outfit.

Alex scanned the village center. There were dozens of people, carrying bags or leading children or just walking swiftly toward some unknown destination. Most of the men wore pumpkin-sized turbans and the traditional white Egyptian gowns known as *galabeyas*. But almost all the women were wearing those same all-concealing black outfits. *It's a perfect disguise*, he realized with both horror and some small bit of admiration. *Mom could walk right past me and I'd never know.*

A bell tinkled as they pushed through the front door of the store.

"Ah!" said the shopkeeper. "Breakfast, yes?" He gave Alex and Ren a quick look and a slick smile. "How is my English? Good, yes? It used to be, but I do not get a chance to practice much out of here."

Alex smiled back politely. "So," he said. "What kind of breakfast are we talking about?"

It was mostly dry, sugary biscuits and tea, but they all wolfed it down at a small table in the back of the store. Then they headed toward the front to pay for the food — and extra for any information. "The shopkeepers hear everything in a town like this," whispered Todtman.

But if this man had heard everything, he said nothing. *A foreign woman?* Not that he was aware of. *Any outsiders at all?* Couldn't think of any. *Anything out of the ordinary lately?* Ghosts and disappearances; rumors of a mummy. Nothing living.

They paid for the meal, a bottle of water, a can of insect repellant, and a cheap backpack, since Alex's and Ren's were still somewhere back in The Order's secret citadel. Alex put the stuff in the pack and the pack on his back and headed toward the door. But that's when he spotted something on a middle shelf: a quick flash of a familiar color. He turned back to the shopkeeper.

"This tea here, with the purple label," he said. "Do you sell a lot of it?"

The man looked up at the tea and then back down at the cash register. "Not much," he said. "It was a special order. Most people around here prefer the Egyptian —" He tensed visibly and swallowed the next word. After what seemed to Alex a very deliberate pause, he continued. "It is neither our most popular brand nor our least. Have a nice day! If you are still around tonight, we also serve dinner."

He slammed the cash register shut, and with it, the conversation.

Alex tapped the metal tea canister. The little bonk he got back told him two things. First, the container was half empty. Second, his mother knew Egypt well — but he knew her better than anyone.

The Buzz around Town

"She's here!" said Alex as they stepped out into the bright, hot morning. "In Minyahur! He sold her tea — he special ordered it for her!"

Ren swatted at one of the many flies buzzing dizzily around the center of town. "How can we get him to tell us where she is?"

"That, he will not know," said Todtman. "She will come in at irregular times, he will say, unpredictable. She will pay in cash and leave quietly, maybe slip out while he is talking to another customer. Sometimes she will head in one direction, sometimes she will head in another."

"How do you know any of that?" said Ren.

"Because that is what I would do," Todtman said simply. "We must search the edges of the village. She would not stay in its center."

They stood on the edge of the sidewalk, waiting to cross the street. There were no cars in sight, but a passing donkey cart was in no hurry.

"Why didn't she buy the whole container of tea," Alex asked Todtman as they reached the other side, "instead of leaving half of it there for me to see?"

"Maybe she did and the storekeeper bought another, hoping for more business," said Todtman with a shrug. "Or maybe she couldn't afford it."

The thought of his mom counting coins and buying only as much tea as she could hit Alex like a punch in the gut. He imagined her eating half of one of those chalky biscuits for lunch, saving the other for dinner. *Hungry, and on her own . . .*

"Ow!" he said, slapping down hard at his neck.

"Yes," said Todtman. "Sand flies. Nasty little beasts — and maybe worse. I think it's time for that insect repellant."

And maybe worse . . . Alex was thinking the same thing: *Could these flies be spies, too?* Alex removed the spray can from his pack, and Ren plucked it from his hands.

"This looks like it's from World War Two," she said, scrutinizing the peeling label on the unpainted steel can. "Half the ingredients are probably banned in the US."

But they took turns spraying themselves. Alex coated his arms and neck and Ren applied it in small puffs, like perfume. Todtman, who had long sleeves, coated his hands and face.

They resumed their search, heading away from the center of town.

"I'll try my amulet again," said Alex, reaching up and

pulling it out from underneath his shirt. He stopped, closed his eyes, and grasped the scarab. The night before he'd sensed a diffuse signal spread across the landscape — death magic everywhere. But something had changed. Alex suddenly felt like he was holding a baked potato fresh from the oven. The sensitive flesh of his palm sizzled, and his vision lit up from the inside in red and orange and gold.

He gasped and dropped the scalding scarab.

He opened his eyes. Color still swirled at the edges of his vision as he looked down at his palm. No physical burns or blisters that he could see.

"What is it?" said Ren, clearly picking up the shock and pain in his expression.

Alex looked at his best friend, who was wreathed in stars.

"It's the Lost Spells," he managed. "They're here."

"Did you get a direction?" said Todtman.

Alex looked at him, his vision just now beginning to clear, and answered as best he could.

"No — I couldn't tell. It was too intense. But they're close," he said. "Very close."

"That is good," said Todtman, "because I think we are about to have company."

At first, Alex didn't understand what he meant, but as the swirling colors subsided, his vision continued to shift and buzz. He looked all around. The villagers were gone, hanging back from the three visitors. In their place, a sea of flies.

Vicious little sand flies buzzed in clouds in the air, and every flat surface within twenty feet was dotted with big black flies.

"Uh-oh," said Alex, and as he did, a fat black fly darted inside his mouth like a filthy drop of midnight.

Where in the World Is Maggie Bauer?

Alex gagged and spit out the fly. It hit the ground like a wet pellet.

"We're in trouble," he said. "Aff Neb is here." He wiped his forearm across his mouth, spat again.

Todtman looked around at the buzzing, crawling swarm. "Yes, or he will be soon. I think they are watching us for him. He will be powerful out here among so many . . . friends. And I doubt he will be alone."

The Order had endless firepower. Alex feared Peshwar and their leader — not to mention a small army of hired guns — were also nearby. *Had they just led an unstoppable force straight to his mom and the Spells?*

His head buzzed inside and out. Flies swarmed around him, one biting his neck while another got tangled in his hair. He felt angry and frustrated — but not helpless. "Hold on to something," he said through gritted teeth.

The wind began behind them and rolled toward them through the wide streets of the little village. It brought with it a wall of roiling sand. The Fly Lord would be powerful out here, but he wasn't the only one with desert magic. The familiar mantra formed in Alex's head. *The wind that comes before the rain . . .*

Alex spread his stance wide and let that wind roll over him. Ren grabbed on to the post of a nearby fence. Todtman speared his walking stick into the ground and leaned forward into it, forming a tripod.

The flies lacked such options.

For a few moments, the whipping wind drowned out all sound and the rolling sand cloud blocked out the sun. When it passed, the air was clear and the flies were gone. Villagers who had ducked into huts and alleyways for shelter began gophering their heads back out for a look.

"That is better," said Todtman, coughing up a little sand. "But it won't hold them for long — nor will it delay their master."

Alex nodded. "We need to find my mom *now*."

Without another word, both Alex and Todtman turned and looked at Ren. "You must use the ibis," said Todtman. "We don't have time to argue."

But Alex stayed silent. He'd noticed something about Ren lately. She was less hesitant with her amulet, less unsure, more . . .

"Ready!" she said, folding her hand around the ibis.

Ren closed her eyes.

A moment later, her eyes fluttered open.

"What did you see?" said Alex, leaning toward her expectantly.

"Same as last time," she said. "Nothing at all."

Alex kicked the ground hard in frustration.

"Well, that is no help," said Todtman, turning away.

"No, wait," said Ren. "You're thinking about it wrong. It doesn't give answers, just information." She turned to Todtman. "Last time I saw nothing you said it meant the Spells were being hidden or protected by some kind of magic."

"Yes," he said. "So?"

"So, they're hidden again," said Ren. She pointed at Alex. "But they weren't when he tried it last time — their signal nearly burned his hand off."

"That's true," Alex admitted. "That hurt."

"Do it again," said Ren.

"What? No way!" he said.

Ren broke into the smallest of smiles and then, imitating Todtman's accent, she said: "We don't have time to argue."

Well, she's got me there, thought Alex. His hand closed around the scarab. He closed his eyes and reached out with his senses, steeling himself for the burning pain and shock to come. Instead . . .

"Nothing," he said. "Just the same little shimmer I got last night. Weak, and all around." He turned toward Todtman. "What does it mean?"

"The Spells were unprotected, briefly," he said. "She must have had them out in the open, and now she has hidden them again . . . Perhaps she has seen the flies, too."

"Or the windstorm," said Alex. "She'd recognize that. This used to be her amulet."

"Either way, we know the Spells are nearby, and they have been concealed again," said Todtman.

"So she's here, and she's watching," said Alex, suddenly looking all around.

"Perhaps getting her attention is not the worst thing now," said Todtman. "We have no more time to waste — and nothing left to lose."

"But why get her attention?" said Ren. "She's hiding from us."

"Hiding, yes," said Todtman. "But also *protecting* the Spells. If there's a threat to them . . ."

"She'd want to know," Alex chimed in, picking up the thought.

"Tell me," said Todtman. "If you saw your mother — even disguised, covered head to toe — do you think you could recognize her?"

Alex thought about it. He considered the million multifaceted memories that made up their history together. He remembered his mom sitting quietly across the kitchen table from him, him half-playing a game on the iPad, her half-reading some thick book, how sometimes they'd both look up at each other at exactly the same moment — who knows why — smile, and look down again.

"Yeah," he said. "I think so."

"Good," said Todtman. "Then we must use the amulets again."

"Which one of us?" said Ren.

Todtman smiled. "All of us, of course."

"On the count of three," said Todtman. "One, two . . ."

They all reached for their amulets. The Order was on the way, and Alex knew they would not be subtle in finding his mom. They would burn this little village to the ground and tear the veils from people's faces. The three Amulet Keepers wouldn't resort to such tactics, but this was clearly no time for half measures.

"Three!"

Alex closed his left hand around the scarab. As soon as he felt the ancient energy crackle through his veins, he began waving his right hand above him in a little circle, like a cowboy twirling a lasso. A whipping, swirling wind kicked up and immediately began picking up the sand that lay all around them in the little desert outpost. A whooshing sound filled the streets, and a tall funnel appeared, the circular air currents made visible as walls of whirling sand.

The people on the street turned to look as the sand devil towered ever higher. Others stepped out of doors or poked their heads out of windows for a closer look. Sand augers and dust whirls were common out here — but not like this.

"Now, Ren!" called Todtman through the whipping maelstrom that now surrounded them.

Ren clutched the ibis tighter and thrust her free hand straight upward.

FWOOP!

A flash of brilliant white light lit up the sky, reflecting off millions of shiny sand crystals. A beautiful wash of splintered white light carried to the very edges of the village.

Alex heard gasps and shouts from the gathering crowd. More eyes turned to the spectacle, and more feet carried them toward it. Finally, Todtman did his part. Alex had seen him use the Watcher to control individual minds many times, but now he needed more than that. He squeezed the stone falcon tight and shouted: "Watch! Look!"

The sound of his voice was all but drowned out by the whipping wind, but his psychic cry carried across the desert. The few doors that had remained closed were flung open now. Suddenly, even the most cautious villager felt the strong desire to see this towering but harmless twister.

Ren lit it with another flash — *FWOOP!* — and the *oooh*s and *aah*s came from a much larger crowd.

Alex's head was beginning to pound and his arm was starting to tire.

"Enough!" called Todtman.

Alex released the scarab and let his aching arm drop. The column of swirling sand collapsed straight down.

"Ack!" called Ren, covering her head.

But the wind had stopped so abruptly that most of the sand fell heavily in a circle all around the friends, leaving them standing inside a sloping foxhole nearly two feet high.

"Look quickly!" called Todtman. "She will be at the edges. The Watcher will not hold a mind like hers. She will stay no longer than is necessary to identify the threat . . ."

Alex scanned the edge of the crowd furiously. There were scores of people now, the entire population of the little village. Most of them stood and pointed and conferred nervously with their neighbors. Alex got the distinct impression that they were no strangers to magic out here. He turned in a circle. The people closest to him blocked his view of those on the edges of the crowd — many of whom were already beginning to leave. The women vexed him in their all-concealing garb. *Why can't I have thousands of lenses in my eyes like Aff Neb?* he wondered desperately.

The crowd continued to disperse, having already sized up these amulet-bearing newcomers.

I'm losing my chance, thought Alex. He needed to concentrate and so he ignored the eyes of the women, ignored their shoulders and walks and any of the other markers he thought he might be able to identify. Instead, he concentrated on just one thing.

He turned and turned and craned his neck around those who remained. And just when he thought he would collapse from dizziness and desperation and one breath held way too long, he saw something.

"There!" he said as the woman disappeared down a side alley thirty yards away.

"Where?" called Ren. "Which one?"

Alex scrambled over the sloping wall of sand in front of him and took off running. He had barely gotten a look at her, and that was fine, because there wasn't much to see. Mostly just a flash of plain black abaya, indistinguishable from two dozen others on the street.

But he *had* seen something. And as soon as he had, any reservations he'd harbored about finding his mom melted away like mist in the desert sun. He picked up speed as he dodged and ducked his way through the crowd, scaring people as he ran up behind them, and leaving his friends in the dust.

An arm reached for him as he ran through the scattering throng, and another, alarmingly, grabbed at his amulet. He shouldered through the first and slapped aside the second. He kept his eyes trained on the approaching alleyway, not even daring to spare a glare for the would-be thief.

"Mom!" he called, his eager voice breaking. "Mom!"

He hit the alleyway too fast and crashed into the far wall before he could turn. He used the impact to bounce himself back in the right direction without missing a beat. He was in a narrow space between two of the village's larger buildings, and at the very end of that space, walking briskly, was a woman in black.

Once she reached the end, she could turn in either direction. Then she could find the next alley and do the same. As small as the village was, Alex had no doubt that she knew it well enough to escape him.

He looked down to avoid a garbage can lid and when he looked up, the woman was gone.

Stupid, he thought. *So stupid.*

He called out again, desperation dripping from his voice now: "Mom!"

He had found her and lost her, and now she knew he was on her trail. Now she could escape again. He'd traveled thousands of miles, only to fall a few yards short. He called out one final time as he neared the end of the alley. And this time there was more than desperation in it. There was sadness, the breaking voice of a broken heart.

And maybe that's why . . .

Because he expected to find nothing as he reached the end of the alley, but that was not the case.

A woman stood with her back to him, halfway to the next alley. Her head was covered in black cloth, but he knew who it was immediately.

"Mom?" he said.

The woman turned and removed her head-covering niqab.

And for the first time in what felt like a lifetime, Alex Sennefer saw his mom. All his doubts — did she still love him, was she mad at him for what he'd cost her — melted away at the simple fact of her presence. After weeks of living in tight-chested anxiety, as if at every point he'd taken one breath too few, his lungs filled with one long, relieved breath.

There was a tear carving a dark path through the dust on his mom's cheek, and it trembled and fell as she opened her mouth to speak. “I couldn’t run from you,” she said. “Not anymore. I couldn’t hear your voice and run.”

Alex opened his mouth but nothing came out.

“How did you know it was me?” she said, giving him a simple prompt, once again making his life easier.

Alex noticed some new gray in her hair, which managed to be both tightly bundled and utterly disheveled. Then he looked down and pointed. He didn’t know if his voice would work until it did.

“I recognized your boots.”

A Door in the Floor

It definitely wasn't the first time Ren turned a corner to find Alex hugging his mom. Back when Alex was a sick only-child and Dr. Bauer was a hardworking single mom, they often hugged before going their separate ways. Toward the end of his life — his first life — they'd hugged a little longer, never quite sure if they'd see each other again.

Ren gave them their space as they hugged hard, with their eyes closed to the world. She was pretty sure they didn't even realize she was there. They were lost in the reunion and defenseless. And suddenly she felt intensely protective of them. Her left hand drifted toward her amulet. She would watch the hostile world for them.

But as she turned one way and then another, she couldn't help but think of her own parents. She remembered her own good-bye hugs at the airport. It felt so long ago now. *Too long.* Her watchful eyes began to brim with tears, and as protective as she felt, she couldn't help but feel a tiny bit jealous, too.

And so when Todtman pivoted around the corner on the tip of his cane, she didn't try to stop him. She knew him well enough by now to know what he would do.

The old curator took in the moment at a glance, paused barely half a beat, and said, "Maggie!"

Dr. Bauer gave her son one more squeeze and closed her eyes a little tighter, as if trying to lock in the moment. Then she opened them and looked over her son's shoulder.

"*Guten Tag*, Ernst," she said, and then, more softly, "Hello, Ren. It's good to see you."

Ren felt her ears get hot — embarrassed to be caught staring — and offered a quick wave.

"The Order is on its way," said Todtman, by way of hello. "They may already be here."

Maggie sighed heavily and nodded. Then she released her son and looked down at him. Alex looked up at her, his arms still held out for a hug that was now over. "Did you do that sand devil?" she said, eyeing the scarab that had once been hers.

Alex nodded.

She reached down and ruffled his hair, something Ren had seen her do a hundred times. "I knew you'd be good with the Returner," she said. "I'm glad it has kept you safe."

"How did you know it would work for me?" said Alex.

"You got your hands on it once when you were very young — and you blew out the windows in the apartment."

"Maggie!" Todtman repeated. "Are the Spells unguarded?"

She looked up at him and nodded. *So she does have them*, thought Ren. "Yes," Dr. Bauer said, her voice hardening as she spoke. "We need to get them out of here. I'm not ready yet."

"Ready for what?" said Ren as they all turned to follow Dr. Bauer down the next alley.

She didn't answer.

Alex rushed to catch up with his mom. "I missed you," he said, so softly that it was nearly drowned out by the steady beat of their footsteps.

And that she did answer. "Oh, Alex, I so wish you hadn't found me yet — but I missed you, too. I left little signs to let you know I was still thinking about you." Ren's mind flashed back to the Valley of the Kings, to an old name penciled into a sun-scorched logbook. "Because the truth is, I missed you every moment of the day."

⟨—+—+—+—⟩

She led them through the little village, leaving her head uncovered. The time for hiding was over. What they needed now was escape.

Alex felt a stinging bite on the soft flesh of his neck and slapped down hard. "Oh no," he said before he even saw the flattened sand fly on his palm. The flies were back.

"What they see, The Order sees," said Todtman, waving at the buzzing cloud.

They were approaching a row of three mud-brick huts on the very edge of the village. The walls were thick, painted a fading blue, and the heavy wooden shutters were closed.

"They'll see," said Alex. "I can create some wind. Maybe —"

"It's okay," said his mom. "Let them."

She pulled open the door of the first hut. "Inside," she said quickly, before turning to her son. "Keep them out, Alex."

He nodded and grabbed the scarab. A quick gust scattered their tiny pursuers as the friends — and family — piled inside and quickly closed the door.

"Uh, Mom," Alex said into the hot, heavy darkness inside. "Do you want it back? Your scarab?"

A gas lantern sparked to life and the growing flame revealed a quick smile on her face. "Not now, honeybear," she said. "But hurry."

Alex had always been embarrassed by his mom's pet names for him, but right now "honeybear" sounded pretty sweet. And then she threw back a dusty old rug that was very nearly the only furnishing in the hut. In the light of the lantern, Alex saw a door in the floor.

"What's —" began Ren, but Dr. Bauer was already kneeling down and pulling the trapdoor up and back.

"Stay quiet and follow me," she said.

Alex heard Todtman throw the steel bolt behind them, locking the heavy wooden door from the inside. The next thing Alex knew, he was following his mom down a rusty old ladder into darkness. Sandy clay hardened into sandstone as they climbed twelve feet straight down. The ladder ended. Alex was surprised to find himself in a tunnel nearly high enough to stand in. Stooping slightly, he followed the glow of his mom's lantern forward.

He heard Todtman slam the trapdoor behind them. Flecks of sand and clay rained down on Alex's head as the others waddled forward like ducklings in the dark. The tunnel seemed none too stable, but Alex felt safer and more at ease than he had in weeks.

Twenty-odd yards later, they arrived at a second ladder. *The second hut*, Alex realized. His mom ignored this ladder, shimmying around it in the narrow tunnel and continuing on.

Finally, they reached the third ladder and ascended toward the third and final hut. "How did you dig all of this?" he huffed at his mom's back as they climbed.

"Most of the work was done a long time ago," she answered. "These huts were built over an old dig site here."

"When you were in school?" said Alex.

"Yes. We left them here as a way to ensure our claim of the site."

She threw back the trapdoor above them. By the time Alex climbed out, the room was already beginning to glow with the soft light of a larger lantern hanging from the ceiling.

The others emerged from the ground like desert gophers and Alex began to look around the hut's one shadowy room. There was a desk, a cot, a pitcher of water, an old trunk, and a backpack leaning against the wall. He didn't see the Spells, but he felt them. His heart was racing and his head was buzzing. Pinpoints and whirls of light played at the edges of his vision.

"Is this what it feels like when you drink those huge coffees?" he asked.

Now and then the swirling lights coalesced into a hieroglyphic symbol. A glowing ankh, the loop-topped cross that meant life, formed in front of Alex. It seemed so real that he reached out for it, but there was nothing there.

"What are you doing?" said Ren.

"You didn't see that?"

"See what?"

"The Lost Spells gave you life," said his mom, once again kneeling down. "You are reacting to them."

She opened the lid of the old trunk and took out a square of black leather. Through the swirls, Alex recognized it as a briefcase his mom used to bring to work for important meetings. She lifted it free and carried it across the room. As she placed it down on the desk and clicked both brass clasps open — *tik! tik!* — Alex felt the sudden need to sit down. He looked around for a chair. There was only one, and it was tucked under the desk.

His mom opened the briefcase and Alex peered inside through a Milky Way's worth of stars. He saw a thin sheet of linen, covered in more hieroglyphs.

"Are those the Lost Spells?" asked Ren.

"No," said Dr. Bauer. "These are the protective spells concealing them. Hiding their signal while I . . . studied them."

"You have been looking for a way to undo the damage," said Todtman, suddenly understanding. "To close the doorways without . . ."

They both turned their eyes to Alex and saw him swaying like a sapling in a windstorm.

"Yes," she said. "I have been looking for some way to undo the damage the Spells have caused without undoing the magic that healed my son. But now I have run out of time." She took one more look at Alex, whose buzzing brain was able to form only one simple thought: *Why does she look so sad?*

"Watch him, please," she said.

And then she lifted the cloth.

Alex saw a slice of yellow light spread outward like a slow smile.

And then he fainted, dead away.

Death on the Doorstep

Alex had seen the pitcher of water in the corner of the room; he just hadn't expected to end up wearing it.

"Puhh!" he said, spluttering some of the water running down his face.

He reached up and wiped his eyes clear with his forearm, and there was Ren, towering above him holding the dripping pitcher. *Towering* was not a word normally associated with his vertically challenged friend, and that's when he realized he was on the floor.

"We have to go," Ren said apologetically.

He sat up and looked for his mom, with the sudden panicked thought that maybe he'd dreamed the whole thing. But the soreness from his fall told him how real this was, and then he spotted her over by the desk. She was carefully folding the linen wrapping back over the Lost Spells in her briefcase.

A powerful image flashed through his mind: his mom, sitting at that little desk, sipping her favorite tea and intensely studying the ancient Spells. Looking for some loophole, some shaded meaning in the hieroglyphic writing that would let her thread the needle, closing the doorways she'd opened to the afterlife without shutting the door on his own new life. *She has always taken care of me*, he thought.

Alex's mind returned to the here and now, and he noticed a small lump under the symbol-covered cloth. He hadn't seen that the first time. *Did she just put something in there with the Spells?* He sat up higher for a better look, but as he did, she slammed the briefcase closed and turned to him.

"Are you okay, hun?" she said. "Because we really do have to go."

He gave a woozy, bobbleheaded nod. He was okay-ish.

"Come out now! And bring the Spells!" called an all-too-familiar voice. "You are completely surrounded and there will be no escape."

Alex stiffened at the sound of Aff Neb's edgy voice. But the voice wasn't as loud as he expected: clearly shouted, but at a distance.

"Where are they?" said Alex, rising shakily to his feet.

Todtman was standing against the wall, peering out a narrow crack in the wooden shutter covering the front window. "They have the hut entirely surrounded," he said. "But it's the wrong hut."

Alex walked over to the window. With the Spells fully covered and the briefcase closed, his revving system had settled down somewhat. Todtman stepped aside and Alex peered through the crack.

Aff Neb looked to be about the size of an action figure, standing close to sixty yards away and bellowing threats at the first hut — the one they'd exited through the door in the floor. A squad of rifle-wielding gunmen surrounded the modest structure, looking like army action figures at this distance. Every once in a while, the swarming flies all around them coalesced into a visible pocket of blackness in the air before spreading out again and disappearing from view.

"They won't wait long," said Todtman.

Alex nodded absently. He was assessing the gunmen.

They had led The Order straight to his mom — and the Spells. They had made the ultimate mistake — *But maybe if it comes to a fight*, he thought, *we can win*. They had three amulets, and the presence of his mom seemed to add to their strength.

But then a man appeared who changed the math. He walked straight out of the desert heat haze, his golden mask glinting in the sun. Alex's breath caught and he jumped back from the window.

"The leader is here, too," he said.

He said it to no one in particular, but his mom turned suddenly toward him. "*He's* here?" she said.

He stared at her, too surprised to answer. The tone of her voice — familiar, fearful — made it seem like she'd met the leader before. *But when? Where?* He had spent his whole life with her — just the two of them — but there was so much about his mom he didn't know . . .

The leader's voice stretched across the open desert, sounding like a whisper in Alex's ears but a barked command in his head. "There is something wrong — step aside!"

The command was meant for the gunmen, but the leader's presence was so powerful that Alex had the urge to step aside himself. He fought it and took one last peek between the shutters.

There was a thick crunch of wood as the leader splintered the front door with a wave of his hand and walked unhindered into the hut. Alex watched as the gunmen streamed inside. He pictured them all, rifles pointed at every corner of the empty room. In a moment, they would find the trapdoor.

A more immediate sound tore his attention from the front window. It was the sound of the shutters being thrown open on the back window.

"We can climb out here," said his mom, ducking down to stuff the briefcase into her backpack. "They will try the second hut next — maybe split their forces and send some down into the tunnel."

"We have a car," said Todtman. "Back in the center of the village."

Dr. Bauer shook her head. "I have a truck," she said. "And it's closer." Then she boosted herself up and out of the window with the grace of a cat burglar.

As the friends rushed over to the open window to help boost the old, decidedly graceless German out next, Ren turned to Alex. "Uh, your mom kind of kicks butt," she said.

Alex didn't know what to say. He'd always known his mom made a mean grilled cheese, but this? "I guess so," he managed. Then they both knelt down and laced their hands together for Todtman to step on.

Ren was too short to boost herself out the window, so Alex was the last one out. He plopped down onto the sandy ground on the shady side of the little shelter. His mom looked back at him, and once again he saw the familiar worry lines crease the corners of her eyes. He didn't like it. He knew he'd given her those lines in the first place. And now she was worried about him again. After all the trouble he'd caused. After he'd left his own cousin in a desert cell. After he'd led The Order right to her . . .

"It's all my fault," he whispered to her. "Everything that's happened, it's because of me. I put you in danger." His eyes flicked around the huddled group. "I put you all in danger."

His mom gave him a sad look. "Oh, hun, don't."

"It's true," he said, barely able to look her in the eyes.

She took his chin in her hand to make him. "No," she said. "It's not."

When he still wouldn't meet her eyes, she began to talk, her voice soft and warm. "We all had a choice," she said. "I chose to save you in that hospital room. I knew there was a risk, and I took it. The only thing you are responsible for is what you did after you woke up. And you came looking for me — to make things right. And that" — she gave his chin a shake — "that makes me proud."

"We had a choice, too," whispered Ren. "That's what I was trying to tell you leaving that pit. It's *not* all your fault — and we're not all your responsibility. We *all* had a choice."

Alex looked over at her, skeptical.

"I *chose* to come halfway around the world," she said, pointing at her own chest. As clear and firm as her statement was, it was her next words that convinced him. Flashing the quickest of grins she added: "Since when do I do what you tell me, anyway?"

Alex crouched in the sand, trying to process it all, replaying the words of the two people he trusted most. "We all had a choice," he said, turning it over in his head. He felt a weight lift, a burden ease. "I guess I can live with that."

His mom smiled, but just briefly. "Not if we don't get moving," she said, reaching over to ruffle his hair. "Now let's go! We should go straight ahead. Stay in the cover of the buildings as long as we can. The truck isn't far."

A voice carried across the desert. "Not here!" called the leader. "Check the next one!"

Alex's mom stopped to listen to the commanding voice, and for once Alex couldn't identify the look on her face. But as the voice fell silent, her determination returned. "They're heading for the second hut," she said, rising from her crouch. "Ready to run?"

Alex took one last look down at the cool, sheltering shade before heading out into the dangers of the open desert. But something was wrong. The ground wasn't shaded gray anymore; it was glowing a rosy pink.

"Don't go," came a thin, scratchy voice. "Stay a while."

Alex knew who he would find even before he looked up.

Peshwar. The three-hut shell game had fooled the rest of them, but The Order's heartless huntress had sniffed them out.

She stood waiting for them ten feet away, gazing out through the eye sockets of the sun-bleached lioness skull. In her hand was a shimmering crimson energy dagger. As soon as he saw it, Alex's elbow ached at the memory of its bite.

Quick as a whip, the hand holding the bloodred dagger shot back and rocketed forward. Alex and Ren dove to one side, Todtman and Bauer dropped to the other, and the brutal projectile slammed into the wall between them with a loud, crackling explosion.

Alex felt little chunks of mud brick spray across the back of his shirt, but what worried him more was the sound. He knew that would carry much farther — and alert the rest of The Order's forces.

As he rolled over and popped to his feet, Alex heard the shouts of men on the move and the metallic clicks and shucks of rifles being readied for action. The hunters were on the way. If the friends were to escape, if they were to keep the limitless power of the Spells out of the hands of their pursuers, it would have to be now.

We all have a choice, thought Alex, *and I choose to fight.*

Alex's hand closed tightly around the scarab, the beetle's wings digging into his palm, just a hint of the pain and danger to come. He turned to face the lethal lioness.

Peshwar lowered her hand and another energy dagger formed, spreading downward and crackling with power. Like an Old West gunfighter, Alex knew she was faster on the draw than he was. But her hand was still down, and his was already on the way up. He pointed his fingers like a spear.

The concentrated gust shot outward with the power of ten sledgehammers, but this time it was Peshwar who ducked nimbly to the side. Her crimson robes fluttered as she tucked and rolled across the sand. In an instant she was up — and releasing her dagger!

It flew not toward Alex, but straight at Todtman. And the old man was not nearly as nimble.

"No!" shouted Alex.

Todtman had one hand on his amulet and the other on his broom-handle cane. Too late and too slow to duck, he swung the cane like a baseball bat. Germans are not known for their baseball prowess, but somehow the awkward swing connected. The wood exploded in his hand.

Todtman released a sputtering shout of pain — "Aaghkk!" — and went down in a heap.

Alex couldn't tell how badly he was hurt — and had no time to ask. He spread his fingers wider to make his next gust harder to dodge. But before he released it, he took a quick look to make sure his mom and Ren were out of the way.

And that's when Ren released another powerful flash of white light. Not looking at her and with her eyes shielded by the sockets of her skull mask, Peshwar barely seemed to notice. Alex, on the other hand, had been standing in the shade and looking directly at it.

"Gaah!" he blurted, suddenly blinded.

And so he only heard the flies descend.

Millions of them.

The living, swarming cloud of hard-shelled bodies and beating wings felt as thick and tumultuous as breaking waves at the beach.

Alex knew the stakes now, understood the sort of ancient power and modern malice they faced. They were fighting not just for their own lives but for the fate of the world itself.

And that fight was not going well.

The insects engulfed him — swarming, biting — and the only sound louder than their buzzing was the burning crackle of the approaching energy dagger.

The Tides of War

Alex was pushed hard to the ground a moment before the energy dagger arrived, taking another chunk out of the wall behind him. He landed facedown, knocking the air from his lungs. He gasped to replace it and sucked in sand — but that was still better than a mouthful of flies. He could feel them swarming all around. He didn't even dare open his eyes to see who had saved him.

The sand flies bit down at the freshly exposed skin on the back of his neck. And the smell was almost worse. The energy dagger had bug-zapped a wide swath of them as it passed. The scent of so many barbecued bugs made him want to retch.

The scarab, he thought. *At least I can whip up some wind and get rid of these bloodthirsty pests.*

But as he reached up for the amulet, he found nothing. He patted his neck and chest furiously. *Oh no oh no oh no!* He reached around to the back of his bug-ravaged neck. He realized in horror that the worst sting he'd felt hadn't been a sting at all. It had been the raking scrape of the silver chain being torn free.

"Don't let her use it!" he heard. "Don't let her put it on!"

There was a rapid-fire barrage of energy daggers — *crackle, crash, boom* — and then there was a louder sound.

Much louder.

KRRAKOOOOM!

The thunder was so close overhead that it shook Alex's teeth. Just as he was scrambling to his feet, a vicious wind shear knocked him back to the ground. Suddenly, the flies were gone, and the rain began to pour down.

Alex opened his eyes into a downpour.

Lightning crackled overhead.

His mom had the scarab back.

The Order operatives had failed. He looked on in awe as she stood tall between him and his attackers. He had managed to summon the wind that came before the rain with the scarab. She had brought the rain itself.

Ren rushed over to him. "Are you okay?" she said through the lashing wind and rain.

Alex felt the smashed bodies of the bugs he'd managed to swat sliding off of him in the rain. "I think so," he said. "Look!"

In front of them, Todtman climbed back to his feet. Alex caught a glimpse of his eyes: They had changed. They looked like two glittering gems, the eyes of his falcon amulet writ large.

He stood shoulder to shoulder with Alex's mom, the wind rippling the back of his white shirt.

Peshwar and Aff Neb took a look at each other and then a shaky step back. Alex and Ren were novice Amulet Keepers, still trying to figure out what the scarab and ibis could do, but in front of them stood two Amulet Keepers in full. They seemed to be feeding off of each other's power, and the Egyptian sky roared its approval.

KRAKOOOOM!

As a flash of yellow lit the dark clouds overhead, Alex felt a glimmer of hope. The Order lieutenants were intimidated, almost transfixed by the display of power, but the spell was broken by a half dozen gunmen rushing around the perimeter of the old hut.

Dr. Bauer turned toward the new threat. The men pointed their rifles but then threw them to the ground and dove for cover. Alex hadn't been holding a chunk of metal, but he felt the sudden electrical charge in the air, too. He grabbed Ren and they sheltered against the battered wall.

This time the lightning hit the open ground near the prone gunmen. They flopped and convulsed like fish on a skillet before rolling over and hugging themselves in pain. Sand is a natural insulator, but the ground was wet, and even though he was farther from the strike, Alex's mouth tingled like he'd been sucking on a battery. He turned to Ren to find her formerly rain-slick black hair puffed out in all directions like an oversized dandelion.

Aff Neb rushed forward to attack. But before he'd made it three steps, he was attacking *himself*! His fists took turns punching his own head. Alex winced as he saw Aff Neb's left fist land smack-dab in his bulbous right eye. Todtman's jewel-like eyes gleamed as he guided the beat-down.

Peshwar tried her luck, flicking her hand down to summon another energy dagger. But almost as soon as the glow appeared, the red energy began to flicker and snap in her rain-slick hand. Even with the sky as dark as gray wool, Alex could see her eyes behind the sockets of the lioness skull, staring unblinking at his mom.

Ren saw it, too. Standing behind and a little to the left of Alex's mom, she raised her hand and pointed her fingers. Alex looked down and away.

FWOOOOP!

The brilliant white light filled the dark day — and Peshwar's unblinking eyes.

"Daa!" she spluttered, and as she did, the energy dagger fizzled out in her hand.

After one more punch to his own jaw, Aff Neb dropped to the ground a few steps in front of his soggy, blinded comrade. Twenty yards to the side, the gunmen still writhed in pain as their guns sizzled on the wet sand.

In a matter of minutes, the tides of war had shifted dramatically. Alex pushed himself free of the old wall, which was suddenly less brick and more mud, and looked around at a battle that seemed won. Joy and relief, strangers to him for so long, began to take hold.

But not all their enemies were accounted for.

The leader walked slowly into view. His thick ceremonial robes trailed just a few inches above the rain-soaked ground, but his body language gave the distinct impression of being far above it all. In the dim light of the storm, his golden vulture mask looked tarnished and fearsome. The iron beak was a pure, slick black. Alex's lungs filled to shout a warning. But before he could, he found himself frozen.

He could only stare at his mom's back as she and Todtman turned their attention to Peshwar. The mighty huntress now looked like a sullen, wet cat, her long-nailed hands held out like claws and her robes clinging to her skeletally thin frame.

Turn around! Alex thought as hard as he could. *Behind you!*

In thrall to the leader's power, he desperately wished he could move — then suddenly, he *was* moving.

And then he desperately wished he could stop.

His feet carried him forward. At first his steps were thick and awkward, but he sped up as the leader became more accustomed to his newest instrument. Next to him, Ren was doing the same thing. Or rather the same thing was being done to her. Alex heard her footfalls in the wet sand.

No no no! he thought.

But there was no denying it. They were running directly toward the others. He could feel his breathing, mechanical and even, but couldn't harness it to say even a single word. *Look out, Mom*, he thought. *Look out!*

But it wasn't his thoughts she heard. It was his wet, slapping footsteps.

Still focused on Peshwar, she risked a quick look back.

Too late.

Alex felt his legs sink lower and — *NO!* — launch him through the air.

As he flew toward his mom, he felt the leader's iron grip slip. He did everything he could to soften the blow, curling back in on himself in midair, but it was too late. He hit his mom in the midsection with a flying body block that knocked her to the ground with a muddy splash. Her hand came off the scarab as she reached out instinctively to protect not herself but her son from the impact.

Todtman saw Ren approaching, but he didn't understand the threat. "Ren?" he said, the jewel-like glow fading from his eyes. Then she launched herself — despite herself — and hit him low. He yelped like a kicked dog as she plowed into his bad leg, and they both went down hard.

The thunder faded and the rain stopped.

"I'm sorry! I'm sorry! I'm sorry!" said Alex, rolling over. The four of them had fallen into a lumpy heap on the ground, and were now turning and twisting as they began to disentangle themselves and sit up. He looked over to see if his mom was hurt or mad. "I couldn't help it!"

Instead of anger on her face, he saw a flash of confusion give way to a steadier glow. A rosy red light washed over her. She reached for the scarab, but stopped halfway as the point of a fresh energy dagger extended down almost to her nose.

"Don't," purred Peshwar.

And as the unnatural clouds pulled apart above them and the strong desert sun shone through, a second shadow fell across them.

The leader surveyed the wreckage wordlessly.

Alex heard the sound of the trapdoor popping open inside the hut. Almost immediately, the remaining gunmen rushed out like ants from a shattered anthill. They pointed their rifles down at the fallen Amulet Keepers.

"The Spells, please," said the leader, breaking the heavy silence.

"We don't have them," said Todtman, sitting up and seemingly daring the gunmen to shoot.

The leader looked over. "Who do you think you're talking to, Ernst?" he said.

Ren was on Todtman's left and Alex caught her eye and mouthed one word: *Ernst?*

"I know exactly who I am talking to," replied Todtman.

"Then you know you cannot lie to me," said the leader. He searched Todtman's face and seemed to find something there. He turned toward Dr. Bauer. "The backpack, please."

"Mom, don't!" called Alex, but she was already taking her backpack off, already handing it over. He could see the square edges of the briefcase through the nylon.

One of the gunmen reached down and took the pack. Alex glared at him as he ripped the top open and removed the briefcase. "Bring it to me," said the leader.

Alex looked around desperately, seeking some means of escape. But they were surrounded by enemies. The leader's eyes gleamed beneath his mask as the gunmen held the case out flat for him to open.

"Are they in there?" came a familiar voice. The smell as much as the tone told Alex that Aff Neb was back on his feet and approaching.

"Yes," said the leader. "I can feel their power."

Alex turned to his mom, ready to follow her lead. Instead, he saw her hand slip down toward her pants pocket.

Pop-pop!

The leader popped the clasps, and all eyes, even Peshwar's, shifted to the briefcase. Only Alex watched as his mom slid a plastic baggie from her pocket and removed a small black device from inside.

His pulse revved and his head swam as the leader slowly opened the case. But he was determined to stay conscious this time. Something was happening. An image flashed through his mind: *His mom folding the protective linen wrapping back over the Lost Spells, a small lump just visible . . .*

The lump was some sort of explosive charge. His mom would destroy the Spells rather than hand them over!

"There's something in here!" said the leader, alarmed. He pulled back the linen and Alex swayed and swooned. If he hadn't already been sitting in the wet sand, he was pretty sure he would've fallen over. But despite the powerful effect of the uncovered Spells, he fought to keep his fluttering eyes open.

His mom raised the little remote.

Press it, he thought. *Press it now!*

But she hesitated. Just for a second. Alex watched as she flexed her thumb without pressing down — and then the chance was lost.

The leader saw it now. He held out one hand, palm up, and the little device tore free from Maggie's grasp and flew to him. He cradled it gently as it arrived, catching it as if it were an egg. A moment later, it disappeared into the folds of his dark robes.

"Take their amulets," he said.

Alex watched woozily as Peshwar plucked the scarab from his mom and Aff Neb took Todtman's falcon and Ren's ibis. Alex bowed his head, helpless and beaten. The leader watched them carefully until the amulets were secured. Then he grabbed a small silver box from the briefcase and tossed it into the sand.

"Incendiary device," he said as it landed with a soft thud. Taking a long, hungry look at the Spells, he added, "They're beautiful."

He covered them back up and snapped the case shut. With the Spells once again concealed, Alex's head began to clear. He leaned toward his mom and whispered, "Why didn't you press it?"

She dropped her head. "I couldn't."

"She spent her whole life searching for them," interrupted the leader, his booming voice seeming to mock their whispers. "The greatest find in the history of archaeology. Not an easy thing to destroy."

"And instead," she said, staring down at the sand, "I have destroyed the world."

"Don't be so dramatic, Maggie," he said. The last word echoed through Alex's mind like one final peal of thunder. *Maggie . . . Who was this man who knew both Todtman and his mom?* "The world will not be destroyed in the Final Kingdom. It will be reborn. You, of all people, should understand that."

Alex's mom finally looked up at the man who mocked her. "A living death, then, ruled by tyrants."

Her tone was so sad and defeated that it tore Alex's heart in half. "It's not your fault," he said to her, trying anything to make her feel less miserable. "He made me run into you. I couldn't help myself."

Alex's mom looked over at him, her eyes softening even as the old worry lines deepened. "I thought I told you," she said. "Don't blame yourself."

"No, don't," said the leader, continuing to intrude on the conversation. "You did as I wished, but then, a boy should obey his father."

Alex stared at the man. *"What?"* he heard Ren say. Alex tore his eyes from the leader and looked back to his mom for confirmation.

"Alex, honey . . ." she began, but she didn't seem to know where to go from there. A moment later, the time for talk was over. They were prodded to their feet at gunpoint. Alex felt a rifle barrel digging into his back and reluctantly complied.

A few feet away, he saw Ren help Todtman to his feet. The friends were wet and battered and bowed in defeat.

Alex looked back at the leader, this man who claimed to be his father, this man whose face he'd still never seen. This man who'd been ready to sacrifice him in that pit. Alex wondered if he'd kill them all now.

The Order had everything: the amulets and their Keepers; the Lost Spells and their power. The Death Walkers would return; the stone warriors would rise. There was no force left in the world that could stop them.

Alex felt the gun barrel dig into his back again.

He shuffled slowly forward. What else could he do?

Enter your code to unlock traps and treasure!

RM2H2TRGW4

Her Ladyship's
Guide to Modern Manners

Her Ladyship's
GUIDE TO MODERN MANNERS

LUCY GRAY

NATIONAL TRUST BOOKS

First published in the United Kingdom in 2005 by
National Trust Books
151 Freston Road
London
W10 6TH

An imprint of Anova Books Company Ltd

Designer: Lee-May Lim

ISBN 1 90540 041 1
ISBN-13 9781 90540 041 6

A CIP catalogue record for this book is available from the British Library.

10 9 8 7 6 5 4 3 2 1

Printed and bound by MPG Books Ltd, Bodmin.

This book can be ordered direct from the publisher at the website:

www.anovabooks.com

Or try your local bookshop

Contents

Who needs manners?

That old saying, 'manners maketh Man', has an old-fashioned ring to it – especially in these days of equality. Maybe it conjures up images of upper-crust gentlemen doffing their top hats at one another in the street – rather an anachronism today! But is having good manners really relevant in modern society? Well, of course – good manners are alive and well, and practised by many of us every day of our lives, without even thinking about them much. But sometimes, when we're in situations we're not used to – a formal dinner with lots of silver cutlery, or even a chance to meet the Queen! – we don't know quite how to behave. But don't be nervous – the information in this book will help you to survive in all *manner* of strange situations.

Perhaps we wouldn't describe our behaviour as 'modern manners', but most of us try to abide by accepted rules in our society, and we also notice when those rules are broken or ignored. More and more, we're encouraged to think of ourselves as free spirits, free to do what we please and be true to our own inner nature. But that kind of attitude only works up to a point. Because, in fact, for society to get along smoothly we need to be able to depend on each other, to understand how someone is likely to behave, and to know the best way to respond without making some dreadful *faux pas.* And good manners provide some unwritten ground rules to help us know exactly what type of behaviour we expect in a certain situation. Sometimes it's hard to spot the subtle difference in behaviour, because social behaviour is a very fine-tuned thing. For instance, if you meet a close friend in the street, you'd know that a hug and kiss is a more than acceptable greeting. But if you bump into your boss in the supermarket, you'd probably stop at a friendly hello. A warm hug would cause embarrassment all round. So we need to know what manner to behave in: that's what modern manners are all about.

Good manners can help us get along with all people in society, however different they may appear to be from us. It's natural to notice the difference between people – perhaps their dress, their skin colour or their physical appearance – because of course we're not all the same. But we can treat each other with the same politeness and decency, and the same good manners all round. Our society has changed so much over the last century, and keeps on changing and evolving. Not that long ago, the telephone was a new-fangled device and people worried about what 'etiquette' to use when they spoke down it. Today, more than a few of us have the some worries about what kind of manners to use when writing an email message to a friend or colleague. Modern manners tackle new concerns, because society is constantly moving on, but all of them are to do with how our society operates. So perhaps this is a good point to have a quick look at how our society got to where it is today.

Good manners can help us get along with all people in society, however different they may appear to be from us.

Class versus tribe

Here's a little potted history of how class-conscious Britain became the society it is today – often called the 'classless society', though some would say that still isn't, quite true.

British society up until the period before the Second World War was very class-conscious. The upper classes, or aristocracy, were relatively few in number. But for centuries, they were the people with most power and influence, who got to decide how the country was run – because they were wealthy landowners who, quite literally, owned the country. They lived by their own social 'rules', which were drummed into them from birth, first in the nursery and later in expensive prep and public schools, where they only met other people from the same social class. As an aristocratic person grew up, this learnt behaviour became second nature. In some ways aristocratic behaviour was quite autocratic – taking action without considering others – but in other ways it was concerned with running society 'properly', in a very paternalistic way. The eldest sons would eventually inherit their father's estate, while their younger brothers would go into the army, the church or the judiciary. Daughters were married off to the sons of other aristocratic families, so as to produce children to preserve the aristocratic lineage. The whole system was self-perpetuating and almost watertight. Outsiders were supposed to 'know their place' and not attempt to put themselves on a level with their betters. This system had been very efficient and had persisted with only minor modifications for hundreds of years. But it was all about to change.

During the 19th century, a middle class of successful tradesmen had begun to grow in wealth and influence. For the first time, factory owners and shopkeepers could become wealthy in their own right, not through inherited riches. When the middle-class merchants began to get rich, they also wanted a share in the power that governed the country. The aristocracy was challenged, and tried to stop the rise of the middle classes in many ways. One small but effective way of trying to keep the middle classes 'in their place' was by adopting complex aristocratic rules governing manners. A middle-class man might be rich but without an aristocratic upbringing, he'd find it hard to grasp the labyrinthine rules that governed upper-class life – having the correct behaviour, or 'etiquette'. Some aristocrats mocked middle-class 'parvenus', who didn't speak with the right 'upper-class' accent, didn't have the right manners and foolishly tried to mix with their 'betters'.

Undeniably, some middle-class people made the mistake of trying to ape gentlemanly behaviour, leading to embarrassing mistakes – like talking about 'serviettes' when an aristocrat would probably say napkins, or saying 'toilets' instead of lavatories. None of that matters today, of course. Silly customs such as crooking the little finger while holding a tea cup were probably middle-class attempts to 'look posh' that didn't come off. One group of people was trying to emulate the learnt behaviour – or manners – of another social class, and couldn't quite get it right.

Lower- or working-class people came further down the social scale. Their role was to work on the estates of the aristocrats, labour in the factories of the middle classes and be domestic servants for both. The many working-class people were poor, ill-educated and exploited, and firmly 'kept in their place' by the classes above them. But, over time, the lack of social opportunity for the working classes led to growing discontent, and slowly a political and social movement began to grow, its object being to overturn the existing system, to establish one that provided the working poor with a fair share of the wealth they helped to create.

After the Second World War, society changed a great deal. Returning servicemen wanted a fair deal from the country they had fought for, and people demanded political change. A Labour government was elected in 1945, the National Health Service was created, grammar schools provided paid-for education for middle-class children: the welfare state came into being. All these measures helped to support the idea of social equality for all. Even though the class society seemed outwardly to be the same as before, subtle changes were afoot. People wanted to 'move up' in life, and indeed it was now possible to change your lot. But still, in the 1950s, many people still felt the way to success in this was to imitate aristocratic behaviour, in accent, dress sense and manners.

The counterculture revolution of the 1960s reacted against those persistent attitudes, and blew them away. Its youthful leaders, some of them barely out of school, were ostensibly rebelling over trivial things like pop music, clothes and hairstyles. But the real revolution was a call to end an archaic social system based on deference and inequality. The United States had a great influence at this time, as it still does today. In Western Europe, America, and many other countries, a younger generation refused to conform to the class system, or to bow to authority just for the sake of it. The 'Swinging Sixties' were a time of liberation, partly a reaction against the postwar years of privation, but also related to more pressing political changes, like civil rights.

Today, in the United Kingdom, the prewar class divisions in society are not so rigid, and some would say they barely exist. Education and the welfare state have given many people opportunities they would not have been allowed in a prewar society.

Manners are no longer anything to do with whether you are rich, had a private education or grew up in a certain social milieu.

The tribal society

How does all this relate to modern manners? Simply this – manners are no longer anything to do with whether you are rich, had a private education or grew up in a certain social milieu. Yes, there are still plenty of rich people around, some of them descendants of the original aristocrats, some of them still owning large country estates, but they no longer have the right to run the country as they once did. And there are probably just as many, if not more, wealthy people who've become rich through entrepreneurship, or running a business – or just by being celebrities (the 'new aristocracy' perhaps?). People are much more likely, in today's world, to define themselves by their work, their interests, or their background than by their social class, and to enjoy socialising with other people who share one of these aspects – or feel free to mix freely with all members of society. Just go into any British pub, and you're like to meet people from all walks of life.

It's still important to feel that you 'fit in' – especially when you're young and perhaps feeling a bit insecure about your place in life. Ever since the Beatles and the Rolling Stones, and before, younger people have defined themselves by their allegiance to a particular type of music – from mods and rockers in the 1960s, to teenyboppers, Goths, punks and heavy-metal music fans – and the clothes and behaviour that go with it. Every young generation finds its own 'tribes'.

But even the more grown-up among us can admit we often feel happier mixing with like-minded people – people that we understand, and feel we know how to behave with. It's natural, perhaps. For many of us, it's still a bit stressful to be in the company of people who have very different lives and interests from our own. Some people might feel nervous and say 'I'm afraid of saying the wrong thing', and what they are really getting at is that they don't know how to behave in this context, and what the social 'rules' are. But the rules really amount to grasping the basics of good manners – they can make you feel far more confident in different social situations and leave you less awkward and embarrassed.

But who decides what good manners are?

We all do. The days are long gone when mysterious aristocratic rules on proper etiquette defined every aspect of good behaviour, although some 'rules of etiquette' are certainly based on sensible ideas of respect and politeness. The relics of upper-class etiquette still exist, mostly in ceremonial and special occasions – like the 'rules' that go with the conventional wedding reception ceremony, on how to word invitations, or who can make speeches and when. But manners, and especially the modern manners that can help us today, spring from simpler and more understandable roots – simply the natural human concern most of us have for other people – and the wish to avoid hurting, embarrassing or inconveniencing others unnecessarily. What some would call 'natural politeness', perhaps – a trust that if we behave well to others, then they'll do the same for us.

In addition, there are what some would call 'formal manners', and these are more like the etiquette of old. When we're in an unusual and formal situation, it's very useful to know a bit about what kind of manners would be in order. But even if you find yourself standing next to the Queen of Spain at a Buckingham Palace garden party, simple politeness and friendly conversation are good manners enough. Even so, for those formal occasions that do still require a bit of ceremony, guidance is – nowadays – usually provided in advance. So, don't worry: if you happen to be knighted one day, somebody at the Palace will be sure to send you some hints on how to behave properly! If you find yourself in an awkward formal social situation, remember that most formal rules – like how to address the Queen – are simply the result of habits and custom built up over time, no more than that. These 'rules' are the last vestiges of that strange aristocratic etiquette, designed to keep the middle classes at bay – but today, you can feel free to revolt!

There are few places today where you won't be admitted unless you're wearing a suit and tie. But, on the other hand, knowing the 'expected' attire to wear at an occasion can be helpful, if it makes you feel more at ease if you fit in. It can also be good manners to show that you respect the nature of the situation and have dressed accordingly.

Are rules made to be broken?

In many senses, yes. The formal 'rules' of etiquette are hardly bothered with by most people today, in normal circumstances. Customs like 'always passing the port to the left' are leftovers from aristocratic dining rules. It seems silly to bother if the person on your right would like a glass – or would like something else to drink! But some of the rules of etiquette – that outdated aristocratic system – carry over into good manners. A lot of them are simple common sense.

Before we leave the formal manners defined by etiquette completely, remember that they had an important role (whatever you may think of it): they were there to help bind a certain social group together – in this case the aristocratic class. And it's apparent, just by looking at the many different ways we define ourselves today, just how much human beings like to feel part of a group – for good or ill. Although today we like to think of ourselves as independent-minded individuals, we also like to fit in with the crowd. And we still, even today, make rules to help us do that.

But I don't need these silly rules!

And, to be honest, there's nothing forcing you to use them, either. Sadly (some would say), bad manners are not illegal. And you don't have to go to society weddings, attend formal parties, get your children christened or wear a tie if you don't want to. But what if your best and truest friend decides on a grand wedding, with all the frills and customs – would you go then? We never know what's coming next, and we can find ourselves changing our minds. Sometimes, it's just easiest to follow a few rather silly formal rules in order to make an event or occasion more pleasant for someone who matters to you – and, you know, that's what good manners are all about.

Have some respect!

How many times might you have heard an older person expressing amazement at a youngster's rudeness? Sometimes they're quite justified, but sometimes it's just a case of misinterpretation. It's easy to forget how much society has changed and how informal and liberated it is today – and still is, in comparison to some less-developed countries. The older generation can think back to days, not too long ago in memory, when society was much more formal. Men were always called by just their surname, bosses always 'Mr' this or that (a female boss would have been almost unheard of). But staff lower down the scale – tea ladies, cleaners and janitors – were referred to by their first name, but in a rather patronising way, almost as if they were comparable to children.

Over the years our society has adopted less formal systems of address as the norm, and most workplaces operate on a completely first-name basis. We're no longer deferential and we no longer put our bosses up on a higher social pedestal (much as some might like it!). On the one hand, the informality we use today helps everyone to feel more equal. But on the other hand, it's sometimes difficult to know how to show your respect towards someone. We call Presidents 'Mr' or 'Mrs' and sometimes Prime Ministers too – almost as a relic of how it used to be. But, on the whole, we tend to quite quickly refer to new acquaintances by their first names, sometimes – in the case of email, for instance – before we've even met them.

We no longer treat going to see our doctor, our priest or our children's teachers as formal occasions, though there was a time when people 'dressed up' to go to the doctor, and no woman would leave the house without her hat on. Life has changed, and we regard these people as equals, providing us with a service or information and to be valued for their talents and skills. But we can still show natural respect to people, simply through the way we treat them.

There was a time when people 'dressed up' to go to the doctor, and no woman would leave the house without her hat on.

And we need to remember too, in such a mobile society as ours, that there are many people who may have come here from a very different social situation in a different country, perhaps one where formality is still more normal. To call them by their first name, especially perhaps someone of an older generation, may make them feel very awkward. Good manners means considering what they are used to, as well.

Indeed, some professions preserve an artificial formality, as a way of keeping a professional distance between people. Somehow it would seem strange if lawyers and judges in the Crown Court referred to each other by their first names, when 'My Learned Counsel' or 'M'Lord' are what everyone expects. Even in ordinary meetings we refer to 'Madam Chair'. And many of us still retain formality when addressing our doctor, or our member of parliament. Forms of address, like other examples of formal manners, or etiquette, often have a helpful purpose – they prevent informality when we *don't* really want it. There are times when we'd rather keep it as professional as possible, because then nobody is going to 'take something personally' when it wasn't intended that way.

Whatever modern manners are, they certainly are not fixed. As society changes, so do manners – because manners reflect the way we act towards each other in our daily lives.

A few basics

Punctuality

Arrivals...

Time is of the essence – and being on time is important, so it gets a whole section to itself. Think about it: being on time for appointments and social occasions is simple good manners, modern or otherwise. Some good advice: for any social occasion, find out when you are expected to be there, and be there on time. Easy! Perhaps that seems obvious to you? Well, that's good. But, if you're always late – or are always left waiting for somebody else who is – see if you recognise any of these types:

First of all there's the 'I just couldn't get my act together' person. Some people are so disorganised that they are always dashing from one appointment to another, late for everything, and always find themselves arriving breathless at the door, apologising profusely. We've all been in that situation sometimes, but if you're always finding yourself saying to your friends, 'Oh, you know what I'm like – I'd be late for my own funeral!', then think about it. Perhaps, like you, your friends think it's just an endearing little fault. Or perhaps they don't – if you've actually made them miss the beginning of the film, or the train they'd planned to catch. Or perhaps you're the friend who always has to wait, and then you'll know how aggravating that kind of behaviour can be.

Then there's the 'I just didn't check the time' person. They arrive very late and, to be honest, don't care when they turn up.

They assume the host will be thrilled to see them, whenever they arrive. They don't think about whether people have been worried about their whereabouts, or whether the other dinner guests have had to sit waiting.

Finally, there's the 'look at me!' attention-grabber, who is well aware that they're late – that's the way they planned it. They want to make a grand entrance and be noticed by everyone in the room. Ideally, they'd like to come down a long flight of Hollywood steps, in a feather boa.

Are you one of those, or do you recognise them? Whichever latecomer you, or the person you're thinking of, may be, being late is, essentially, just being rude. Not good manners at all.

Good manners when it comes to punctuality aren't difficult to acquire. Be on time – it's only considerate, after all. Even the simplest party has taken a bit of an effort, and your hosts are looking forward to seeing you. Even if there is a later showing of that film, why should your friend wait outside in the rain for twenty minutes, wondering what happened to you this time. Put yourself in the other person's position, and good manners become an easy matter. And just think – you won't have to make excuses for being late, and they won't have to get stressed out waiting.

Be on time – it's only considerate, after all.

What if you're the host of that party – how can you help? Well, always make sure to be quite specific about time when you invite someone, unless you really don't mind when they turn up (and then tell them that). But you can't be too school-marmish about it – it's helpful to allow a bit of leeway, to allow for some guests getting caught in traffic or being unavoidably detained. So, if you say something like 'do come 8 for 8.30' (meaning, we'll eat at 8.30, so come some time before then, but after 8pm) if you want to ensure that people won't be late. And if you're a guest, make sure you allow time for that unexpected eventuality, like a pile-up on the motorway ahead. Things can, and often do, go wrong – so makes sure you plan ahead.

What if you really can't avoid being late?

Sometimes there's nothing you can do about it – if the babysitter didn't turn up, or you got delayed at work, or the trains weren't running. If you can, phone ahead and warn your friend or host that you've been delayed, and why. Let them know what time you expect to be there and apologise briefly. When you do arrive you can make a proper apology but for now keep it short – don't forget they may be looking after their other guests, or waiting in the rain, depending on the situation. Always give the reason why you're unavoidably late – if people have already been waiting half an hour to eat, because you weren't there, they'll at least appreciate knowing why. If you're the host of a dinner party and someone 'calls in late', you should never let your impatience show – even if your guest has no real excuse, and you think they've just been very inconsiderate. It's good manners to rise above it, and not let your annoyance show. Why should your other guests have to deal with your annoyance, or the tension in the air when your guest arrives? Keep the atmosphere pleasant, don't embarrass your guests – save it for after they've gone!

Being late is one thing. The other gaffe you can make is arriving too early. Arriving early at a dinner party or drinks is only acceptable when the hosts are very close friends, and they have let you know they could do with some help getting things set up, or keeping the kids occupied. In other circumstances, being early can be just as inconsiderate as being late, and not good manners at all. Your hosts are probably looking forward to having time to change, and a five-minute breather before the hordes arrive. Don't be the one who spoils their moment of quiet relaxation!

...and departures

When is it time to leave? Many people find it difficult to know just when to go, and either leave too early or outstay their welcome. It's good manners to choose your moment appropriately but also, if you're the host, it's good manners to let your guests know without appearing rude. For instance, if you want an event to finish at a particular time, it's quite in order to make this clear on the invitation. It's not at all unusual to do this when you have booked a public venue, or the event is an 'at home' or, perhaps, in honour of someone who is frail or older, and needs to rest. On the other hand, it can look rather eccentric, and even rude, to tell dinner guests that the evening will finish at a certain time – normally you have to rely on your guests to make their departure tactfully, even though you can drop a few hints (offering coffee for a second time or yawning discreetly sometimes help!).

If you're a guest, choosing the right moment to leave an event can be awkward. You're not alone if you're one of those people who just doesn't know when to say 'I must be getting off now.' If you genuinely have another appointment to go to, make sure you tell your host right at the outset, when they invite you – they won't think you rude if you explain that you'd love to come to lunch, but will have to leave early to get to a previously planned engagement. But they will think you rude if, later on in the evening, you suddenly 'remember' another appointment, as an obvious excuse to get away.

Who's going first? It's always a problem at a party – nobody wants to be first to leave, because it seems as if they're keen to go. Eventually somebody will take the plunge and offer their farewells, and then usually others seize the opportunity to join them. A mass exit of this sort is quite acceptable. If you're the host, don't be offended if some people have to leave early, either – some people need to get back home for various reasons, or may have an early start tomorrow. But, as a guest, whatever time you leave a party, you should seek out the host or hosts, let them know that you're off now, and thank them for their hospitality. One obvious item of tactful good manners: tell them you had a good time, even if you didn't. And however much you long to slip away unnoticed from that really boring party, don't. Apart from the fact that it's just not good manners, you'll probably not get away with it – Fate always steps in at such moments, and your host will probably catch you in the act of sneaking into the coat room and out of the back door. Be polite: it doesn't take long to say goodbye, after all!

But, even if the party is amazingly good, don't outstay your welcome. Unless you've been asked to stay the night, assume that your hosts would quite like you to leave before the cock crows for tomorrow. Judging this is a fine art – it depends on the kind of party, and the kind of hosts. Some friends are quite happy to stay up nearly all night, chatting and enjoying each other's company. In that case it's obviously fine to stay into the wee hours. Other hosts may have small children, or be obviously exhausted. Use your intelligence – if you find yourself in the middle of a long monologue, and your hosts are asleep on the sofa, it's time to go. Actually, it was time to go quite a while back.

If you're a host stuck with a guest who just won't take the hint, it's quite acceptable to stifle a yawn and say 'Oh well, must get to bed now. We've got an early start tomorrow.' Some people need a good dig in the ribs before they'll take the hint and leave – help them out a little.

The truth and nothing but the truth

When is it good manners to tell the truth? And when is it good manners to tell a few white lies? Good manners involve more than a bit of diplomacy – in essence, your considerate good manners help create situations where events turned out as desired, with the least amount of friction. Sometimes a few fibs help that along – it's up to you. It was the young George Washington who said he 'couldn't tell a lie', admitting to his father that he'd cut down the cherry tree – but how many of us could say we are compulsive truth-tellers in that league? Not many. Most people don't want to hear the 'unvarnished truth' about themselves, especially if it's not too pleasant. That's not to say we have to go around flattering everyone and telling them how marvellous and wonderful they are, but it can be good manners to avoid awkward subjects, and tell a little white lie on occasion. If it saves someone's feelings, and does no other harm, there isn't much cost to you – and it will help someone to feel good about themselves, perhaps.

Most people don't want to hear the 'unvarnished truth' about themselves, especially if it's not too pleasant.

Sometimes, however much people ask for it, they don't really want your advice. Beware of being too direct in your opinion, especially if being 'outspoken' may hurt someone. Put yourself in the other person's position and, especially if you have a negative opinion in mind, perhaps keep it to yourself. In general, the only time for a really straightforward opinion is if you have been hired to give professional advice, of a factual nature. However much a friend genuinely appeared to want your opinion, bear in mind that they may not be expecting what you could say – and your friendship could be damaged as a result.

Manners and snobbery

In theory, manners are a way to help us behave in a civilised way towards our fellow members of society. Anyone can have good manners. In our so-called classless society, however, there's still a great deal of snobbery around. And there are still public-school-educated folks with 'cut-glass' accents, and many less privileged members of society – some of whom may have accents that others deem 'common' or 'working-class'. These distinctions are hard to eradicate, and are often ingrained. Good manners involve rising above such snobby behaviour as calling those you deem less cultured than you 'oiks' or 'chavs', for instance, or – on the other hand – reverse snobbery, such as calling the landed gentry 'hooray henrys' or 'public-school twits'. Perhaps it's human nature to feel more comfortable among those who share our own values, but that doesn't mean that we have to avoid the company of people from other parts of society, and doesn't give us, or them, any right to feel superior. Eleanor Roosevelt once said: 'No one can make you feel inferior without your consent.' She was, as so often, very wise. If you are confident of who you are and what you are worth, you will be able to walk with kings. You don't have to treat people from other walks of life as enemies to be guarded against. You merely have to show them that you are quite comfortable in your own skin and that you assume the same respect from them that you give to others.

Not in front of the children

Unless you choose to join an enclosed religious order, you're going to meet children in a variety of social situations. If you're invited to a social occasion, it's only good manners to ask your host if your children are welcome, and to understand if the host indicates that it's not really an occasion where children would be happy. Listen carefully to your host's answer and judge for yourself whether they mean children are really welcome or that they are merely tolerated. Don't take offence if it seems that, on this occasion, it's really an adult affair – some events, like a formal dinner party for instance, just aren't suitable for kids, who'll probably be bored and tired anyway, and may spoil it for everyone else, including you. You may be used to your kids creating mayhem, running around playing and generally doing what children do. But, if it's not a family event, your hosts – and the other guests – may find this rather distracting. Yet your children are of course part of the family, and you may want them to come along – especially if you know they are capable of behaving politely and not being disruptive to others. There are plenty of kids who can be relied upon to enjoy a grown-up party and even to help by refilling glasses and taking round plates of food. Bear in mind that you might have to bribe them with some extra pocket money though!

There are plenty of kids who can be relied upon to enjoy a grown-up party and even to help by refilling glasses and taking round plates of food.

If you are the host you have a couple of options when it comes to inviting guests with kids. A good one, if you have the stamina, is to throw an extended party in which Part One takes place in the afternoon or early evening and is for families with kids and Part

Two is held later and is for adults only. Alternatively, you can go out of your way to have a children's room and provide toys, games, videos or whatever to keep the children happy. This can work well but it does mean that adults will have to keep an eye on the proceedings.

Both parents and hosts should bear in mind that kids don't necessarily all want to play together – especially if they have never met before. Don't force your kids to 'join in' with all the games and other children's activities: if they're happiest reading a book in the corner, or staying with you, let them. Our considerate good manners need to extend to the kids as well!

At some of the more formal occasions, like weddings, children can become a bit overwhelmed, especially tiny children and babies, who might start crying at just the wrong moment. Although everyone loves to see that tiny bridesmaid, or the adorable little pageboy, it's good manners to make sure there's an adult nearby who'll take charge if the occasion becomes too much, and bawling commences. A hug and a kiss is often all it takes, and can do a lot to keep the day special and happy for everyone.

In the same way, it's important to consider other people in public places, such as restaurants, where wandering or wailing kids can really spoil other people's enjoyment. Even though you might be longing just to relax and enjoy your meal, it's good manners to think about the other diners. Don't let small children run around bothering people who may find them a bit of a nuisance, and don't take offence if other people don't seem thrilled to be surrounded by small toddlers. Children are children, of course. But they're also quite capable of sitting and enjoying their meal without too much hyperactivity – and it's the way to learn the good manners that you'll be teaching them by example. But you can only do your best, and most fellow diners in a family restaurant will probably sympathise – they've almost certainly been in the same boat.

One tricky question is whether children should attend family funerals. In the old days the answer was 'of course', then received wisdom swung the other way and at one point it was deemed quite inappropriate. Now the pendulum has swung back quite a long way and the feeling seems to be that, as long as the children understand what's going on, they should be allowed to say goodbye with everyone else. It is a decision that should be based on the maturity of the child, and whether or not they want to attend.

Another difficult issue is that of children and medical treatment. Attitudes have changed a lot and now by the time the children reach secondary school it is likely that they will be treated as responsible people able to speak for themselves. While they are pre-teens you will still be welcome to attend the consultation, but as they get a bit older you may find it suggested that they should see the doctor alone. They can even go to get medical advice and treatment without your knowledge and consent. Many parents find this deeply troubling. They feel that their role is being undermined by outsiders. But if you ensure that your relationship with your kids is close enough that they feel they can confide in you, they are likely to tell you about any medical problems that concern them, or even ask for you to accompany them to see their doctor.

Sorry seems to be the hardest word

We all end up in situations where an apology is necessary. Sometimes it's simply making a tactless remark, or putting our foot in it. Or perhaps we lost our temper for a moment and snapped at someone – friend or family – or did or said something we now regret. None of us are perfect, and all of us have the ability to say 'sorry', and mean it.

Saying 'sorry', and meaning it, is not a sign of weakness. Far from it. It's a sign of good manners and consideration. That mythical person who said, 'Never apologise and never explain', was trying to sound tough, but succeeded only in being insensitive, and really rather crass. What on earth is wrong with trying to make amends if we have done something thoughtless or hurtful?

Saying 'sorry', and meaning it, is not a sign of weakness.

How to say sorry depends on the nature of the apology, and what it's for. Barging into someone in the street because you weren't looking where you were going can usually be put it right with a simple, 'I'm so sorry, I didn't see you', and a big, apologetic smile. If the apology is for something a bit more 'serious', you'll need to say sorry in the most appropriate way. For example, if you said something hurtful or did something thoughtless that offended a friend, then a quick, 'Whoops, sorry!' just won't do the trick. They may think you're mocking them, and are unlikely to believe your apology. Sometimes a little present can go a long way to helping an apology along, but don't think you can necessarily buy your way to forgiveness. Above all, you need to talk with the person you inadvertently offended, and try hard to put matters right. You can't rush this sort of thing and it's no good hoping that just saying the right words will get you off the hook. You have to mean them, too.

Not all apologies are of the personal variety. If you mess up at work – perhaps forgetting to deliver something with an important deadline, or losing a vital file – the only thing you can do is 'own up' and say sorry. Don't try to conceal the problem, because people are bound to find out eventually and will respect you far less if you didn't come clean in the first place. Usually a problem can be solved and the quicker the better – explain what went wrong, say sorry, help to rectify the situation if you can. Just remember how little we respect some of those particularly evasive politicians who try to avoid answering difficult questions, or are insincere in their responses. Don't be like them – your manners are better than that!

One situation in when it pays to stop and think before you say 'sorry' is when a formal letter is required or a legal situation is implied. Then it's best not to say 'sorry, my fault' straight away, even if you want to help smooth things out. If you and another driver have a prang at a crossroads, don't leap out of your car and immediately start offering profuse apologies. It may not have actually been your fault, even if you are trying to be nice! In this case you want to keep things formal, so that you can go through the proper insurance procedures. Exchange details, ask any witnesses for their name and contact number, and check that everyone is okay. But hire a lawyer if apologies are required.

Finally, sometimes we are in the position of having to apologise for something that was not our own fault. If someone has taken offence at something for no reason you can see, or if someone blames you for something that was, by rights, caused by a colleague's action, what can you do? Where the problem is trivial, often the simplest, and most well-mannered route is to quietly apologise to defuse the situation.

Oh, don't mention it...

Receiving an apology can be almost as difficult as offering one. Good manners call for you to be gracious when someone makes you a heartfelt apology. Rubbing someone's nose in their mistake will make you look petty-minded and vindictive. Just as the apology needs to be sincere, so does the acceptance. It is pointless to say that you forgive someone if you don't, but you can still be civil in your response, and listen to what the person has to say. If the apology is personal, it is important that the person understands how hurt you were – but don't go on and on about it: just say your piece, and stop. Don't use an incident to gain some kind of emotional sway over a friend and never bear grudges.

If someone has made a mistake, remember that nobody's perfect, and everyone makes errors or tactless remarks sometimes. We are all human and fallible and every now and then everyone manages to drop a really heavy brick. That can hurt, but if someone has the decency to explain and apologise sincerely you ought to accept. But on the other hand, of course you're under no obligation at all to let someone off if they are just anxious to get out of an awkward situation or if they make a habit of being thoughtless. With friends like that, who needs enemies? And it might be time to cool it towards that particularly thoughtless person.

Saying 'sorry' almost seems to be an unconscious 'tic' for many Brits, and quite a few foreigners get rather confused by the amusing British habit of apologising for things that are not their fault. When an American asks, 'Is this the train for Kings Cross?' we reply, 'No, sorry, this one goes to Kings Lynn.' Why on earth are we sorry, they wonder? We didn't make the mistake and we've just saved someone from a long journey in the wrong direction. So, perhaps it's best to concentrate hard on not saying sorry unless you've actually done something wrong!

The golden rule

Is there anything more important than fitting in with the crowd? Although people have many different ideas about how to behave and some of these ideas may be contradictory, there is a general consensus among most people that kindness and consideration for others are basic values to which we all must aspire. No matter what else you may get wrong, as long as you stick to these two things you will never be far wrong and it's unlikely that you will ever get into a situation that cannot be salvaged. Your considerate good manners will see you through. In fact your consistent respect and thoughtfulness will probably mark you out to others as someone deemed to have 'natural politeness' and 'a good nature'. And, even if you've put a lot of work into your manners, you should take that as one of the highest compliments going!

Party people

We're all social animals, aren't we? Some of us are more outgoing than others but, on the whole, few people object to a good party with friends. What's more, we need to meet and interact with people – often a wide variety of people in different social and work-related situations. All these social events help to 'oil the wheels' of the society we live in. So we meet in all sorts of ways – parties, conferences, business meetings, cultural events and nights out with our friends – and we can be very inventive in our reasons for getting together. 'Let's get together for a drink!', 'Come over and we'll play a round of golf with Jack and Mary', 'We should hook up to go to a play together some time', 'Fancy a coffee next Saturday?'. And when we meet up, we get on with all sorts of social activities, depending on the situation. We may make friends, do business, plot and plan, select new sexual partners, exchange gossip and just strengthen the bonds that hold our various social 'tribes' together. For most of us, socialising is both a pleasure and a necessity and knowing how to behave makes every event easier and more effective. Having a good grasp of the modern manners suitable for a variety of different social occasions will help them to go well for you, and what manners to use depend slightly on the social occasion.

Invitations

How do you send them, and how do you respond to them? Today, an invite can be as formal as a gold-edged card covered in fancy copperplate writing, or merely a hastily scrawled note, a text message or a quick message on the answerphone. Really there are no strict rules on what form an invitation should take, although it's unlikely that your invitation to attend that Buckingham Palace garden party will arrive by fax. The more formal the occasion, the more formal the invitation is likely to be.

Send...

If you're not the sort to give big formal parties all the time, deciding what sort of invitation to send, and what it should say, can be a bit daunting. But don't worry – you can get a lot of help on this. If you go along to your local printer or copy shop, you'll find they have all kinds of samples you can look at, as well as suggested wordings. You can even look for samples on the Internet, and order them that way. The simplest advice is that you should keep your wording clear and concise, with details of time, place and, if it matters, dress code. Make sure you explain clearly what kind of event it is – a wedding or baby-naming ceremony, or an 18th birthday, or whatever. If it's a formal occasion, it's probably best not to try to be funny or too 'original', as people may misunderstand. You may want people to RSVP – so that you can get a good idea of how many people to expect. Incidentally, the letters RSVP at the bottom of an invitation stand for *Répondez s'il vous plaît* (meaning 'Answer, please'), and are a leftover from the days of aristocratic etiquette, when French was the most fashionable language. If you put RSVP on the invitation, you must provide an address, or perhaps just a phone number or email address, which people can reply to.

...and receive

When you receive an invitation the most important rule of all is that you must reply, and promptly – not at the last minute, even if you don't intend to go. And even if there is no 'RSVP' on the bottom of the invitation, you really should let people know whether you are able to attend, if there is a way. Think about how difficult it is to cater an event if you're not sure how many people to expect, or when – it's good manners to help lower your host's stress levels if you can! Also, if you have said you will be coming and then find that something has come up that you just can't get out of, it's good manners to call your hosts and send your apologies, as soon as you can.

Replying to an informal invitation is easy – usually you can just phone or email. For formal invitations, it's more usual to reply in writing, and to write in the third person. So, if you get an ornate wedding invitation that says something like 'Mr and Mrs John Smith invite you to the wedding of their daughter Julie to Mr Alan Jones', you'd probably write back 'Mrs Jane Evans thanks you for your kind invitation and will be delighted to attend.' And remember to write back to the person who sent the invitation – in this case Mr and Mrs John Smith, rather than the people who are actually getting married. But, actually, even formal occasions are getting more and more flexible in the way they invite people, so don't be surprise or put off if the invitation indicates that a phone call would be acceptable. And, similarly, when many people are hosting their own marriages or other formal get-togethers, they are likely to send out the invitation in their own name, rather than Mum and Dads'.

Playing host

There's an art to being a good host. Some would say that if you're enjoying your own party, then you can't be doing a good job as host. That's not necessarily true, but perhaps what they're getting at is that you have to do a lot of work to make a party go well. You need to be seeing to your guests, making sure they have refreshments, introducing them to people they might like to meet and, just as important, keeping them away from people that might rub them up the wrong way.

If the party is an informal 'walk about' (or even dance about!), your job as host is to keep circulating, because it's your job to make sure that people are happy and interested and not feeling unwanted. Remember that you're probably the only person in the room who knows a bit about every guest present, so you can introduce people to each other and start the conversation between them. Try and find something they might have in common, or something unusual or interesting that might start them chatting. But don't reveal personal secrets or embarrassing information! 'Jack, you must meet Bob – he's got the most wonderful house, quite near where you used to live' is fine. 'Jill, you must meet Joan – she's in therapy for depression too' is probably not! Once you've got a conversation started, move on after a few minutes. Don't monopolise people and don't let them monopolise you. Your job is to make everyone feel wanted. If you see someone who is clearly feeling a bit left out you need to introduce them to someone they might get on with. If you see cliques forming you should try to break them up as tactfully as possible. The sort of party where all your friends from the office, for example, take over one room and chat to each other while freezing out any interlopers is to be avoided at all costs. It helps if you have activities that get people talking to each other. If it's a fun event, like a Christmas party, you can even have some silly games.

It helps if you have activities that get people talking to each other.

At formal professional or work gatherings, such as conferences or business parties, it can be helpful to give people name badges.

This saves everyone the trouble of having to ask names and then perhaps mishearing them or forgetting them and then having to bluff their way through the rest of the event. If it's a professional meeting, you can also include the person's job or company, which helps to provide a conversation opener, so guests can approach each other. Remember that your job as host is to make everything as easy and comfortable as possible for your guests. Anything that might cause a guest difficulty or embarrassment should be dealt with swiftly and smoothly. Little things like where to park the car and where they can safely leave coats can cause guests a problem right at the beginning of an event, so make sure you have that sorted out already. And during the party, small embarrassments – like a dropped glass of wine – should be cleared up quickly with a smile and a quick 'don't worry about it!' A good host thinks ahead, to put their guests at ease.

Some people just love throwing parties. Others don't. That's fine: if you don't feel up to being an extrovert and capable host, then consider hiring staff to help you out, especially for a larger, formal do. You can also hire caterers to do all the cooking, serving – and the washing up. And why not – it may cost a bit, but many people think that it's money well spent, especially for a once-in-a-lifetime party. Today it's not just big wedding receptions that have caterers: some people hire a caterer to provide the food for the small dinner party at home, or for an informal birthday bash.

And while we're on the subject of food and drink: do always make sure that everyone has enough. But also, as host, don't force food and drink on people, even if you can't understand why they wouldn't want more. And lastly, if alcohol is being served, watch out for people who may have had 'one too many'. Try to make sure they stop drinking if you can – quietly removing their glass or the bottle can be more polite, and effective, than getting cross –

and certainly don't let them drink or drive. Offer to call them a taxi, arrange for them to be dropped off by a sober guest who's going the same way – even offer them a bed for the night, if that's the only option.

Safety first

Your final duty as a good, well-mannered host is to make sure that everyone gets home safely, as much as you can. Make sure that younger and older guests, especially, have a lift home. Know which guests you can trust to take people to their front door. It's simple common sense, but can do a lot to make your guests leave feeling happy.

How to be a great guest

You may feel that being a great guest just involves turning up and enjoying yourself. Actually, that's not strictly true. First of all, for most private parties it's good manners to bring a small present for your hosts. Safe, if rather uninspired, choices are a bottle of wine, a bunch of flowers or perhaps a small flowering plant or a box of chocs. That's more than acceptable for most situations. If you know your host very well and have an idea of their taste, you could bring something a bit more adventurous – a rose bush for that gardening-fanatic friend, or some scented candles that match your friend's newly decorated bathroom. But keep to safe choices unless you know your hosts well.

Once you've arrived, it's good manners to think about the other guests. If most guests know each other, look out for any newcomers who may feel a bit left out. Make a point of chatting with them and helping the social situation along. If conversations are getting a bit 'cliquey', try to steer them to more general areas where everyone can join in. There's nothing more bad-mannered than a group of guests who stand around gossiping and making in-jokes that the other guests can't understand. Help your host out by making sure all guests are involved in the social interaction.

If the food is a buffet or other informal situation and there are no professional waiting staff, you can help a bit by handing round snacks to the guests near you, or keeping glasses topped up. You don't need to spend the whole time doing these things but it is polite to lend a hand when it is needed. And actually, if you are yourself feeling a bit shy or awkward, it can be a good way of keeping yourself occupied and being 'part of things'.

At the end of the evening, if you're driving, you might ask if anyone is going your way that needs a lift. You may save a grateful person a taxi fare and also have some company on the way home. If you need a lift yourself, it's quite in order to ask if anyone's going your way, or to ask your host if you might phone for a taxi.

Some people like to send their host a note thanking them for the party and telling them how much they enjoyed it. This custom is becoming rare these days but it is a nice one. It is always touching to receive a little thank-you card, or even an email or text message. All you need to say is how much you enjoyed the evening and add some pleasantries about the food or the company. Two or three sentences at most will do the job.

Meeting and greeting

What are the rules when it comes to introducing yourself to strangers at a social event? It can be awkward to find yourself in a situation where you don't know anyone, or would like to make yourself known to someone, but there is no host around to do the introductions. But things have changed. It used to be the case that rules for introductions were strictly observed as part of social etiquette. Men had to be introduced to ladies, and young people were introduced to their elders. People were very formal and addressed each other in ways befitting their status in society. None of that now applies, you'll be very glad to hear, but that doesn't mean that there are no longer any rules. There are unspoken 'rules', but they are different and less clearly defined. In order to play the social game these days you have to employ some common sense and a little psychology. If you spot someone you'd like to talk to there is nothing wrong with going up to them and introducing yourself. You don't have to be clever, or word your introduction in a particular way. You can just say something basic like 'Hi, I'm Tom, I don't believe we've met,' while holding out your hand to shake. The other person will most likely introduce themselves then, but if not you can say something like 'and you're…?' to encourage them to do so. Remember to smile and use a friendly tone of voice. 'Clever' introductions and smart chat-up lines usually make you look like an idiot. If you don't feel confident enough to go straight up to someone, you can attach yourself to the group they are in and take an opportunity to contribute to the conversation when a gap arises. Sometimes this is hard though, especially if you're a bit shy, or all the other people are deep in conversation. It's often better to seek out the host, and ask them to introduce you to the person you'd like to meet. This way you stand to get a bit of background information about them in advance, which will help ease you into a conversation.

In order to play the social game these days you have to employ some common sense and a little psychology

Shaking hands may seem a bit formal to some people, but

when you meet someone for the first time, it's quite in order – whether it's a business or personal social situation. You don't have to do more than give a firm, friendly handshake. Quite brief – no need to pump someone's arm up and down enthusiastically! It goes without saying that you should have clean hands – that may sound pretty obvious, but at a buffet lunch you could find yourself inadvertently covered in salad dressing, so wipe your hands on a napkin first. It's actually quite acceptable, if you are busy balancing a glass and plate of food, to say 'Nice to meet you,

The days are long gone when only men could initiate a handshake, by the way.

Eye contact

In Western culture eye contact, and how we use it, is extremely important in social interaction (things are different in some other cultures). In British society we tend not to look 'straight on' at someone too much until we know them well, although we do make eye contact quite a bit. In North America it's much more normal to make and keep eye contact with anyone you are talking to – so don't be put off if an American seems to be staring at you hard while you converse. In general it's not only good manners but good psychology to look at people while you speak to them. People really will trust you if you give them a lot of eye contact. In fact, you'll often notice that salesmen and woman may look straight into your eyes all the time you're talking with them. They've been trained to convey sincerity (even if some of them aren't sincere!).

I'm afraid my hands are full at the moment,' or something similarly friendly and cheery, if it's impossible to put things down.

If somebody doesn't initiate the handshake, remember that you can. Hold out your hand in a friendly way towards the other person and say 'Pleased to meet you!'. The days are long gone when only men could initiate a handshake, by the way.

The art of conversation

Unless you're a natural chatterer, happy to talk about anything and everything, making conversation at social events can be a bit awkward. What should you talk about, and how? There used to be an unwritten rule that sex, politics and religion were subjects to avoid, except with good friends. But nowadays it's quite all right to talk about these topics in serious conversations with people you've just met. Many people enjoy the cut and thrust of an intellectual or political debate, or like to debate an issue of the day. If you do too, make sure that your companions are genuinely interested in this kind of 'heavy-duty' conversation before you wade in. You wouldn't want them to feel you were directly attacking their beliefs or views and inadvertently get involved in a full-on row. Good manners call for tact and diplomacy and even if someone starts spouting off about something in a way you find quite disagreeable or, in your opinion, wrong, try to react calmly and with restraint. Other people will respect you for it.

Social chitchat, or 'small talk', about day-to-day subjects is usually best unless you are sure you've read the situation correctly. Usually you're well advised to spend a few minutes of conversation with a new acquaintance generally getting to know them and exploring what views and values you may have in common, without getting in too deep. If you end up talking with another guest who, it quickly becomes clear, holds views that are so different from yours you just can't bear to continue the conversation, choose a pause to make an excuse to leave – to get yourself another drink, or go to the cloakroom, for instance. When you come back, find somebody else to converse with. Above all, be gracious about any differences of opinion, and keep the atmosphere civil – you may have to accept that not everyone shares your opinion on certain matters, and also accept that you owe it to your host, as a well-mannered guest, to treat everyone there with respect.

Joking apart

Humour and laughter can help any social conversation to run smoothly, but have to be used skilfully. Don't start telling a joke unless you know that you're good at it – it's very embarrassing to find that you've forgotten the essential punchline. But humour can be useful to get a serious point across in a light way – just don't overdo it. Teasing can be a good way of gently disagreeing with someone you know, but don't tease someone who obviously can't take it. Never tease someone you don't know at all – you may find you've caused deep and permanent offence, but they're just too polite to show it.

Quite a few people are actually very offended by dirty jokes or 'lavatorial' humour, and will be shocked or seriously offended.

Rude or 'dirty' jokes are also a no-go area in the vast majority of social situations. Think twice (or more) before telling any dirty jokes in public, however funny you find them – and however funny other people might too. Quite a few people are actually very offended by dirty jokes or 'lavatorial' humour, and will be shocked or seriously offended. They won't think much of you and you're unlikely to be able to change their opinion. Only use the more 'earthy' jokes in your repertoire when you are absolutely sure that everyone present is likely to share your sense of humour. Never, ever tell sexist or racist jokes: they're not only inexcusable, they are also very likely to cause great offence.

We Brits have a tradition of dealing with difficult situations by making a joke of them. Sometimes those jokes are in appallingly bad taste. It's a kind of coping strategy that most people brought up in Britain have probably encountered. But it's not something that should be tried out on people you don't know well, and certainly not on people from another culture. Although your friends may know that usually you're a caring, sensitive type, the strangers you've been chatting with will only know you as the person telling all those tacky jokes. They may not give you the benefit of the doubt.

There are a couple of things that are real 'no-no's in social conversation. One is using the occasion to ask for some free advice from a professional. Don't sidle up to a guest who happens to be a doctor and ask him how to deal with your piles, or worse. Don't corner the local builder and ask him all about building an extension to your house. When people are at a party they are, most definitely, 'off-duty'. Of course they may chat about their work, often to tell you funny stories about things that have happened there, but they don't want to put on their professional hat, especially to give unpaid advice. If you seriously do want their advice, you can ask for a business card, or ask if you can phone later in the week to make an appointment.

The other thing that you really mustn't do is be a bore. That's a tough one to watch out for because, unfortunately, most boring conversationalists tend not to be the ones who notice they're boring! If you're considerate of others, you're hardly likely to fall into this category. But do make sure that you don't talk compulsively and at length about your work, or insist on telling a stream of stories without letting anyone get a word in. If you haven't heard anyone else talking for a minute or two, or haven't asked anyone a question, consider the possibility that you might have been talking too much yourself. Some people start talking compulsively when they are feeling shy and nervous, but there's nothing wrong with listening for a while. And do remember to change the subject occasionally.

If you really can't think of anything to say, or any subject to talk about, just ask a few interested questions of the person you are with. Most people enjoy being asked about their lives – it can be quite flattering. What do they do for a living? Have they got children, pets, hobbies? How long have they lived in the area? How do they know the host? Listen hard to their responses and you'll almost certainly find some information that you can respond to, or use to ask a follow-up question. 'Ah, you live in Markham Road – I used to live there when I taught at the school. Do they still have that wonderful park at the corner?' Avoid simple yes or no answers to any questions you are asked, as well. It's good manners, however nervous – or even bored – you may be feeling to help out the conversation by offering as much as you can.

Usually you can easily 'feel' your way around a conversation with a new acquaintance at a party or other event. If you have a lot in common and 'get on like a house on fire', you'll know quite quickly. In those circumstances, you may quickly get into quite a chatty and detailed conversation, telling each other about your lives. Other people find it very interesting to chat to people whose lives are very different from their own, even if they are similar in other ways. If you are getting on well with someone, it is quite okay to offer to exchange phone numbers or email addresses.

Body language

Psychologists tell us that human communication is 20 per cent verbal and 80 per cent non-verbal, so if you want to know whether you have clicked with someone, take a look at their body language and be aware of your own. In a social situation you can use body language to convey a positive impression – maintain eye contact with the speaker and stand squarely without fidgeting too much. Turn towards people while they are talking and smile when appropriate, to show you are interested in them. If you adopt a physical bearing that appears confident, you'll be surprised how confident you will actually begin to feel. On the other hand, if you stand in the corner slouching over your glass, or sit hunched up with your arms curled around you – well, you'll be very unapproachable and people will find it hard to know how to talk to you. We all feel nervous at parties sometimes, but we can help ourselves out a lot with careful body language.

If you adopt a physical bearing that appears confident, you'll be surprised how confident you will actually begin to feel.

There are lots of theories about how our body language can indicate what we are really thinking. If someone scratches their nose, or pulls at their ear, it can – some say – indicate that they disagree with the speaker. Of course, they may just have an itch! But we all know that someone whose eyes wander while we're talking to them is not really interested in what we are saying, or that someone who backs away from us is trying to get away from our 'personal space'. At crowded parties, it's sometimes hard to maintain your personal space, or to avoid getting too physically close to other people. Bear in mind that some people may be very nervous if you seem to be crowding them, and even interpret it as a sexual 'come-on'. Unless you meant it that way – and even if you did – do be considerate of how other people may feel. If you get a clear indication that the person doesn't appreciate your closeness and is not interested in that kind of interaction, politely move out of their personal space and chat from more of a distance.

The office party

Ah, the office party – there are few social occasions quite like it, and quite so fraught with peril! Actually there are several kinds.

Office party Type One is the party to which clients and suppliers are invited. This isn't really a 'let your hair down' occasion, but a civilised get-together to thank outside people for their contribution to the firm. These kinds of occasions can be very friendly and chatty, but probably not too informal – after all, these are your customers.

Office party Type Two is the kind often thrown by larger organisations such as banks or corporate businesses. These kinds of parties can be intimidating – you don't want to get drunk and make a fool of yourself in front of your boss, or the people you are boss of. So keep it polite and friendly, and don't overindulge. It's good manners to talk to people in a friendly manner, but don't get too personal or opinionated unless you know your colleagues well.

Some people use big corporate parties as a chance to try and get ahead. It's entirely up to you – if you feel you'd be confident going up to the top brass and introducing yourself, now's your chance. But judge the occasion carefully and make sure that your approach would be welcome at this kind of party. It might be better just to enjoy the event and make an appointment to chat about work with your boss at another time.

Office Party Type Three is perhaps the most 'dangerous' one, the traditional office knees-up. The trouble is that the line between business event and informal party isn't clear. The boss and directors seem to be off-duty and joining in the general fun. There is often free booze and people get carried away. We all know the awful things that happen at some office parties: getting drunk and trying to photocopy your bottom, snogging someone in the cupboard, not to mention becoming 'unwell' after a few too many beers. Watch out – some people you work with may be not so much your friends as your competitors and any gossip they spread will last a while. And, of course, the boss may have a rather long memory about what happened, too. Perhaps this is a bit cynical, but it always pays to behave in a civilised and in-control manner – you can still have fun and a drink or two, just watch it!

Formal occasions

There are many gatherings that are truly formal and serve a serious purpose. These may be business, academic, political or diplomatic functions and they are all subject to quite rigid 'rules of etiquette'. If you are going to dine in an Oxbridge college, a regimental mess, or as a guest of the Worshipful Company of Wig Makers (okay, that one's made up!) you really need to do your homework in advance. These places absolutely reek of tradition and there will be a hundred things you need to know. If what people think at such events matters to you, follow the accepted rules of their traditions. You can do so, even if you only follow them to help you feel more at ease. Happily, nowadays most of these bodies are well aware that their traditions appear somewhat arcane – not to mention stupid – to outsiders, so are helpful in explaining what's expected and not offended if you don't play the game.

What to wear

What do you wear if you're suddenly invited to some social occasion that is completely new to you? Does it matter? Well, ultimately no – it's you that's been invited, not your frock. But, naturally, it helps to feel that you're dressed for the occasion and not going to stand out like a sore thumb. There's nothing worse than turning up for a social occasion or a business meeting wearing very different clothes from the rest of the crowd – unless you like to create a stir of course! If you've seen the film *Bridget Jones' Diary*, you'll probably remember the scene where she turned up to what she thought was a tarts-and-vicars fancy dress do, only to find it was a formal reception.

Novelist Anthony Trollope once observed, 'I hold that gentleman to be the best dressed whose dress no one observes,' meaning that, in his opinion, the person who blends in with the crowd is the one who's dressed well for the occasion. Think about it: wearing clothes that fit the occasion will put you at your ease, but is also a courtesy to the host, who is no doubt anxious that things should go well, and that the whole event should be a success. That being said, only the most pompous host would complain if someone wearing jeans turned up at a formal wedding reception – it's the occasion that matters more than the clothing.

It seems to be a feature of film-star chic these days to blend casual and smart – jeans and diamonds, evening dresses and denim jackets. Not many people can get away with it and it's probably not a good idea to try for this look unless you're very sure you can carry it off. Play safe unless you have a model figure, and a budget to match.

Here are a few hints on what, in general, is considered acceptable dress for various situations. But you'll find plenty of situations where these 'rules' no longer apply, since life is much less rigid than it used to be only fifty years ago. But if you are worried about inadvertently causing offence, especially to people of an older generation, it might be worth considering these:

Gear for the men…

The suit – sometimes called a business suit, or a lounge suit – is the default 'smart' men's outfit. It's really a kind of unspoken 'uniform' for doing serious business and most suits are either dark grey or blue, sometimes with a pinstripe or chalk stripe to liven them up a bit. Green or brown suits are not generally very fashionable for conventional business wear. A suit can be a very expensive item, but need not be. If you're starting work in a big company, like a bank or law firm, you'll almost certainly be expected to wear a suit, even in this day and age. You'll probably have been told that normal work attire is 'suit and tie'.

The tie is not optional in a formal setting where 'suit and tie' is required. What the point of a tie is, nobody knows. It seems designed to be difficult to put on properly and then spend its time getting in the way. At least ties are a bit more adventurous today than they were a couple of generations ago when sober patterns and stripes were about all there was to choose from. Now you can get ties with silly cartoons, funky patterns and very 'loud' colours. But be careful – if your workplace is a serious one, a tie bearing a picture of Marilyn Monroe will probably not go down too well. Some people wear a tie indicating which school or Oxbridge university college they attended, but that is really rather a snobby and old-fashioned habit. But that's where the expression 'old school tie' comes from, a bit like referring to the 'old boys' network'.

Bow ties are a bit of a pain to get right. About the only time you'd be required to wear one is a formal wedding and then only if you are the groom, best man or one of the official ushers. The easiest way to tie a bow tie is to get somebody else to do it for you, or to get one that is ready tied, and attached to elastic!

Socks seem to be rather inoffensive wear, don't they? Well, clean ones, that is! But be careful in your choice – at a formal work place it may not be considered appropriate to wear brightly coloured socks, or socks with logos or pictures on them. Don't wear anything too flamboyant unless you are sure that it's acceptable.

For formal business wear, shirts should be white or blue, or a muted shade of pink also works. In general plain shirts are best for very conventional offices, but in others it may be quite okay to wear patterns and even very bright colours.

As a general rule of office-dress 'good manners', spend a few weeks getting the feel of how the office 'dress code' operates before you get out your silly socks and that tie with the flashing light on the end. (And in any case, you'd probably best save them for the office Christmas party.)

Evening wear

If you get an invitation to a formal dinner, it will usually say if 'evening dress' or 'black tie' is required. That's all very well, but what does it mean exactly? Both these mean that men should wear a dinner jacket (sometimes known as a tuxedo) and a black bow tie. Though actually, today, it is by no means essential to wear a black bow tie. Many people jazz up this rather sombre ensemble by wearing a colourful or patterned bow tie. In a tropical clime you might wear a white jacket instead of the more usual black, but this isn't usual otherwise.

So, that sorts out the gents, but what about the ladies? Formal evening dress for women is usually, but not always, long. You don't have to wear a fancy ball gown, but should make the effort to wear something quite smart. A formal knee-length dress is usually acceptable, if it is definitely the sort of thing you could class as 'evening wear' (usually made from something silky or velvety).

What other kinds of dress are there? Very rarely, today, you might be asked to a 'white tie' event. This means wearing tails – black, not white – and a white bow tie, for the men. Usually there's a special kind of white starched shirt, with a winged collar and a waistcoat. Many formal weddings adopt this dress – partly for the fun of it, more than convention! – and it is easiest to hire the lot for the evening. If you go to any gentlemen's outfitters or wedding-clothing hire place, they'll give you a great deal of helpful advice on what exactly to wear. For a 'white tie' event such as a state ball or similarly grand occasion, women would always wear long evening dresses, and often wear long white gloves as well.

For a 'white tie' event such as a state ball or similarly grand occasion, women would always wear long evening dresses, and often wear long white gloves as well.

Other types of dress sometimes specified are 'lounge suits', 'smart casual', 'informal' and 'business attire'. These are really to inform you that it isn't a very smart 'black tie' event, but you should just wear a suit (for 'lounge suit' or 'business attire') or a sports jacket and trousers, or something similar, if the event is casual. Jeans are probably not a good idea: a little bit *too* casual! For women, a suit or smart daywear for a 'business suit' event, and something smart, but more relaxed in other cases. In a way these invitations are most daunting, because there's no formal uniform

– just keep it smart but not too grand. If you wear a suit for a 'casual' occasions, that's not going to matter at all.

It certainly isn't deemed rude not to wear a hat, and very few occasions 'require' one – apart from a hard hat on a building site, of course!

An invitation may also indicate that 'decorations' may be worn. This, of course, refers to medals and other hardware you may have – military or civil awards etc. If you have any decorations of this kind, wear them on the left breast of your dinner jacket, when the occasion demands. If you are a woman, the left side of your evening dress or, if you are wearing a jacket, on the left breast. Incidentally, at some grand occasions women may be offered a corsage – this is simply a small spray of flowers.

Well, we hope that clears up what to wear! But, what if there is no indication of what to wear on your invitation? If you are any doubt, the best thing to do is to phone the host, or somebody else who is attending, and ask them. Then you can turn up confident that you're in the 'right' outfit for the occasion, and concentrate on enjoying it to the full.

Hats off – and on!

Not that long ago, all men wore hats, and you could actually tell quite a lot about a man by the hat he wore. Posh businessmen wore bowlers, less 'exalted' folks wore trilbies, and ordinary working-class people in more menial roles tended to wear flat caps. Of course, that's not the case at all today – you don't see many businessmen in bowlers and flat caps are all the fashion in some circles. It certainly isn't deemed rude not to wear a hat, and very few occasions 'require' one – apart from a hard hat on a building site, of course!

But there are a few simple rules of politeness if you do decide to wear a hat. If you're wearing a hat and go inside, you should take it off, especially if you are entering a house of worship (except in a synagogue or mosque, where the opposite applies, and you should keep your head covered). On very formal occasions, like smart society weddings and the Ascot races, top hats are still worn, by custom. You'll also need to wear a 'topper' if you're collecting an honour of some kind from the Queen. But apart from that, how you wear your hat, and if you choose to, is up to you – just take it off if you're in front of someone at the cinema, or you'll make no friends! It's no longer the case, as it was once, that men raise their hat with their left hand on meeting a lady (simultaneously extending their right hand to shake, quite a feat of co-ordination).

A word about healthy hat wearing. Sunhats in the burning sun, and woolly hats in the freezing winter winds are definitely a good idea. Other hats – especially the more 'amusing' or informal ones sported by the younger clientele, clubbers and snowboarders alike, may be best left to the young – but that's entirely up to you, you're as young as you feel, after all! In general, though, a multi-coloured velour clown hat with integral strobe lighting is probably inadvisable for picking up your OBE from the Queen.

Flat caps, panamas, bush hats and the rest are all perfectly acceptable in informal settings. The panama even makes it to the more formal settings of bowls, cricket and croquet. However, on the whole men are not expected to wear hats except on very formal occasions. So, if you're at all worried, it's probably best to leave your hat at home.

For the women, ladies' hat-wearing manners are a bit more of a challenge. Anything involving a religious ceremony may require a head covering of some kind for all the women, so a hat is advisable.

Certainly, today, you would not necessarily have to wear a hat at a Christian or civil ceremony wedding, for instance, but it depends on the formality involved. You would be expected to wear a hat at a formal event like racing at Ascot, or rowing at Henley, although the good news is that there's no strict 'rule' on what style it should be. Some women really go to town at this kind of event, and wear very grandiose confections, but you really don't need to. Most large department stores carry a wide range of hats suitable for more formal occasions, so just go along and try them all on for size.

The bling thing

Jewellery, and how and what to wear, is a difficult one – for those of us with strings of diamonds and reams of pearls to choose from! On the whole, what jewellery you wear for an occasion is simply a matter of your personal taste. 'Less is more' is usually a good rule, as a touch of understated but smart adornment can make its point, and look elegant and smart. There is no need to wear jewellery at all, unless you want to, but most women would probably wear a necklace and earrings for an evening 'do'.

Many men wear a wedding ring, and perhaps a signet ring too. Others wear a chain or medallion or perhaps a gold bracelet. None of this is 'required' or considered 'polite' (or not). Perhaps men loaded down with gold chains and medallions are more likely to be regarded as a bit of a 'medallion man' (not a compliment, generally) but, again, it's a matter of personal taste.

Rites of passage

Some call them 'hatches, matches and dispatches' – our social rites of passage are those formal occasions (such as christenings, engagements, weddings, funerals) that mark stages in our progress through life towards the inevitable. These important events are always formal in some sense, and have their own little rules of behaviour, which often come from long tradition. And we often like to preserve them, because it helps the event to feel special, after all.

Rites of passage can involve some sort of religious service or other expression of spiritual belief. In today's multi-cultural society that can be a bit intimidating for some of us, especially if we are unfamiliar with the faith involved. Quite often, only family and close friends are actually invited to the religious part of a ceremony and then a wider group of friends is invited to the evening party, or reception, that follows. That's one good way of helping everyone to feel at ease, and has the benefit of allowing people who feel uncomfortable with religion to miss that bit out.

If you get invited to a ceremony that is quite outside your own culture, you need to do a little research so that you'll know what to expect and how you should behave. For instance, at a Hindu ceremony men and women will not sit together. At a Jewish ceremony women should wear a hat or other head covering. If you're unsure what to expect, just ask the person who invited you: you'll find that most people love to tell you all about their customs and you may well end up with too much information, if anything! Usually you won't have to do anything too complicated other than observe the ceremony – remember, you were asked because your presence was valued. If the ceremony is being conducted in a foreign language, then you can either sit through it patiently, or get someone to translate.

Birth

The celebration of a baby's birth is generally an occasion of great joy. It gives not only the new parents, but all their friends and relatives, a chance to express their pleasure, show their support and wish the new offspring well as they embark on life. But even before birth, there's cause for celebration when a couple knows that they are 'expecting'. For reasons of both tradition and caution, however, it is usual not to throw a big 'baby shower' party to tell all your friends and relatives that you're going to have a baby until the first few months of pregnancy are past. Unfortunately, not all pregnancies make it past the three-month stage so, rather than get everyone excited and then have to give them bad news, it is usual to wait until the pregnancy is really going well. But of course, simply sharing the joy of your pregnancy with close friends and relatives is a different thing altogether.

Baby's here

All cultures are different and all individuals too. In some cultures women go into seclusion to give birth, while in others – like ours – the dad is fully able to take part in the delivery, and expected to as well. Some people even video the baby's birth. Who is present at the baby's birth, in addition to the medical staff, is more or less up to the parents.

Once the baby has been born, the new parents are likely to be inundated with friends and relations who wish to meet the new arrival. It can be a difficult time when sensitivity – basically good manners – towards the couple and their child can really help. If you're a friend, don't go rushing round immediately – your friend may need to spend quite a few days getting used to the experience. It's good manners just to send a card or a bouquet and get in touch a little later. And it's not just friends that need to be thoughtful – imagine that you're the new grandma and your daughter has just had her very first baby. You're overjoyed! And you have loads of experience of bringing up baby, so you just know that you'll be able to offer so much help and support. You'll be able to provide an expert hand in the baby's early days. But be careful: don't go taking over the situation. Your daughter (or son) now has a new family and needs to get used to the experience. Of course they are likely to appreciate and need your help – but they also need time for themselves and to learn how to look after their baby. And they may have some different ideas from you – remember to respect their wishes and bite your tongue if you would personally do things in another way. So take a back seat, be there when and if needed and express your love through respect and caring as much as child-care help.

New parents need to think about the feelings of the grandparents as well, of course. Think about it – it must make you feel rather strange to find your little girl or boy is really 'all grown up' and now has a baby of their own. They may suddenly feel very old indeed! Most people just love becoming grandparents – all the fun of young babies, without all the sleepless nights and nappy changing – but it can also be a rite of passage for them as well. They may even feel a bit 'useless' all of a sudden. Giving grandparents a role in the christening or naming ceremony can help make them feel better about any inner turmoil that may be going on.

Finally, perhaps you have a friend who's about to have a baby. Even if you personally aren't so keen on all that baby stuff – not everyone is – it's only good manners to show some interest in your friend's big event. Try asking when the baby's due, whether the parents know if it's a girl or boy (and, if so, whether they are telling), and if they have names they're thinking of. Your friend will appreciate your good manners in showing an interest, and giving them a chance to chat about what, for them, is a hugely significant event. And after the baby's born, it's normal to send greetings cards, flowers and cuddly toys for the baby, if you know either or both of the parents quite well.

Making the announcement

If you're the one who's expecting, feel free just to give out as much information as you're comfortable with. You don't have to involve everyone in your choice of names, unless you want to, or tell them if it's going to be a boy or girl. But it's good manners to make an announcement of the birth – usually in your local paper, where there's a special section that doesn't cost much and is sometimes even free. And of course, do phone family and close friends to let them know about your happy event. It's also quite acceptable to send a 'round robin' email to work colleagues, or a wider circle of friends – or even, if you're that way inclined, put together a little web page with pictures of you and your new baby (but probably not clips from the video of the birth!).

Christenings and baby-namings

It wasn't that long ago that a christening was a ceremony almost every new-born British baby experienced – some of them crying throughout as the 'holy water' was administered. Today christenings are far less common and it's no longer a sign of social stigma not to be christened. Indeed, many people who are not practising Christians think it rather hypocritical to have their baby christened in a church. Other people like to have the ceremony, despite not being Christians, and many churches are sympathetic. Many other people, of course, have their baby named in a ceremony appropriate to their own, different religion, while people with no religious views can choose to have a non-religious, secular baby-naming ceremony, like that of the Humanist Society.

Whatever the ceremony is like, there will be certain expectations of how people behave and it's likely to require informal but smart attire – perhaps a suit and tie, or something similarly dressed up, for the chaps, and maybe a smart dress or trouser suit, even a hat, for women. Life, and the ceremonies that go with it, is so varied nowadays that it's best to go for smart but not too formal, unless the invitation says otherwise.

Perhaps you have been asked to be a godparent? In the Christian religion, the godparents are expected to be confirmed in the Christian faith, and their role is to guide and support the child's religious upbringing. Godparents are usually longstanding friends of the child's parents and, in practice, don't get 'tested at the door' to see if they are Christian through and through. It's more important to be someone who'll offer support, love and friendship. So, if you are not a Christian but are asked to be a godparent, don't feel you have to say no.

Most people regard the request to be a godparent as a great honour and are delighted to accept. If, however, you don't feel willing or able to be a godparent, you need to be very careful how you decline the invitation. As it's such an important request from the parents, it needs a serious-minded excuse. It's good manners to explain that you maybe don't feel you can, on religious or personal grounds, although you are extremely honoured to have been asked. Whatever your reason, make sure that you speak in person with the parents, and thank them for thinking of you.

A christening is a good excuse for a party and it is usual for the guests to bring the baby a present. Christening presents are usually rather formal and are often things that the child will need in later life. Bibles and prayer books used to be popular, as did silver christening spoons (thus giving rise to the expression 'to be born with a silver spoon in your mouth'). But really, any thoughtful and appropriate gift will be fitting – usually, people buy something that lasts. If you go into any large department store you'll find a gift section expressly for christening and baby-naming events – just ask a member of staff to guide you through what's available.

First communions, confirmations and bar mitzvahs

These religious ceremonies – the first two Christian, the last Jewish – are examples of ceremonies that mark a stage at which a child is considered, in some sense, to have become grown up. First communion is a Roman Catholic ceremony and usually takes place at the age of eight. Confirmation is particularly popular in Protestant churches and may take place at any age, though it is most popular for children in their early teens. A bar mitzvah is a ceremony by which a Jewish boy of thirteen is formally accepted as an adult member of the community. There is a version of the ceremony for girls known as a bat mitzvah but it is far less common.

As a guest at one of these ceremonies, or any other informal version of the same kind of event, you'll need to bring an appropriate gift. How much you spend is entirely up to you, and if you are not a very close friend of the family, you shouldn't feel you have to purchase an extremely generous present. But a box of chocolates won't cut it here! Some events may even have a 'gift list', or you can give some money in the form of a gift certificate, or book token perhaps. If in doubt, ask somebody else you know who is going what sort of thing they recommend, or ask in a shop that sells gifts.

What do you wear? Well, usually these kinds of occasions are pretty formal. Suits for men, smart trousers or dresses for women, possibly hats as well. Remember, if you aren't Jewish but are invited to the synagogue bit of a bar mitzvah you will need something to cover your head. For women, buying a hat is perhaps still more usual, while men may not know what kind of hat is suitable – a baseball cap isn't going to work here! You will need to find something sufficiently dignified. At a Jewish ceremony you can wear a *yarmulke* (the skull cap worn by Jewish men), even if you're not Jewish yourself – that's fine, and will be seen as a sign of respect, not an insult. You may even be offered one if you arrive without headgear. No one will mind that you are wearing one if you are not Jewish; in fact people will be happy that you made an effort to join in. You can even put a (clean!) hankie over your hair if that's all you have – as an accepted emergency measure!

Fortunately, guests at these kinds of 'growing-up' ceremonies don't have much to do except stand around watching the proceedings, and enjoying the party. However, there are things you should know beforehand, so that you show good manners. For instance – what is the attitude to photography or video recording? In many places of worship this is not acceptable inside, and certainly you should always ask beforehand in any case. Also, make sure you don't get in the way of any professional photographer who may have been hired to record the occasion. At all formal family occasions, it's best to check with the hosts – in advance, not at the time – if they mind, especially during a ceremony. This applies as much to weddings.

Engagements and weddings

It's a long while since the time when being an unmarried couple 'living out of wedlock' was considered quite unacceptable in British society. Today you can marry, in a civil or religious ceremony of your choice, or you can live together as common law man and wife, or as a gay couple, male or female. That's up to you, and you don't need to feel that society is pushing you into an arrangement that doesn't suit you, or fit your beliefs. However, the Christian tradition of marriage persists as both a genuine religious ceremony, for many, or more of a superficial celebration for others. And both religious and civil marriages are often followed by formal wedding receptions, which have quite traditional social rules and formats.

The Christian tradition of marriage persists as both a genuine religious ceremony, for many, or more of a superficial celebration for others.

It used to be that the young man asked his sweetheart's father for his daughter's 'hand in marriage'. If you find anyone who's actually done this recently, do let us know! Most prospective father-in-laws today are hardly expecting to make decisions on their daughter's behalf (and most daughters probably wouldn't let them!).

Another rather old-fashioned formality is that of going down on one knee to ask the girl to marry you. That one does still happen, as a romantic gesture that's maybe a little self-conscious. It's certainly not compulsory.

'Popping the question' used to be the man's job, and it's still, traditionally, that way. Women only got a chance to do it during a Leap Year, traditionally. Things are changing and women are just as able to ask a man to marry them. Every couple is different, and who asks who is less important than deciding that you want to formalise your loving relationship and celebrate this choice with friends and family.

The 'manners' required for asking someone to marry you are simple – ask, lovingly and sincerely, in whatever way is natural to your relationship. Perhaps the only difficulty is how to say 'no' to a proposal. Saying 'no' doesn't mean that you don't care for a person, or don't respect them – spend time explaining, gently and carefully, just why marrying is not for you. Remember, asking someone to marry you is a huge moment, that takes a bit of nerve – if you're the one who's saying 'no', say so with consideration.

Once the question has been popped and accepted, there is still usually a period of engagement before the wedding happens. And engagement conventionally involves the giving of rings. Traditionally the man gave the woman a ring when he made his proposal, but it's more normal to choose an engagement ring together, or even to buy and exchange rings so that you can both wear one.

Informing people of an engagement is a fairly relaxed business and many people are content to let the word get around on the grapevine.

You can, if you want, announce your engagement by a notice placed in a newspaper. However, informing people of an engagement is a fairly relaxed business and many people are content to let the word get around on the grapevine. Some people hold an engagement party to announce the happy news to all their friends and relatives. This can be a jolly, relaxed occasion at which people do pretty much as they wish. It isn't nearly as formal as the average wedding party.

What if things go wrong, and you and your partner decide to break off the engagement? It's actually not that unusual for a relationship to get a bit shaky once the engagement has been announced and the pressure to organise a wedding is on. It can feel very awkward if your parents and friends are all rooting for you, and you don't want to disappoint them. They may even have spent money on your behalf, booking the reception or arranging the food. But think about it – this is one case where your future happiness is more important than the inconvenience you may cause. Talk to your family and explain that the marriage is going to make you unhappy. But if the engagement is called off, you should let people know. If they have already sent you presents, you need to send these back, with a brief letter of apology. You don't have to go into great detail about what went wrong, simply say that you are sorry for any inconvenience and hope they'll understand. And true friends will, of course.

In general, once you're engaged, wedding preparations begin. A wedding, or other similar celebration, is probably one of the most emotionally charged occasions most of us will go through. It involves not only the happy couple but their immediate families, relations and friends. It is an occasion when emotions are not only heightened but also very mixed. The formality of the conventional wedding and wedding reception can actually help this very powerful event to go well.

Wedding preparations

Let's assume for the moment that the wedding will be held either in church or a registry office. There are plenty of other possibilities, among them mosques, synagogues, temples and civil ceremonies in exotic venues at home and abroad. If you get invited to a ceremony that is in a faith you don't have experience of, try to make discreet enquiries of your host, well in advance, about the nature of the ceremony.

For a conventional Christian-tradition wedding, one of the first jobs for the bride and groom is to choose the bridesmaids and best man. It is important to find your bridesmaids early on because you will need to buy or make dresses for all of them and this can take time. Bridesmaids are traditionally any age from small children up to young women; if married they are called a 'matron of honour'. Wearing a pretty dress is more or less what the whole ceremony is about as far as a bridesmaid is concerned. She doesn't have to do much except follow the bride into the church (carrying her train if she has one). As she is likely to be a relative or close friend of the bride, she will also be valued for the moral support she provides on such a big day.

The prospective husband, or groom, has the 'best man' to give him support. Unlike the bridesmaids, the best man has quite a few duties to perform, in the traditional role. The groom can choose anyone to take this role, usually a very close friend or a brother. It can be quite a difficult choice, for which diplomacy is needed. Since your best man is going to have to make a speech, look after some of the organising and also produce the ring during the service, you don't want somebody who – however good a friend – might be a bit unreliable. If you're choosing a best man, bear in mind the other male friends and relatives who may, even at the back of their mind, be hoping you'll choose them – and find a way of easing the situation. 'You know, I chose Bob because he's also a friend of Carrie's,' or 'Jack's one of my oldest friends from school, and I promised him years ago I'd do the same for him.'

Who pays for the wedding? That's something that is likely to be on your mind, if you're about to get spliced! Traditionally, the bride's parents used to pay for the whole wedding and reception. Often, today, both the bride's and the groom's parents split the cost, or the bride and groom pay for it themselves – especially if they are older and both working. If you're going to get married and pay for it yourself, do bear in mind that actually your parents might like to feel involved and contribute financially – offer them the chance to pay for something like the dress, or the honeymoon, or whatever you feel would be within their means.

Who wears what? The traditional 'white wedding' used to be only for virgin brides, but that's certainly no longer strictly enforced. Some second marriages, and some very obviously pregnant brides, are still white. It really doesn't matter, although at a very traditional church you might find the vicar has strong views. Some brides, especially at winter weddings, go the other way and choose rich colours like dark red, or blue.

The groom and male guests at a traditional wedding tend to wear suits. At a formal wedding (or even an informal one, where you want the fun of it), top hats and tails might even be worn by the groom and his best man – what's sometimes known as 'morning dress'. In this case the father of the bride, and the male ushers, would wear morning dress as well. You don't have to buy it of course; that sort of outfit can be hired for the day.

Normally, if you have chosen a traditional Christian church wedding, you would meet with the vicar in advance. This is only good manners, as a courtesy, but is also so that the vicar may talk with you about your spiritual and religious beliefs. Some vicars may give you advice on marriage and what it entails, after the big day. Most vicars will understand that you may not be a regular church-goer, but have beliefs that concur with the Christian religion, and would like to mark your commitment in church. When you meet the vicar you will also choose the music and hymns to sing at the ceremony. You'll also need to meet to have a 'rehearsal' at the church, about a week before the wedding, usually with all the 'principal players' – the parents of bride and groom, bridesmaids etc – but not 'in costume'. It's good manners to turn up, on time, and to take it seriously – because it's designed to help your big day go smoothly.

Wedding ceremonies

Wedding 'manners' are quite carefully defined by tradition. It won't be the end of the world if things don't go quite to plan, but here is the traditional order of progress for a Christian church wedding and it's often the same for a more formal civil wedding.

The bridegroom and his best man should be first to arrive at the wedding venue and take up their places at the front of the church or room. Ushers, chosen from close friends and relatives, help guide arriving guests to their places. Traditionally, they will ask guests whether they are there for the bride or the groom. Today, many people are likely to be there for both – so feel free to say that, if asked. In a formal wedding, the bride's friends are seated behind her (usually on the left side of the church) and the groom's behind him (on the right side of the venue). But it's far more usual today for people to sit wherever they wish, especially in civil ceremonies. If you have small children that might make a noise, it's good manners to ask if you can sit near the back, or on an outside aisle, perhaps – so that you can make a quick escape if little Johnny begins to wail just as the vows are being made.

The bride traditionally arrives a little late, just to make sure everyone is ready, really. At a traditional church wedding, she comes 'down the aisle' on her father's arm and he leads her to stand before the altar then takes a step back. The best man should normally have charge of the rings and make sure that he is ready to hand them to the groom when he needs them. When the vicar or celebrant asks who is giving the woman in marriage, the bride's father indicates that he is the one.

If you're the one getting married, do make sure your answers can be heard. It's not a private moment as much as a public declaration that you are sharing with your friends and families. It's quite in order to look happy, and smile – but it isn't good manners to interrupt the vicar or celebrant (or to break into nervous giggles). Services today are very flexible and often the bride and groom write their own vows and read them to each other – these can be personal, and informal, and need not be religious. So if you have spent a long while thinking of what to say, make sure everyone can hear it.

If you're the one getting married, do make sure your answers can be heard. It's not a private moment as much as a public declaration.

At a church wedding, the ceremony ends when you sign the register. There's a similar moment in a civil wedding. After that, you're married and can either walk down the aisle happily, or go to mingle with your guests, or whatever is appropriate. Remember, if you have hired a photographer, it's good manners to let them do their job properly. This will probably be the time when they want you to pose for photographs in various groups. However excited you are, take the time to do this well – the photographs will be with you for a long time!

A well-known wedding tradition is for the bride to turn her back and throw her wedding bouquet over her shoulder, towards the bridesmaids (usually). The old wives' tale attached used to be that the person who caught it would be next to get married. It isn't compulsory today and may happen instead at the reception. If you're the bride, throw it towards someone who'll appreciate this special memento – perhaps the chief bridesmaid, or even your mum. If you're a guest, don't make a rugby tackle for it!

Receptions and speeches

The reception is the place where things can, and often do, go wrong, so it is important to know the rules and make sure that the other participants know them as well. First, it's only polite that the happy couple should get to the venue before the guests so that they are there to welcome them on arrival. Many people have a formal receiving line in which the bride, groom and immediate family members line up to shake hands with each guest as they arrive, but don't feel obliged. If you want to be really grand you can have someone call out their names as they approach the line. This may seem rather too formal, but it does ensure that each guest is welcomed personally. If you are the bride or groom, or one of the parents, just behave as any good party host would – circulate, make sure people are happy and looked after. Don't forget, wedding parties are unusual because there will be many people there who don't know anyone else. It's a little daunting to socialise for such a long period with complete strangers, so take time to work out a good seating plan or to introduce people to each other. At a buffet-type meal the family members should circulate to ensure that all the guests are being looked after. And do keep an eye on Uncle Stan, who gets a bit boring once he's had a drink or two – rescue his latest 'captive audience' from him occasionally!

Presenting the presents

At a formal wedding, the guests will, normally, bring or send a present. You won't be expected to open them then and there. Instead, write every single person a thank-you letter, very soon after you return from your honeymoon (if you have one). In this case good manners dictate that you should send a handwritten note, on attractive paper or a note card. Make sure to say you much you liked the gift (whatever you thought of it!) and provide a few words about your honeymoon, or the event itself. Say how nice it was to see the person, if they came to the wedding.

As a guest, it is good manners to provide a nice gift, wrapped and with a congratulatory card. Something useful for the home is always a good bet, and need not be too expensive – perhaps a set of wine glasses, or a tablecloth. You can send this in advance, normally to the home of the person who invited you (the parents of the bride, traditionally) or bring it to the reception, where there will probably be a table to leave gifts on. Do make sure to say who the gift is from!

Once people have eaten and drunk enough, the speeches begin. At a traditional wedding they go in this order:

- Father of the bride (who also toasts the happy couple).
- The groom thanks his father-in-law (and others) and proposes a toast to the bridesmaids.
- The best man replies on behalf of the bridesmaids and also reads out any messages from those who could not be present.

Although this is the traditional order, it is quite permissible to vary it – today, many brides would like to make a speech as well, and there's no reason why they shouldn't!

If you're one of the people required to give a speech, don't panic – there are quite a few books on wedding etiquette and speeches, so pop down to the library.

Basically, the bridegroom's speech is a simple thank-you to everyone for everything. Don't miss anyone out – you'll hurt their feelings. Remember to sneak in a 'my wife and I' at some point – you're bound to get a cheer!

The best man has a more difficult job, since he needs to say something gently amusing about his old friend, the bridegroom – perhaps a story about a childhood jape, or some other anecdote. Above all, don't really embarrass the groom – or the bride – and don't reveal any really personal secrets.

And now for the fun – if there's to be dancing, the bride and groom should start things with a dance together, after which everyone joins in. Formal dances are rare nowadays, so really there are no rules on what is good manners (stay upright, don't drink too much!). But it is traditional for the bride to dance with her dad at some point.

Near the end of the reception the bride will disappear to go and get changed, and then the happy couple will leave, usually to go off on honeymoon. The best man and other friends of the groom usually take this opportunity to decorate their car with shaving foam and streamers. Once the bride and groom have left, the party often continues for a while and people then start going home. But, again, today there are no strict rules – many couples don't see why they should leave early to 'go away', and enjoy staying on to the end of the evening with everyone else.

As bride and groom, it's essentially good manners to buy a little thank-you present for the bridesmaids and the best man, something bigger than a box of chocolates – perhaps a bottle of good wine or Scotch, or silk scarves or jewellery for the bridesmaids. And perhaps something more modest for all the people who helped out as ushers, or volunteered to help with food.

Today, church wedding receptions and civil ceremony receptions are often identical, it's only the ceremony itself that differs slightly, although there can certainly be singing and music at both. For a church wedding, it's good manners to invite the vicar to the reception. You can also invite the registrar, in a civil ceremony, but there is less obligation to do so.

Although we've concentrated on how a traditional church or civil wedding and party proceeds, there are of course many other different kinds of religious ceremonies. All weddings are similar in that the two people getting married are the centre of attention and are there to publicly make vows as to their commitment to each other. Whoever the people are, and whatever the religion, enjoy the ceremony as a time of joy shared with friends and family. And, even if you don't know what is going on – or don't personally agree with it – it's good manners to follow the accepted protocol and kneel or stand when everyone else does, join in the hymns (if you can) and generally take the whole thing as seriously as it is intended.

Lastly, don't forget that however happy the occasion, it is a time of great emotion. Many new 'mum-in-laws' are actually feeling mixed joy and sadness, at losing their son or daughter to a 'new life'. So respect that people may be feeling rather tense or emotional and use your good manners to be calm and respectful to all, without taking offence at any unintended words.

Significant others

Modern manners entail understanding modern lifestyles. Don't forget that, however traditional your own family might be, others may come from very different situations. Many people divorce and remarry today, and there is no stigma attached to that at all. People of the same gender set up home together, some people choose not to have a family, some have large 'blended' families from different marriages. Good manners today means being sensitive to the fact that not everyone will have the same family situation as you are familiar with, and that doesn't make their lifestyle better or worse than yours. In general, if you are not sure how to refer to someone, ask tactfully – if you are close enough to one of the family. But it's easiest to avoid blunders simply by referring to 'partners' or 'significant others'.

Don't forget that, however traditional your own family might be, others may come from very different situations.

One of the problems is that, as we have observed elsewhere, we now tend to deal with almost everyone on a first-name basis and it means that we have no clue as to the precise way in which people are related. To make things even more complicated, there may be children, step-children, half-brothers and half-sisters all living under the same roof. The trouble is that if you ask all the questions to which you may urgently need answers, then you risk looking nosey. If you don't ask, you risk making assumptions that prove not only incorrect but embarrassingly wrong. There are no rules about this, but I can give you, from personal experience, a very good tip: ask your kids. They usually have far fewer hang-ups about it all, and know just who's living with who, and whose kids are whose.

If you are in an unconventional relationship – or one that might seem unconventional to someone of an older generation – it's good manners to make sure that they have some help. 'Jane's my partner' or 'well, we don't use "step-children", they're all just "the kids" to us'. If you are recently divorced, it's particularly important to ensure that people you may not have seen for some time are aware of this, to help them avoid a blunder. And if they do assume you're still married, don't take offence – they just didn't know. And never ask your friends to choose between you and your 'ex'. Why on earth should they?

Funerals

Unlikely though it may seem, there are good funerals and bad funerals. A good one demonstrates the love that those left behind feel for the deceased. It also gives everyone a chance to express their love and support for those who are bereaved. The ceremony needs to be dignified and well organised. This means that all the participants know what is expected of them. It may be a staple comedy situation on TV, but in real life there are few things more upsetting than a funeral that goes wrong.

There are practical and legal requirements that you will need to investigate separately, but here are some of the things that good manners require:

- First, if you are the next of kin you need to tell people the sad news as soon as possible. Relations and close friends of the deceased should be informed by phone or, if that is not possible, by a handwritten letter. Email should only be used in dire emergency.
- If the deceased was still working then, of course, the employer should be informed by phone at the earliest opportunity.
- Once those most closely concerned have been informed it is usual to place an announcement in the national and/or local press. This should not only give the information that a death has occurred but should also tell people where and

when the funeral will be held. If you want flowers to be sent you must state where they are to go. If you would prefer people to make a charitable contribution instead of flowers you should tell them which charity you are supporting. You might want to appoint someone to collect all the money and send it as one sum in memory of your loved one.

- You should also write to any social organisations (clubs, associations, charities, etc) with which the deceased was connected. This is not only polite but it will minimise the risk of you receiving upsetting mail and phone calls in the months to come.
- Some people hold a viewing at which people can go to see the deceased and pay their last respects. This used to be done in the deceased's home but that custom is now rare, except in certain communities. Usually the viewing is held at a chapel of rest.
- All practical aspects of the funeral will be organised by the undertaker, but he will need some help from the next of kin. For example, some people regard it as essential that the hearse should start its journey to the funeral from the deceased's home. They will also hire funeral cars and close relatives and friends will be invited to ride in the cortège. It is vital that people are told in advance whether they are expected to go in a funeral car and, if so, in which one. Traditionally the closer you were to the deceased, the nearer your car will be to the hearse. Nowadays, however, some people prefer not to have a cortège and for the hearse to arrive at the funeral straight from the undertaker's premises. There are no rules about which approach you take – it is entirely a matter of personal preference.

- Funerals can take many forms and it is essential that you let people know what sort yours is going to be. You don't need to do this formally, but you should let your friends and relatives spread the word. If you are attending a funeral and aren't sure what to wear, simply wear smart clothes in dark colours – black, nowadays, is not essential, although it's traditionally the colour of mourning. Full mourning dress – black tails and hat, formal dresses – is rarely worn, and the invitation would say if it was required. If the funeral is an especially tragic one (that of a child or young person, for example) it is unlikely that people will be feeling anything other than wretched. However, where the deceased has had a long, fulfilled and happy life there may well be an element of celebration involved. So it's as well for people to know how they are expected to act. I went to the funeral of a man who had led a full, active life, had been happily married twice and had loads of nice children and grandchildren. His passing was seen as the inevitable bittersweet end of his life and people celebrated it as such.
- The actual service can take just about any form you wish. You do not have to have a religious service. Instead, you could have close friends and relatives sharing their memories of the deceased and readings from favourite poems. The only thing you can't do is to have no ceremony at all. If you don't provide a ceremony the duty vicar will be called in to say a few words. There is absolutely no right or wrong way to organise a funeral. All the decisions are entirely personal and depend on the view of the next of kin.
- As a guest it is essential good manners to treat the whole occasion with seriousness and respect, whatever you may think of the ceremony, or the deceased. Even if you are

nervous, refrain from whispering with your neighbours, or breaking into giggles if a particularly awful choice of music comes up.

- It is usual for the mourners to gather at the church or crematorium. The closest relatives and friends will go around welcoming people and thanking them for coming. Someone will remain with the deceased's partner to give moral support. When you are summoned for the funeral to begin you should walk quietly into the church and be seated. Sometimes, a man may offer a female guest his arm, to walk in with her. This should be taken for what it is – a traditional and slightly old-fashioned example of supportive good manners.
- The deceased's closest family and friends will occupy seats nearest the front and others will fit in behind as best they can. If you are not a close friend or family member, don't sit near the front.
- After the ceremony, it is usual to thank the vicar or whoever else performed the rites. Some people may have travelled a long way to the funeral and will be feeling wretched and quite probably cold. Therefore, guests (including the vicar) are normally invited to take refreshment somewhere. This can be at the deceased's home or it may be at a local hotel or in a room hired in a pub. At this point the conversation can become less gloomy. There is no hard-and-fast rule for how to behave on this occasion and you will have to take your lead from those around you.

If you were not close enough to the deceased to attend the funeral, but you are acquainted with the family, you should send a card of condolence or, better still, visit to give your condolences in person. A small gift, such as flowers or a plant, is customary.

You may be daunted about talking with someone who has suffered a recent bereavement, and even want to avoid them, but do take the trouble to give them your support and show your considerate good manners in just popping round to see how they are doing. Remember that they may well be feeling extremely lonely and wretched, and even a few minutes' conversation may be a great comfort to them. As always, good manners are a case of putting the other person first, even if you feel a little awkward.

Eating Out

Eating out – especially on unusually formal occasions – can be a surprisingly nerve-racking activity. That's a shame, because it should, after all, be a pleasure. So here are some clues on the 'rules' of good manners in some of the grander situations you might find yourself in.

Formal dining

Taking your place

At many formal parties, such as a wedding or a retirement meal, perhaps, there will probably be some milling around before people proceed to their seats. This period is sometimes called a 'reception' or simply 'drinks', and drinks are usually served – most likely by people coming around with trays, or perhaps glasses of wine will be laid out on a table for you to help yourself to one. Really, this time is a chance for the guests to mingle informally and get to know each other. It also gives you a chance to have a quick glass of something, if that helps you feel less nervous – but don't overdo it, the evening has only just begun! There may be a seating plan on display and, if so, you should take the opportunity to work out where you are sitting. At some point you will be invited to go into dinner and, if the affair is really old-fashioned, gentlemen will offer a lady their arm to hold while they lead them in. But more likely, everyone will meander in informally to take their seats.

If there is no seating plan then you may find that name cards have been put at each place setting. Try to find your card with minimum fuss. It is certainly not good manners to rearrange the place cards to sit next to someone you'd rather talk to. You should sit where you have been placed, and show your good manners by saying hello to the people on your table, making introductions if you don't know them – you don't have to wait to be introduced, just say 'Hello, I'm John Baker, I don't believe we've met,' and offer your hand to shake. A thoughtful host will have spent time on arranging the seating so that people with interests in common, or who might well like each other, are seated together.

When you've found your seat, it's quite all right to simply sit down when it seems everyone else around you is settling. It's no longer the case that men must wait until all women present are seated, or stand and pull back the woman's chair for her to sit on. You can certainly follow these old-school customs if you like, but they are a little outdated, and might even cause offence.

Don't talk with your mouth full

Formal dinners are as much about conversation as they are about food, so a general rule is to cut your food into small chunks that can be chewed easily and swallowed quickly when required. However good the food is, don't simply concentrate on eating and ignore your companions. Make sure that you are eating slowly and carefully enough to be able to make conversation with others on your table. It's good manners to include everyone near you in any conversation, and be especially careful to speak to anyone who looks a bit left out or shy, perhaps on their own. Ask them occasional questions: 'so, Elspeth, what do you do for a living?' or 'Jim, have you been working at Barnards' for long now?'. Similarly, try to steer the conversation to other topics if someone seems to have taken it over with talk about themselves. Treat the table as a mini-dinner party, where you are an attentive and interested guest.

Do make sure you have introduced yourself, or been introduced, to everyone seated with you. If you forget someone's name, as often happens when you meet several new people at once, you can say 'I'm sorry, your name just slipped my mind…it's…?' and the person will usually take the hint and tell you.

Saying grace

In some places, especially the colleges of the older universities, it is customary for grace to be said before the meal begins. Grace is a Christian (usually) custom in which God is 'thanked' for the food and company. This may be in Latin, if you're at one of the grander Oxbridge colleges. Whether you are a believer or not, you should bow your head slightly until it is over. Bear in mind when you first approach the table that you may need to remain standing and wait for grace to be said. Just watch what everyone else is doing.

Conversation

Formal dinners are far more than a chance to have some good food. They're an opportunity for people to relax and socialise in pleasant surroundings, in a kind of civilised bonding exercise. So keep conversation light and friendly: it's not the place for talking shop with colleagues.

At a large dinner, the host doesn't have a hope of keeping track of the conversation and steering it away from boring or even controversial topics. As a guest, your good manners can help you to assist here. Always talk to both the diners either side of you, not just the one who you get on best with. Don't sit in silence, however shy you are. Anyway, you'll enjoy the event more if you make an effort to take part, even if you dread small talk. Just smile a lot, ask general questions of your fellow diners, about their lives and interests, and be prepared to chat a little about yours. Don't feel that your life is uninteresting or boring, simply because it seems so different from the person's next to you. And show interest in what people tell you about themselves: you may be surprised what you learn about life!

Bread and rolls

In more formal dinners and restaurants bread is either brought to your table by the waiter, or is already on the table, usually in a basket in the middle. Or you may find a bread roll placed on your side plate (that's the small plate to your left). You can eat it as soon as the starter is served. It's good manners to offer the basket of bread around to your near neighbours before taking one yourself.

If you're being fussy about 'etiquette', it's normal to cut a slice of bread into pieces with a knife but for a roll (or bread if you wish), you should tear it into conveniently sized pieces, which you butter as you eat them. But that's just custom: whatever you choose is fine. Usually butter will be on a plate with a butter knife to take some with. Don't use this knife to cut your own bread – simply take the butter and put the knife back.

Don't throw your bread rolls at your neighbour, unless it's a very good party!

The staff

A big formal dinner do will probably have waiting staff. Their job is to be as near invisible as possible, and just make sure everything you need is there. It's a little different from a restaurant waiter, who may be keen to give you lots of information and advice on what to order or drink, and will hope for a nice tip too. You don't have to tip staff at a formal dinner, or even speak to them much as they serve you, although the occasional word of thanks as they deliver your next course or fill your glass is just fine, and good manners after all.

If something is wrong, don't make a big fuss. Simply speak quietly to the waiter nearest you. There's no need to be angry or speak loudly, just say 'I'm rather sorry, but this fish isn't quite done – do you think you could cook it a bit more?' or something similarly polite.

Special meals

Perhaps you are a vegetarian, or allergic to seafood or gluten, or have a religion that doesn't permit you to eat certain foods. If so, it's good manners to make sure your hosts know well in advance, so that suitable arrangements can be made. Don't leave it until you arrive, or even the day before – it will cause the host embarrassment if they can't produce a meal for you, and even a vegetarian meal is still an unusual option to some people, especially perhaps the older generation. So, think ahead and give the host a quick phone call or drop them a note to say 'I'm vegetarian, so thought I'd better let you know now' or 'By the way, just to let you know I only eat halal food, do let me know if I can suggest anything simple the caterer could provide'.

Incidentally, it is perfectly acceptable to refuse food on dietary or ethical grounds, but it is not okay to decline a whole course simply because you don't like the look of it. Even if you have an extreme dislike of apples, and an apple pie turns up for the dessert course, you'll have to make a stab at it, to be polite. Eat a few mouthfuls (a glass of water can help you get it down!) without showing any dislike, and perfect the art of 'picking' a bit at the rest, and moving it around the plate until the course is over and you can put it aside.

Navigating the place setting

Cutlery

A fully laden dining table groaning with cutlery, porcelain, silver and flowers is a magnificent, and, to some, intimidating, sight, but there is really no need to feel dazzled by all that silverware. Even if your normal meal of choice is a double cheeseburger with fries, you can still easily find your way around the formal dining table.

Like everything else, it's simple once you know how. Look at the cutlery and you'll see that everything will have been laid out for you in the right order – all you have to do is work your way inwards from the outer items. At the outside, there may be a small knife for you to butter your bread and then a small knife and fork to use on the starter. There may also be a soup spoon (more rounded than a normal spoon) in case you need it. Your main knife and fork will be closest to where your plate is set down, so if in doubt, look at those and work outwards. Cutlery for desserts might be at the top of your place setting or might be supplied by the staff when your dessert is brought. If you drop an item of cutlery, you can simply ask the waiting staff if they could please bring you another. In general, don't go grovelling under the table to pick it up unless it is very near (and the floor is very clean!)

The 'correct' way to hold a knife is in your right hand with the handle tucked into the palm of your hand; your thumb extends down one side of the handle and the forefinger points down the back (not touching the blade), with the remaining fingers curled around the handle. When a fork is used with a knife, it is held in the left hand with the tines – that's the prongs – pointing downward. Hold the handle near the tip rather than near the base. When using a fork by itself, it can be held the other way, with the tines pointing upward. The American custom of cutting up all one's food and then using the fork to shovel it up may be frowned upon by sticklers for dining etiquette in very grand establishments, but is usually acceptable otherwise – more and more of us eat that way nowadays. When using a spoon and fork to eat pudding, the fork should again be held tines down. Like forks, spoons are held near the tip of the handle. There, that's how to hold cutlery in very grand style!

Napkins

The napkin that's for your use will be on your left, probably on your side plate. Or it may be in the middle of your dinner plate, or in your water glass, folded into a fancy arrangement. As soon as you sit down, take it and spread it across your lap. Do not, in any circumstances, tuck it into the neck of your shirt, even if that seems much more sensible and you always do that at home! The exception is that if especially messy food (such as lobster) is to be served you may be provided with a suitable bib to protect your clothing, or alternatively everyone may tuck their napkin in. In this case only, if in doubt, look to see what everyone else is doing. But in more usual formal dinners you only use the napkin to clean your fingers and dab excess food from around your mouth. Don't make a big fuss of it. At the end of the meal it is usual to leave the napkin unfolded – just crumpled up and on, or near, your plate. It's one way of showing the waiting staff that you have finished.

Too many glasses!

At a very classy dinner there may be all kinds of glasses on the table by your plate. But there will also probably be all kinds of waiting staff, and they will fill your glass for you – so, don't worry, they will choose the right one for you. But sometimes at big meals the wine is left on each table for diners to serve themselves. Then, it can be helpful to know what kinds of drinks go in what kinds of glasses. Here are some pointers:

- Red wine glasses are usually larger and rounder than those used for white wine. You should not fill more than one third of the glass. The glass is only large so that the aroma, or 'bouquet', of the wine can be appreciated more fully.
- White wine is poured into rather slender glasses. Again, you should not over-fill your glass. White wine is usually served chilled and you will be supplied with a container of ice to keep the wine cold. Return the bottle to the ice after you have poured the wine.
- Champagne is served in tall, narrow glasses called 'flutes'.
- Port is drunk from small wine glasses and brandy glasses are very big and balloon-shaped. Again, you shouldn't fill a brandy glass up – a small amount in the bottom is sufficient.
- There will also be a water glass somewhere. It might look like a tumbler, but some places will just give you a spare wine glass.

It is polite to keep an eye on your fellow guests' glasses and offer to refill them from time to time, but if you don't feel confident about doing this, you should not feel obliged. If bottles of wine are placed out for all to share, be careful not to hog them – it's okay to help yourself, but always offer to fill other glasses first – ask 'would you like some wine?'.

If you end up using the wrong glass, don't worry. You'll hardly be shot for it. You can simply ask the waiter for 'another red wine glass' if you need a replacement.

The finer points of dining

Sneezing, coughing and burping

Well, we all do them in the privacy of our own homes, but try not to make a big event out them of when dining out. If you have to, turn your head away from the food, cover your mouth with a clean handkerchief (try not to use your napkin), and get it all over with as quietly and quickly as possible. If you really can't control that terrible cough, say something 'I'm sorry, I'll just go and sort out this cough,' and go outside until the tickle has disappeared.

Awkward items and troublesome food

There are some dishes that are just plain awkward to eat. Anything with small bones, such as fish, needs to be treated with caution. Place the bones on the side of your plate. If by any chance you do get a bone stuck in your throat and really need help, don't let good manners stand in your way. Similarly, if someone else is obviously choking, help them out or ask if anyone can assist.

Any other items that you cannot swallow (pips, stones or pieces of gristle and bone) should be removed from the mouth with as little fuss as possible, perhaps by using your napkin over your mouth, and placed on the side of the place. Do not ever spit anything out enthusiastically and yell 'yuck, a bone!' or similar!

Some food is eaten in a particular way. Caviar, for example, is often served with small, plain biscuits. You put a little caviar on the biscuits with your knife and, depending on the size of the biscuit, you take a bite or pop the whole thing in your mouth. However, if you are dining with people who really know their caviar, there is a different ritual you need to know. You put a little pile of the eggs on the web of skin between the index finger and thumb of your left hand and lick it off. Don't try this unless everyone else is doing it – otherwise you'll get some very funny looks. In fact, don't try it at all unless there's no alternative!

Some foods seem designed to embarrass us at posh occasions. Take garlic, for example. Many of us love the taste, but garlic does leave us with a problem in the fresh-breath department. If everyone else has eaten garlic, that's fine. If it was just you, don't get too up-close-and-personal to other people for a while, or have an after-dinner mint.

Peas are famous for being hard to eat. Technically, the rules of high-class manners say that you are not supposed to turn your fork upside down and use it as a spoon. So use other food on the plate, like potatoes or rice and stick the peas to it. This should avoid the problems of stray peas rolling around your plate as you try to persuade them to go onto your fork.

If in doubt, use your common sense. Most people today are less hung up on the sillier rules of dining, although it always helps to know what they are.

Finger foods

It can be difficult to know just which foods it's okay to pick up in your fingers at a more formal dinner. Watch what other people are doing and copy them. If nobody is picking up their asparagus, you'd probably better not either – even if you know it would be so much easier. Shellfish is usually eaten with the hands, and can be rather messy – usually you'll get some special sharp forks and other tools to help you tackle things like mussels and snails.

Other food just shouldn't be let out in a formal setting. Corn on the cob, for example, is almost impossible to eat politely. Probably best to leave it alone, unless the occasion is an informal barbecue, where everyone is just diving in.

Strange as it may seem, pizza can be another problem when it comes to finger food. At home, we all eat it with our fingers, don't we? Preferably straight out of the pizza-delivery box on a Friday night! But in a restaurant, you would eat a genuine Italian pizza with a knife and fork. It can be a bit of a battle. It may be simplest to cut it into portions and then pick it up in your fingers, and most people will be glad to follow suit – judge the occasion and make your choice.

If nobody is picking up their asparagus, you'd probably better not either – even if you know it would be so much easier.

You can find yourself having the same problem with fruit. At home, you'd crunch straight into that apple, but at a formal occasion you should cut it into pieces and may even want to peel it first. A small, sharp knife is usually provided for this purpose. At a very formal do, you'd use a fork to get the pieces to your mouth. Again, see what everyone else is up to.

The French are especially particular about the correct method to eat cheese. It is not so much the eating that matters, but the way you cut the cheese to begin with. Those produced in round cakes (such as Camembert, for example) are cut by slicing outwards from the centre so that you get a small wedge. That's the best policy with any round cheese, and makes it easier for the next person to serve themselves a similar portion.

Twiddling your noodles

Finally, we need to take a quick look at awkward foods. Pasta, for example, is hugely popular but people are often a little confused about how to handle the long, stringy varieties such as spaghetti and tagliatelle. At a formal dinner you should be given a spoon and fork for this sort of pasta. You pick up a few strands with the fork, hold them against the bowl (the inside surface) of the spoon and wind them around the fork until they form a neat little bundle that you can pop into your mouth. Well, that's the theory! It can take a few goes to get the knack. It's also not such good manners to suck up a string of spaghetti until it pops into your mouth with a 'splat' – not at a formal do, anyway. (And even if it is fun.)

Eating Indian and Chinese food

In Indian and other ethnic restaurants in Britain we use knives and forks as normal. Only if you get invited to a very authentic Asian or Arabic meal will people eat with their fingers, in the traditional manner. Use some rice or bread to help scoop up a ball of food and pop it all into your mouth. Traditionally the left hand is considered 'dirty' by many Eastern cultures, so always use your right hand.

If you are eating Chinese in the west no one will mind if you ask for a spoon or a fork instead of using the chopsticks that are usually provided. If, however, you get invited to a dinner where everyone is eating with chopsticks you might feel foolish if you can't join in. This is one way to do it:

- Take one stick and lay it across your hand so that it rests in the bit between your forefinger and thumb. (If you're right-handed, your right hand).
- Let the end of the stick rest on the inside of your middle finger. This stick does not move.

- Now take the second stick and lay it on top of the first.
- Grasp the second stick between thumb and forefinger. You can now move the stick up and down using it to trap food against the stationary stick. It's easy with a little practice. Incidentally, people from Southeast Asia generally use a spoon and fork and keep chopsticks for eating the noodle course.

In many parts of the world you are expected to eat with noisy enthusiasm (in Japan, for example, slurping appreciatively is quite normal). Watch others and copy what they do. If you insist on western-style good table manners you might look as though you are not enjoying the food – but don't go overboard!

If you are a guest then you have no option but to struggle with difficult food, but if you are the host take pity on your guests and avoid foods that will cause problems. Try to choose foods that are easy to deal with, and won't be regarded as too unusual.

How to eat

Here are a few common-sense suggestions on what makes good manners when eating out in public:

- Eat quietly, taking only small bites at a time.
- Eat with your mouth closed.
- Don't blow on hot food to cool it. Wait until it cools naturally – use the time for conversation.
- What goes into your mouth should not, except in case of dire emergency, come out again. If you have accidentally put something inedible, such as a bone or fruit stone, in your mouth then you should remove it with your fingers as unobtrusively as possible and place it on the side of your plate. Don't spit it out.

Soup

However wonderful it tastes, don't slurp! Old-fashioned rules of etiquette say that it's good manners to eat soup like this: half-fill your spoon (and it is best to aim for a half-full spoon to avoid slurping) by dipping it into your soup and tipping the spoon away from you, so that the soup flows into it. When you get near the end, tip your bowl slightly away from you. That's if you really want to bother with old-fashioned manners, which very few people do. Just eat it quietly, that's all we ask!

- The purpose of a formal meal is to socialise, not to satisfy hunger. Don't ever give the impression that you would rather be eating than talking.
- If you are a naturally fast eater, try to slow it down a bit, so you don't finish before everyone else.
- If you like to chew everything 32 times, try to speed up, so that you won't find everyone else waiting for you to finish.
- If you want to pause, place your knife and fork on the plate, but not together. Only place them together (side by side) if you want to show the waiting staff that you've finished and they can take your plate. Here's an interesting fact: in China, the way to show you have finished your pot of tea and would like some more is to turn the lid upside down on the pot. I've tried this and it works.
- If there is something on the plate you don't like it is quite acceptable just to leave it, or perhaps try a mouthful as a token effort.

After the meal

All the plates are cleared away, and the meal's over – what next? That depends on your hosts really. At some very formal dinners, port or brandy may be brought to the table. At others coffee is served. It used to be the habit that the ladies left the room at this point, leaving the men to their own conversation and cigars – but you wouldn't find that happening today!

> **The elbow question**
>
> The traditional rule used to be 'elbows off the table!', and it was thought rude to lean forward on your elbows while eating. But things have changed, and today it's quite normal to do this, especially if you are dining informally with friends and having a good conversation. But if you're at a very formal occasion and not sure, it's good manners to play safe, until people have obviously relaxed and eating is over. Usually the more formal rules get quickly abandoned once people have got to know each other and are simply having a good time.
>
> If you're seated at a rather cramped table, keep your elbows in and try not to dig other people in the ribs – and hope they'll treat you to the same good manners!

At some formal dinners it is usual to signal the start of the after-meal activities with a loyal toast (that is, toasting the health of the Queen and some members of the royal family). Alternatively, there may be a toast to the person who is being honoured, or simply an announcement that dinner is over and you are welcome to circulate. You are not supposed to smoke before the loyal toast has been drunk. After that you can smoke once invited to do so – but only if the restaurant or venue allows it. If you are a smoker, do think about the other people near you. It may be best to refrain, or to go outside, or into a 'smokers' area.

Speeches

Sitting through after-dinner speeches can be a great pleasure, or a complete bore, depending on how amusing the speaker is (and how sober, in some cases). If you are called upon to give a speech, do make sure you speak up – a common problem is that the speaker is just too quiet for the audience to hear the finer points of the speech.

If you are listening to a speech, stay awake and look interested – even if you would rather be at home clipping your toenails than hearing this old rubbish. It's incredibly bad manners to start talking to your companions, even if they are far more interesting. If the speech contains jokes, laugh a little (even if they're only mildly amusing) and generally help the speaker to feel as if they're doing okay.

Some after-dinner speeches are informative and can be almost like a small lecture. But if questions from the floor are invited, try not to be that annoying person who keeps asking questions when it is quite clear that everyone else wants to get back to their own conversation, even if you harbour a genuine interest in the speaker's subject. Perhaps you'll be able to catch him or her on their own later, or get hold of their card.

In the later stages of a meal it is quite usual for people to move places in order to talk to special friends from whom they have been separated. There are always people who have to leave early to catch trains and so on, so there should be plenty of spare places. At this stage you can be much more informal and talk about things

In the later stages of a meal it is quite usual for people to move places in order to talk to special friends from whom they have been separated.

that interest you and your friends rather than feeling that you have to entertain the people you have been seated with. A chance to relax, at last!

Paying up

If you are eating in a restaurant, rather than simply being an invited guest at a formal banquet, there comes the awful moment when you have to ask for the bill. Asking for the bill is a strange ritual, and one that many of us find quite difficult. The first difficulty is catching the attention of the waiter, who's often really busy getting food to some other diners too, and keeps whizzing by without seeing you. Try to catch the waiter's eye, and if all else fails, do raise your hand a little in the waiter's direction and ask 'could we have the bill, please?' as the waiter passes. If that has no effect, you can always stand up, looking a bit lost – and go and find a waiter to ask if necessary.

Even if the evening out was your idea, your guests may still insist on paying, or in sharing the bill. What you decide with them depends on the situation. It's quite normal today to say 'let's split the bill', so that nobody has to pay for the whole thing. But even if you really want to pay for the whole meal, don't get into a heated 'tussle' if your guests insist on chipping in. Accept graciously and leave it at that. On the other hand, if your companions don't offer to share the cost and the event is not one that you are 'host' for in particular, it's fine to say, in a friendly manner, 'shall we split this?' or 'let's just go halves, shall we?'

Check your bill to see if a service charge has already been added. It may have been, especially if you were dining as part of a large group. In that case it is up to you whether you leave a little extra tip on top, for really outstanding service. Otherwise you will see a notice on the bill that says 'Service not included'. You'll normally see that the final amount on the credit card slip has been left blank so that you can add a gratuity – that's another name for a 'tip'. Traditionally in Britain the usual tip is between 10 and 15 per cent of the bill. So add that amount, or leave it separately as cash – tucked under a plate perhaps. If the service was terrible, well there's no obligation to tip – but it's good manners otherwise.

In much of Europe, you can get coffee and a light snack at a streetside café, served by a waiter, which happens less in Britain. Here the waiter would certainly appreciate a tip, but you only need to leave a small amount, in cash, when you leave.

Drink up!

Drinking usually goes with eating, and alcoholic drinks feature at most social occasions. Alcoholic drinks can help to make the situation more relaxed and enjoyable and can give people confidence and make them more extrovert. In moderation, that can be very helpful in a rather intimidating social situation. And at a banquet or big do, the booze is usually being paid for by someone else, so what could be better? But, even if you are normally a very responsible drinker, do be careful – it's so easy to have one too many and get a bit more than 'tiddly'. And there's not much you can do about it by that point. However shy you may be feeling, it's good manners to keep your drinking well under control, and not to lose too many inhibitions – you may regret it!

Of course every situation is different. At an informal large party with very good friends and family, it may be more acceptable to have a bit too much, get a bit merry and generally behave in a slightly silly way. At a large banquet, in the company of strangers, you would be ill-advised to behave in the same way. One problem

Leaving

Invitations to very formal dinners or events might state 'Carriages at 10.45 pm' which is an old-fashioned way to let you know when the proceedings will wind up, partly so that guests can sort out trains and taxis beforehand. It would have to be a very formal dinner to have actual horse carriages arrive at the end! Very few formal dinners or events have leaving formalities, but it is obviously always good manners to thank your host briefly as you leave. Keep it simple – remember they have other people to say goodbye to – and follow up with a thank you letter if you think it's appropriate. At very formal events there is usually a member of staff – perhaps a porter or a hotel doorman – who can call you a taxi, or you can even do it yourself from the telephone at the hotel reception desk.

is that once we've had a bit too much we tend not to notice how our behaviour has changed. If you're at all worried, it's best to keep to soft drinks – there's nothing rude about saying, 'I'm not drinking tonight' or 'I really would prefer an orange juice, thanks.' People are likely to think you are driving and simply being sensible. And of course, you may not ever drink alcohol – if you don't, either because you don't like it or on principle or for religious reasons, you can simply politely refuse.

One last important point about getting drunk: getting more than tiddly is generally a bad idea, and it is extremely bad manners to get drunk if you are the host of the party. That's because it's your job to look after everyone and to make sure that all guests are happy. If you're under the table, you're going to find that difficult.

At a large party, it may also be necessary to make sure there isn't too much noise or rowdy behaviour – you have a duty to remain completely sober, so that things don't get out of hand.

Wine

Some people get in a real tizzy about the ins and outs of wine, and all that expert knowledge that you're, apparently, supposed to know. But really, don't worry about it. All that intimidating language about 'bouquets' and 'a nice nose' is fine, but you don't need it to appreciate a nice glass of wine and enjoy sharing wine with others. Good manners do not hide behind pretentious language, they are found in simple concern for other people's comfort and enjoyment.

But here are a few little tips when it comes to dealing with buying and knowing about wine. Though many of us buy a bottle of wine from the supermarket, you can also buy your wine by the case from a wine merchant – the more expensive and 'classier' wines are sold this way. And in an upmarket restaurant there may well be a wine waiter – a member of staff whose sole job is to help you choose the best wine for your meal. Some wine waiters can be a bit snobby – you can laugh at them, quite justifiably, when you get home, but when you're there it may help you to know at least a little about all the different kinds of wine.

The wine ritual

If you are the host, your wine waiter (called a *sommelier* in the more expensive restaurants – which is just the French word for the same thing) will bring you the wine list to study. If you have someone in your party with a real knowledge of wine you can hand over the job of choosing what you are going to drink to them. However, don't feel you have to. Take the list and study it. You need to know what sort of wine you want. There are no hard-and-fast rules (for example, people used to say you should only drink white wine with fish and poultry, but that's not the case today); you can order what you like. But make sure you know the basics – there are a great many wine guide-type books that can tell you the difference between a chardonnay and a sauvignon, or a pinot noir and a merlot.

When the waiter brings your wine to the table, he will show you the bottle first. You are supposed to read the label and make sure that he's brought the one you ordered. Also have a quick look to check that the capsule (the bit of foil or plastic that seals the top of the bottle) is present and unbroken. It is not unknown in seedier restaurants to sell off leftover wine by putting it into a new bottle. Then the waiter will remove the cork and pour a very small amount of wine into your glass. This is so that you can taste and make sure that it's okay. If you want to do taste the wine thoroughly and 'professionally' you should swill the wine gently in the glass and then stick your nose right in and take a good sniff. But most people feel too self-conscious to do that, and really all that matters is whether the wine is 'corked' or not. If it tastes terrible, a bit like vinegar, it probably is corked – this means that it has reacted chemically with the cork, not that there are bits of cork floating in it. If the wine tastes as if it is corked (and it will usually smell nasty too) tell the waiter, firmly and politely. It's quite in order, and the waiter should replace the bottle without question.

If the wine tastes fine, you don't need to do more than nod at the waiter, or say 'that's fine, thank you.' He will pour a small measure into each glass and then he'll leave the bottle and retire. If you are having white wine, he will put it in some form of cooler and will leave you a cloth so that you can pull it out again without getting wet. By the way, if we're being fussy it is usual with white wine to pick the glass up by the stem rather than the bowl. This is so that your hand does not warm the wine. But it is only important to remember this at parties and wine tastings where you might be holding the glass for some time.

If you are serving the wine yourself, at your own dinner party, obviously you won't want to taste it. You may want to pour a little into your own glass first, in case there are any little fragments of cork in the wine, before serving wine to your guests.

If you are invited to a wine tasting it is polite and practical not to swallow the wine that you are given to taste. You will probably be offered quite a few wines to taste and if you drink them all you'll quite soon be drunk. And that's not the idea! In such surroundings spittoons will be provided and you will be expected to spit the wine out into them – this is one situation where it is good manners to spit in public. You will also be offered small snacks such as little bits of French toast. These are not to keep your hunger at bay, but to clear your palate, so that your tastebuds will be ready for the next wine you taste.

It is usual with white wine to pick the glass up by the stem rather than the bowl. This is so that your hand does not warm the wine.

Incidentally, if you don't drink or don't want to drink any more, it is quite okay to hold your hand over your glass when the wine waiter is doing refills. You don't have to drink another glass. If it is your host who is re-filling, then a few words of explanation ('no more for me, thanks, I'm driving tonight') would be polite. Don't let yourself be pressured into drinking more than you want. Some people may get a bit pushy, because they want to be a 'good host' and can't believe you don't want any more – but they'll understand if you smile and say 'no thanks!'

Champagne

Champagne is a drink for special occasions, for most of us, and it can be difficult to know how to deal with it. We've all seen racing drivers shake up a bottle and splash it all over the podium, but that's not what you should do if you actually want to drink it. Instead, remove the wire retainer around the cork carefully, and put a clean napkin or tea towel over the top of the bottle. Twist and pull the cork carefully, making sure to release the gas pressure gradually. Have a glass ready just in case the wine spurts out a bit. To serve your guests hold the bottle by the bottom. This looks awkward but you'll find it gives you more control than you'd think and it means that you won't warm the bottle with your hand.

There are all sorts of champagnes at a wide range of prices so, as with other wines, it pays to do a bit of research. There are also fizzy wines that are made by the 'champagne method', like cava – they can also be very good, and not quite so expensive. Remember, it is not always the most expensive wine that tastes best. Look out for champagne-style wines from countries you might not expect, such as Australia and New Zealand, or Spain.

Fine wines

Very old, fine wines are likely to have quite a bit of sediment in the bottom. After all, they've been around for a while. If you are serving a wine like this, it's best to decant it – transfer it to a decanter – well before the dinner. There's a traditional trick to spotting the sediment – you are supposed to put a lighted candle behind the bottle to help you spot any that might escape into the decanter. If you feel that it is safe to serve the wine straight from the bottle, it is usual to leave the bottle open for some hours before the wine is served. This gives it a chance to 'breathe'. Even a less expensive red wine can benefit from being opened a little earlier.

Spirits

The Scots/Scandinavian custom of drinking spirits as a beer chaser is becoming increasingly popular, and carries the risk that you will get very drunk very quickly. Schnapps is often drunk cold, with the effect that the alcohol doesn't take effect immediately – so you may not realise how strong it is for quite a few minutes.

Whisky is an equally potent spirit. Most popular brands are blends of several different malts. But more expensive whiskies are single malts – which means that they are not blended. Savour them as you would a good glass of wine – they're expensive, but worth it.

Brandy is another drink that needs to be savoured rather than swigged. The balloon-shaped glass allows you to swirl it around and warm it with your hand, releasing a delicious bouquet and making the spirit less fiery to drink. When it is really warm it should slide over your tastebuds like silk – a very nice sensation indeed!

Pub customs

For some people the British custom of buying a round in a pub is confusing, because it isn't done in all countries. In many places everyone buys their own drinks, and only buys other drinks for close friends and family. This isn't seen as rude at all. So if a visitor doesn't offer to buy a round in the pub, they are not necessarily being bad-mannered, they just don't understand British ways. Part of the reason that buying a round is popular is to take the aggro out of getting the drinks in. It's far less inconvenient if one person takes on the chore, and everyone takes turns. But if you are buying a lot of drinks there's no reason you shouldn't ask to 'share the round' with someone else.

Going to stay

Being the perfect guest – or the perfect host

Know your limits

Being invited to stay with someone opens up a whole range of possible 'foot in mouth' situations, but these can easily be avoided if you're well prepared. The main thing to remember is that when you go to stay with someone you're going to be 'invading their space' while you're there and you need to be sensitive to this, so that you don't get on their nerves. However much they are looking forward to your visit, even the best of friends can find guests a bit stressful at times – and you don't want to ruin a friendship.

First of all, get an idea of how long the visit is supposed to be – if they've said 'come for the weekend', then it's obvious. But if someone says 'do come and stay, for as long as you like,' you need to think about how long that really means. It may need a bit of flexibility on your behalf – often you can't really tell how long to stay until you get there. But, be certain – 'as long as you like' doesn't mean, 'for months on end'!

Don't expect too much

It's easy to get very excited about visiting someone, or having someone to stay with you. With everyone wanting everything to be 'just perfect', it's likely that the visit is likely to feel slightly disappointing – you, as host or guest, were probably just expecting too much. And remember, if everyone feels that they've got to make the visit perfect, they'll be under a terrible strain from the word go. And even the most well-prepared host is probably going to crack under the strain of looking after guests for 24 hours a day, for several days on end. As a guest, the effort of being 'on your best behaviour' for such a long time isn't going to be easy either. Really, it's best if everyone just tries to relax and have a good time. If you're the host, remember that guests don't require looking after all the time and might even like some time alone to read the paper or just hang about doing nothing. Having good manners with regard to your guests doesn't mean that you have to run after them all the time. And, as a guest, your good manners will make you sensitive to the host's need to put their feet up for a while, and have a bit of private 'breathing room' without worrying if you're okay all the time. And, remember, if little things go wrong, or a few stressed-out words get said, just ignore them. However much you enjoy having guests, being 'on guest alert' all the time can leave you a little exhausted!

On the other hand, if the visit does seem to be going very badly, take your cue as a guest to tactfully bring it to an end – find a sudden work commitment or a family problem that requires you leave, perhaps. A few white lies are better than staying in a situation where both host and guests are extremely unhappy. But be good-mannered about it, and depart on as friendly terms as you can manage.

Making a good impression

As a guest, you should arrive bearing gifts for your hosts. If you're simply coming to stay for a couple of days, something simple is fine – perhaps a bottle of wine, or some flowers and chocolates. If you're coming for rather longer, you could bring something a little more grand – toys that would appeal to any of the family's children are a good choice (but make sure you have brought something for all the children, or something they can share). But if you are not extremely well off, don't worry too much – you can also ask your hosts in advance 'is there anything I can bring?' or 'shall I bring some starters for dinner?', giving you a chance to bring some home-made food or something simpler.

Once you've arrived, do make sure that you show interest in all the family – including the kids, and even the family pets. If you're not too used to talking with children, just asking what they did at school today, or to show you their favourite toy, is a good opener. And don't forget that many small children find adults a bit 'scary', so don't think they are being rude if they run off to mum or dad! Whatever you do, try not to find yourself saying 'how much you've grown!' to the kids themselves – it won't do much for your street cred. If there are dogs or cats, or other pets, do stroke or greet them if you are comfortable with that. Conversely, if you are a host with pets, be considerate to the fact that not all guests are thrilled when Rover jumps up to say hello.

If you're the host, remember that guests don't require looking after all the time, and might even like some time alone

Above all, it's good manners to take everyone as they come. You may be spending time with people different from you, with different kinds of jobs or lifestyles. Don't be judgemental, be interested. You never know how well you might get on with someone who has a very different kind of life from yours.

Play by the house rules

When you stay with someone, you have to fit in with the way they live their lives – and that can bit a bit hard. Even if people's habits, like meal times or when they go to bed, are very unlike yours, you'll need to do the same. If a family follows little observances you're not used to – like saying grace at a meal – simply accept it. If you say grace, but your guests don't, live with it rather than complain. If you're the host, bear in mind that your guests may also have little quirks that you can easily accommodate, if you take the trouble to ask – for instance, a guest might be used to making themselves a hot drink if they can't sleep, or getting up early to go for a run. Show them where the hot chocolate or the breakfast cereal is, and ask them to make themselves at home.

Mainly, for both guest and host, remember that it's good manners to say in advance if there is something you would appreciate, like a hot water bottle in bed perhaps, or some family ritual, like letting mum have the shower first because she has to get to work, that your guest needs to know.

Make space and time for your guests

As already mentioned, everyone needs time for themselves occasionally, some more than others. If you're the host, make sure that you have provided space in the day for your guest to relax. Don't crowd them all the time. If your guest is not used to the hustle and bustle of family life and yours is a very hustle-bustle family with lots of kids and dogs, try to keep the kids away a bit, some of the time. Look out for signs that your guest is a little overwhelmed by it all.

Know when to say nothing

For guests, this next bit of 'good manners' advice is obvious really, but even so, many of us are guilty of falling at the first hurdle on this one. You are the guest – so, not a word of criticism about your friends' way of life. Don't wander around saying 'hmm, wouldn't have gone for this wallpaper myself' or 'gosh, don't you ever discipline your children, they really are out of control.' This is just as true if you are visiting relatives and a lot of really big family rows start just because one person has decided to give their opinion on how their relative chooses to run their life. However much temptation beckons, keep your opinions unspoken.

Remember that your host is letting you into their private domain, and they are letting you share all the things they value most in their life. So don't hurt them with insensitive remarks. Ignore the décor that makes you, personally, feel a bit ill. Perhaps they'd hate your place just as much. If their kids seem a noisy lot, and yours are little angels, feel glad – but don't go on about it. Just be happy to share the company and hospitality of friends. This holds just as much if you're the host – just smile, and laugh about it later if you have to.

Keep it friendly

Same thing applies here, when you're conversing with your hosts. If you keep the conversation light and friendly, you should be able to steer clear of any contentious areas, where you and your hosts might violently disagree. Even so, you are likely to have some longer and more serious conversations, if you're staying for a while. You may end up watching the TV news together or reading the newspapers, so topics of the day are likely to come up. Well, if you know your hosts even slightly – and most likely you will – you'll have an idea of the political opinions they're likely to hold, and what they may feel about news items. So avoid areas where you are likely to conflict, or at least keep it tactful. And don't assume that everyone holds the same views as you – it's an easy mistake to make. Even friends you've known for some time can surprise you.

Religion can be a very hot topic, and if you hold very different religious views from your hosts (or guests, according to which you are), or have no religious belief, while they do, it may be best to keep away from the subject if you can. If religion comes up in conversation be non-committal or open-minded, and don't get into a deep discussion. If a topic comes up that you really feel strongly about, and fear will start a raging argument, the best thing may be to say 'well, let's not talk about that – it'll only get me over-excited' or some other such tactful way of stopping a row from starting. If necessary, find a sudden need to go to the toilet, and hope that the subject will have changed by the time you return!

Clear up

If you're a guest, remember that you need to respect your hosts' home and keep it tidy, even if you are a complete slob in the privacy of your own place. So, when you get up in the morning, make the bed and tidy up your room. If you have books or papers out, clear them up. Mess can really get on some people's nerves, so be sensitive to that, even if you personally don't mind mess a bit. It also works the other way – if you're a very untidy host, with a neat and natty guest, you may stress them out completely if you don't clear up some of those books, clothes or piles of CDs. It doesn't have to be a palace – just a bit of a clear-up helps.

Lend a hand

As a guest at someone else's house you should offer to help 'make yourself useful' often. Offer to lay the table, do the washing-up, or pop to the shops for any food items needed. Most hosts are grateful for a bit of assistance when they've got guests, even if they initially say 'oh no, don't bother!'. Ask again, and only sit down and do nothing if you're completely sure if they don't want you to help at all. Hosts – it's not bad manners to let your guests help out a bit, and don't be ungracious if someone offers to wash up or some other useful chore. Smile and say 'thanks'.

Don't make yourself too much at home

When you go to stay with people they will often say 'treat the place as your own', as a way of inviting you to relax. But don't do that literally – it would be very bad manners to use their things without asking, or help yourself to the contents of the fridge. Another complete no-no is using the telephone all the time, and running up expensive bills. And don't invite your friends to phone you there non-stop either – that's just as rude. If you'd like to use the phone, ask – and if it's long-distance, insist on paying for the call.

In general, fit in with the 'rhythm of life' at your friend's house. If they go to bed early, follow suit – don't force them to stay up late, just to be polite, when they're obviously tired and used to getting a good eight hours' sleep each night. Just try to read the situation – Saturday night may be fine to stay up into the early hours chatting, but on Sunday night they may have work the next day. Good manners here are just a common-sense thing.

If you're particularly old friends with one of your hosts, you may have a wealth of stories about silly and embarrassing things they did in their youth, or with other partners. Don't tell these stories unless you're absolutely sure your friend won't mind – there may be some his or her partner, or kids, just don't know. And they may want to keep it that way. Don't be the guest who caused red faces all round.

And so to bed

Things can get a little awkward here. If you're a guest who came with a friend, your host may not be quite sure whether you sleep together or not. Help your host out – it's good manners to make the nature of your relationship quite clear early on, so that everyone is comfortable with what's what. Just drop it into the conversation if you can, ideally when the invitation is issued, although you can do it once you've arrived. 'Steve's my partner' or 'Jane's my girlfriend' are often sufficient. Or, you may prefer to have a quiet word with your host – 'so Jane and I are quite happy bunking up together, no need for separate rooms' – if it seems confusion might arise. Bear in mind that older relatives, or people with strict religious views, may decide to provide separate rooms – don't take offence, it's their home after all. Just grin and bear it. You won't be there forever.

As a host, don't be afraid to tactfully ask, if the situation doesn't seem clear. You can say something like 'John, I've put you and Steve together, hope I've got that right – plenty of room though if you want to go separately', or you can just ask outright. Usually the situation is fairly clear from early on in the visit.

What guests should do

It's good manners to show that you are appreciative of your host's hospitality and that you're enjoying yourself. But you can't go around saying 'thank you' all the time. Instead, admire the home, or say approving things about the garden or the children. Show interest in your hosts' hobbies. Generally make them happy by showing them your pleasure in their life and family, and also do take time occasionally to say 'thank you so much for inviting me, I'm very much enjoying being with you and your family' or something similar. If you are feeling generous, you could show your thanks by offering to take them out for a meal.

In general, fit in with the 'rhythm of life' at your friend's house.

Or if you're a great cook, you could offer to cook breakfast one morning. When you leave, you should buy your hosts a little present. Having got to know them better, you probably have an idea of something they might especially like – 'Jack, I thought you might like a couple of new books on fishing to add to the collection', or something that all the family might enjoy eating or drinking (after you've gone!). And don't forget to follow up with a thank-you note, especially if the visit was during a holiday season and your hosts had gone to a great deal of trouble. Last but not least – if it's appropriate, perhaps you can invite them to stay with you some time?

Gracious hospitality

What the host should do

Here is a bit of advice on being a good host, and making your guests feel at ease. Do give your guests a short guided tour of the house, so that they know where the bathrooms and loos are, and where they will be sleeping. If there are any strange quirks – a door that's likely to stick, or a window that is a bit fragile – try to mention them early on: 'I'd watch that bathroom door, it has fallen off the hinges when I've yanked it too hard, once or twice' or 'now, just to say be careful with the window in your room, and you need to unlock it with this key.' Sometimes we get so used to 'working' our home that we forget about all those funny little bits and pieces, or that step that everyone else seems to fall over.

Think about little luxuries that might make the stay more pleasant for your guest. Perhaps a TV in their room, or tea and coffee things and a kettle?

Think about little luxuries that might make the stay more pleasant for your guest. Perhaps a TV in their room, or tea and coffee things and a small kettle? It will help them to feel more at home and would mean they don't always have to ask. Make sure they have some books and magazines in their room, and – if you have spares – a dressing gown or robe. And don't forget to provide bath towels and any other necessities. Say something like 'now, just ask if there's anything you need', and most people will let you know if they need something like a glass for some water, or some tissues, or whatever. No guest will expect you to offer the swanky luxuries of a hotel (well, no polite and well-mannered guest will!) but a little pampering goes a long way.

Getting around

Many of us spend quite a bit of our time travelling – for work, for pleasure, to get from A to B. And there's no two ways about it: despite the glut of budget airlines, the faster trains, and the many different ways we can travel nowadays, we still have to put up with delays, overcrowding and other annoyances. Sometimes it seems as if travel is no fun at all, especially when you're stuck in a traffic jam. Sometimes travel is exhilarating, but sometimes it's boring, frustrating, claustrophobic, noisy and dirty. It's quite easy to get stressed out by it all and to take it out on our fellow travellers. So, bear in mind that good manners are an essential when it comes to getting through our tricky travel moments.

So, let's start with an obvious point of 'travel manners': when is it good manners to give up your seat to someone else? In days of yore, a gentleman or a boy would always offer their seat to a lady, no matter how old or young. That's no longer true. Today people are treated more equally and a woman might even find this a little annoying. But, common-sense good manners say that you should offer your seat to anyone who seems more in need of it than you – a pregnant woman, an older man or woman, someone who is disabled, someone with young children in tow. It doesn't matter whether you are a man or a woman, anyone who needs a seat will be grateful of the offer. If they choose not to take it, at least you've offered. If they have the bad manners to appear cross about it, then take it in your stride – although that's a rare occurrence.

In general, don't take your travel frustrations out on employees of the travel company, who can't possibly be directly responsible for the fact that your train's delayed, or your flight has been cancelled. It's good manners to be civil and as pleasant as you can be – although of course you can tell them that you are unhappy about a situation and be firm in insisting that they help you to resolve any difficulties that have arisen as a result. Don't bully or hector staff – bad manners and also not very effective!

Don't rage on those roads

It's hard not to get cross, isn't it, when that idiot in the other car has come just 'that near' your bumper and has then flashed his headlights to try and intimidate you further. Not much you can do except keep a wary eye on him and make sure nothing that you are doing is likely to upset other drivers unnecessarily. Angry drivers are dangerous drivers, apart from anything else. So here are a few tips on driving behaviour to avoid, things that police and motoring organisations like the AA always say are designed to wind up other motorists:

- Be polite, and don't get too close to the car in front. This kind of 'tailgating' is rude and dangerous if the person ahead needs to stop suddenly.
- Don't cut up other drivers. 'Nipping in' in front of someone can be very aggravating and doesn't really save you much time.
- Don't stick in the middle lane of the motorway. It's supposed to be for overtaking only.
- Don't beep the car horn to express anger or frustration: it's only there to signal danger and caution. Behave, now!
- Always try to indicate well in advance. It can be easy to forget to indicate if you know a route well, or are lost and turning suddenly. Think about the person behind.

Of course these are just a few hints on sensible, safe driving. Here are a couple of common-sense tips that are to do with good manners on the road: if you're in a heavy, slow-moving stream of traffic and people are waiting to get on, be considerate and make room if possible. And when you're parking, don't just leave your car anywhere, or straddled over two spaces or blocking an entrance.

And for goodness sake, don't make a fuss if cars choose to park outside your house at the curb. They have every right to, as long as the road allows parking and they're not blocking your drive. However much you might prefer to have an unobstructed car-free view, you can't decide where people can or cannot park. Sorry!

Get on your bike!

Cyclists occupy a strange position – not exactly a vehicle, but not a pedestrian. When surrounded by motor vehicles, cyclists are vulnerable and when surrounded by pedestrians they can be dangerous. So good travel manners are particularly important here. Cycling without thought for others is rude because it can cause harm to pedestrians and alarm to motorists. Besides, if you get knocked off your bike by a driver, you are far likely to come off worst. However much you hate cars, as a cyclist you have to respect the rules of the road and also respect that you may be virtually invisible to some less observant drivers.

As a cyclist, it may seem easier to ride along the pavement with the pedestrians, but that's a rather impolite way of cycling, and you could easily injure someone who wasn't expecting you to come along. If you do end up cycling on what is really a footpath, be careful – keep your distance from pedestrians and ring your bell when need be. But don't ring your bike bell loudly and frantically if you want to get through a crowd of pedestrians – just get off and walk.

When cycling on the road, make sure that you're wearing appropriate clothing, especially at night or in bad weather. And use lights. Always give clear signals, to indicate to motorists what you're about to do (and never give rude hand signals, how ever clear they may be!). Even if you are a very adept cyclist, it really isn't good manners to dash across traffic or make sudden manoeuvres, just to get to make a turn. If you're stuck, get off the bicycle and walk across the crossroads at the lights with the pedestrians – there's no shame in it, after all!

If you're part of a cycling group, it's very bad road manners to cycle in a spread-out and rambling mess. You should always cycle in single file, leaving plenty of room for cars to pass. Never block the road, unintentionally or otherwise. Lastly, don't park your bike just anywhere – make sure it isn't blocking a pavement or footpath and always make sure that it is okay to lock it up where you've chosen.

The horse brigade

There's something very nice about seeing someone riding their horse along a country lane, but a bit of common-sense good horse manners is needed to avoid problems. For a start, horses are not machines – they're animals that can at any moment act unpredictably, especially if something suddenly frightens them or startles them from their happy trotting. A rearing, lunging horse is a sight to behold and not one you particularly want to behold through your car windscreen, either. If you are the rider, make sure that you know how to control your horse before you take it out on the public highway, for everyone's safety.

When riding, it's good manners to keep your distance from people on foot. Also, just because you don't have flashing indicators doesn't mean you shouldn't give any warning of where you're going. Give clear indications and also wear high-visibility clothing – and a riding hat, of course.

If you're driving past someone on a horse, give them a wide berth and slow down, well before you reach them, to give the horse some warning. As a rider, wave or smile to thank the passing motorist and if the road is narrow, it can help to give the driver behind you an indication of when it's safe to pass you.

I'm on the train…

It's not just people shouting loudly on their mobile phones that annoys train passengers. Here are a few things that can really get up people's noses, quite rightly too:

- Leaving luggage in the aisles, or on the seat beside you, even though the train is full.
- Putting your feet up on the seat in front of you, especially when the train is crowded.
- Taking up all the leg room so that other people have to sit in a cramped position.
- Insisting on having the window open or closed when it clearly bothers everyone else.
- Using the sort of headphones that let the sound escape. No one wants to listen to a couple of hours of tinny percussion while sitting next to you. Really.
- Forcing your company on people who would rather not talk.
- And of course, treating everyone to a free listen to your phone conversation.

That list is pretty obvious really, isn't it? Except perhaps for the one about talking to people who aren't interested in having a conversation. Some people just hate chatting to strangers, or have other things they want to do – like read, or do some work, or just enjoy looking out of the window at the scenery passing by. So, be considerate. Even if you personally can't think of anything better than chatting to your neighbour to fill the time, make sure that the feeling's mutual. A friendly smile and a polite remark (often involving that old British favourite, the weather) will usually help you to 'test the water'. If your companion seems encouraging, you can expand the scope of your conversation. If you get a brief or even chilly response you will know better than to force the issue.

Going underground

The London Underground, known to all Londoners as 'The Tube', is a great place to get really annoyed, especially when the train is hot, packed, and late again. A real test of good manners! A few reminders, here:

- Just because you have been pushed into a position where your face is six inches from the person next to you, it doesn't mean you are now best friends. If you catch someone's eye, perhaps a quick sympathetic grimace is okay, but starting a long chat isn't going to be appreciated by most people, who'd rather pretend they were the only person on the train and get the journey over with.
- When the Tube train pulls into the station, do wait until everyone who's getting off has, before getting on.
- If you have a rucksack on, take it off when you get on the train. It's so easy to forget you are wearing it, and bash half the other passengers behind you.
- Don't hold the doors open to prevent the train leaving; it just delays the train and can be very dangerous.

- Don't block the escalators. On the London Tube it's the custom to stand on the right (keeping your luggage in front of you) and let people in a hurry run up or down the left-hand side. People in London are always in a hurry and rather short on patience, so if you block the escalator, they will try to push past you and this is potentially dangerous.
- If you're really lost people will usually give you directions, but do try to use the plentiful maps and diagrams first, and you can also approach uniformed station staff.

Move along the bus, please!

Most of the things that apply to the Tube also apply to travel by bus or coach. There is always a place to store luggage and baby buggies, so use it and don't leave them blocking the aisle or occupying seats. Pushing and shoving to get on or off will also make you unpopular.

Sometimes it is hard to gauge where the front of the queue starts, especially when there is a large crowd of people waiting for the bus. But there *is* a queue, however ramshackle it may seem – so don't be tempted to try and push into the front, or side, when the bus arrives. You'll only get some very cross looks.

When travelling by bus try to have the right change for the fare – it will speed up the boarding process and will make the driver happy. For many bus services you can also buy tickets in advance – in London from streetside machines, Tube stations and many newsagents. That can make things run much more smoothly, and is likely to make your driver (and you) much more happy. Handing a £10 note over to the driver for a 50p fare is not going to make him or her too pleased.

Up in the air

Air travel has its own unique stresses. For a start, delays are common at the airport and you just have to try to stay calm and take it in your stride. Yelling at airport staff doesn't really do much to help the issue, or endear you to your fellow passengers. Play nice, and be as good-tempered as you can, even if you are feeling tired and dejected, with three even more tired and dejected kids in tow.

Today you can often book your seat on a scheduled flight ahead of time – even when you buy your ticket. Even so, the nicer seats are often gone and you may not get the window or aisle seat you'd hoped for. If that matters a lot to you, try and get there very early so that you are more likely to be successful, especially if you are a family group. The budget airlines sometimes offer flights where the seats are not allocated and it's just a case of getting on and picking a seat. However much you want it, it's not good manners to fight over the last remaining window seat, okay?!

Taking a great deal of hand luggage is unlikely to win you friends and may cost you money. Once on the plane, the worst thing about economy air travel is the cramped conditions. You'll have to be considerate of those around you – don't kick the back of the seat in front, elbow your neighbour or hog the armrest. When you recline your seat, be aware of the person behind you. It's simple consideration in the face of awful conditions that makes for good air-travel manners!

Children can be very annoying to other passengers in a plane, because there is little they can do to escape rowdy or over-excited kids, however much they'd love them in normal circumstances. If you have kids with you, watch that they aren't annoying fellow passengers by running around, or banging the seat backs or trays. It may seem like nothing much to you, and at least it's keeping them occupied. But the person next door may already be exhausted and just longing for some quiet. It's a good idea to come well prepared with toys and simple games to keep your children occupied – colouring books and jigsaw puzzles, or some new comics or books. On the other hand, if you're the one who's scowling at your neighbours' noisy kids, do remember that for most children the flight is a very exciting adventure, and a quick game of peek-a-boo from behind the headrest might be all you need to do to keep the youngster amused for a few minutes.

However much you want it, it's not good manners to fight over the last remaining window seat.

As with train journeys, and perhaps more so, don't assume that the person next to you wants to spend the journey chatting to you. Everyone's different, and while you may be an interested extrovert, other people just want to curl up and go to sleep and try to forget that their cramped legs have already gone to sleep some time ago. Try to take the hint if someone smiles, says a few words, and then gets back to their book.

Ship ahoy!

Going on a cruise? The nearest most of us get to life at sea is a cross-Channel ferry or, at best, a tourist cruise. Both of these are really no more than a floating train, or a floating hotel, respectively. There are no special rules, except that on the grander cruises you might be asked to 'dress for dinner' – that is, wear smart cocktail or evening wear. In that case, you'll have been given full details beforehand, when you booked. But today there are no particular manners that you need to observe. Even the captain – who used to have to 'go down with the ship' if it sunk – is allowed to get into the lifeboat with everyone else these days! About the only thing that might happen is that, on a cruise, you can be asked if you'd like to dine at the captain's table – treat this as a formal dinner and you'll have a good idea of how to behave and dress.

By the way, it is a myth that the captain of a ship can perform marriage ceremonies, so don't ask!

Communications

Today we can pick up the phone, send an instant message, text a message, tap out an email, even set up a webcam and send live pictures. Or even if we don't know how to do all of those, you can bet our younger relatives probably can. It's hard to imagine how people survived, in the not-too-distant past, when writing was the main form of communication over a distance, later to be followed by those new-fangled gadgets like the telegraph and telephone. Digital technology and especially the internet, of course, has been responsible for much of this huge expansion of communication, which affects our world in every aspect, not least our informal communication with each other. And with new forms of communication come new ideas of what is polite and what isn't – what makes good communication 'manners'. Indeed, the 'rules' of how to communicate politely on the internet even have a tongue-in-cheek word that people use for them – 'netiquette'. If you are diving into internet communication and email for the first time, there are a few points that might help you feel less worried about the whole experience.

Email

Those of us who maybe only use email for the occasional message might be surprised to realise that it is probably the most widely used form of communication in the world. Even developing nations are now gaining more access to email. It's an amazing way to communicate with people who may be thousands of miles away from you, and to send them documents, pictures or even music electronically. You can send a whole book at the touch of a button. And, with a few clicks of the mouse, you can send your message to as many people as you want, or as few.

The advantages of email are obvious. However, one of the big disadvantages is that it's hard to make them as personal or obviously friendly as a letter in your own handwriting, or a tone of voice down a telephone. So don't assume that someone is being rude if their message seems terse or cool, it is probably 'just the email talking'.

An email from a work colleague, or from somebody emailing in a work-related capacity, might come across quite like a letter, even if it is brief:

> Andrew
> Do you think you could bring that spare case of widgets over when you make the delivery on Wednesday?
> Stephen
>
> Stephen Pearce
> Area Sales Manager
> Grummet & Widget International plc
> www.grummetnwidget.com
>
> This email and any files transmitted with it are confidential and intended solely for the use of the individual or entity to whom they are addressed. If you have received this email in error please notify the system manager.

However, there's no real need to imitate a formal letter, like that. More often you can be more informal; you can start your message with 'Dear…' or even a simple 'Hello' or 'Hi'.

Hi Andrew,

Could you bring over that box of widgets next time?

Thanks so much,

Stephen

On the whole, the tone and content of an email is more likely to work if you keep to the same format you would use in a phone conversation with the person you're emailing.

Partly because computers used to be much slower, and longer emails took more 'effort' to send, a system of abbreviations developed, to make messages shorter. Someone might write 'AFAIK' instead of 'As Far As I Know'. This soon became quite a trend, and today lots of people use abbreviations as a kind of clever, jokey way of making messages more informal. You certainly don't have to use them, but you may see some, like 'BTW' – 'by the way', or 'IMV' – 'in my view'. If you search for "Internet Lingo" on Google (another internet success story that everyone uses all the time) you're bound to find some information on others. Some of the abbreviations are formal, simple shortcuts, others are intentionally funny, like ROTFLOL – 'rolling on the floor laughing out loud!', in response to a joke

In addition, many people use strange little signs, made up of punctuation marks, which have come to be called 'emoticons'. They're yet another way that people try to make email seem more informal. Two of the most familiar are the smiley face – :-) and the wink – ;-). If you don't get it, turn this page around 90 degrees and look at the page again! Today, many email programs are very clever and if people type one of the well-known emoticons, the program translates it visually into a little yellow smiley face – the right way up as well.

:-) smiley face (humour)
:-)) laugh
;-) wink (light sarcasm)
:-| indifference
:-> devilish grin (heavy sarcasm)
8-) big-eyed smiley
:-D shock or surprise
:-(sad
:-C really unhappy
:-P wry smile
;-} leer
:-X big wet kiss
:-O yell

It may all seem very silly to you, but it's simply a kind of optional internet humour, used not only by 'geeks' – those folks who just love computers – but many internet users.

When you write an email it's entirely up to you whether you use lingo and emoticons. People won't expect them. However, there are a few general rules of good manners in email that people have come to expect:

- Don't write in capitals. This is known as 'shouting' and is considered to be VERY RUDE.
- If you are replying to someone's message, or if you are reply to a message on a newsgroup or other email bulletin board that you may be on, always 'quote' the message when you reply. That is, have your program set up so that the original message is quoted as part of your reply. Your email program should do this automatically: if it doesn't you need to go to the 'preferences' part of the program, or

similar, and 'turn on quoting'. It's considered a bit rude to reply like this:

Hi Mark,

Yes, that would be fine.

All the best,

Jennifer.

Why? Well, busy Mark may have sent out several messages, and received quite a few back – he can't necessarily remember what on earth you're talking about. This is far better:

Hi Mark

Mark Battley wrote:

>Can I come over on Tuesday at 10am to fix that pipe that's leaking?

Yes, that would be fine.

All the best,

Jennifer.

- Think before you send – and never send in ire! Sending very angry or rude responses to an email is known as 'flaming' and people find it very rude, especially if you do it to a group or 'list' that you are on. Remember how hard it is to convey emotion in an email – your irate message may sound much more offensive than you intend. Always calm down before you respond and read through the message before you send it – because you won't be able to get it back.
- Don't email any message that you wouldn't mind the world reading. Because no message is completely private:

messages can end up stored on backup servers, saved on hard drives, or sent to the wrong person. A private message might be sent on to a whole crowd of your work colleagues, intentionally or by mistake. Always use discretion. Imagine you are on the phone in a public place – sending email is a little like that.

- It's especially important to think about how you want to come across in a business email. Don't be too jokey and informal if this is a business relationship where you need to keep the usual professional distance. You may find it hard to be more formal with the person 'in the flesh' if you have sent them lots of silly messages.
- Sometimes you will accidentally end up with information, such as the email addresses of other people, that has been sent in error. It is, of course, polite to delete this information and on no account should you make any use of it.

The internet

The internet is an amazing way for people to communicate in real time. Not only can we find out amazing amounts of useful (and not so useful!) information, with search engines like Google, but we can 'talk' to our friends, and people we may never have met, in real time. Instant messaging and chat rooms abound on the internet – there are chat rooms for almost every human interest, from archery to zoo-keeping. This little book can't explain the ins and outs here, but there will be many resources in your local computer book shop, or on the internet itself.

Chat-room 'good manners' differs, depending on the chat room. In some you have to ask to 'enter', in others you can simply join in the discussion as soon as you start, or 'log on'. You usually have the option to remain anonymous if you want, and that isn't considered rude. Someone who joins an email list, or a live chat group, and remains an interested observer rather than joining in is called a 'lurker'. Contrary to how it sounds, this isn't rude at all! It just means someone who isn't an active participant in the discussion – and that's perfectly okay, although other members of the group may be pleased if you 'de-lurk' and introduce yourself eventually.

Many chat rooms and email lists have a 'moderator'; this is someone who has voluntarily taken on the role of looking after the list and making sure there is no rude or aggressive behaviour. Someone can be barred from a list if they 'flame' abuse, or keep writing messages that are 'off topic' – that is, not related to the subject that the list or chat room supports. Anyone sending spam, electronic junk mail in the form of adverts and promotional emails, will be barred almost immediately from well-run groups.

Lastly, a word of advice on internet communication – be careful out there! There are lots of people who are not necessarily who they say they are and you should act as cautiously as you would with a stranger who knocks on your front door. It is quite polite to go only by your first name, and it is sensible internet security to NEVER put your home address and phone number in your personal email messages. Many people make the mistake of doing this, and end up with a lot of junk mail – or even suffering identity fraud – as a result.

Making a call

The phone has become second nature to us now. Most of us have at least one telephone in our home and may also have a mobile as well, or instead. We're used to being completely informal and chatty on the phone, as well as using it for communicating serious or informative matters. Few of us need help in knowing how to use one, but there are a few hints on good phone manners that can help smooth a conversation.

If you call someone, and it is not a completely informal call to family or friends, it helps to announce who you are and, if the person who answers is not who you wish to speak to, to ask for that person by name:

"Hello, this is Sophie Price. Is Janey Griggs there?"

If the person who answers says that no, she isn't there, ask 'may I leave her a message please?' (if you want to) or politely finish the conversation. It's common sense really, but so often we forget to say who we are, what we want, or to thank the person who bothered to pick up the phone in the first place (and may have put down a pile of books, hurried across the office, and be rather puffed out by now, just to pick up the phone for you).

And, think about the time of day you phone. It's so easy to pick up the phone and call, day or night, but do remember that it is rude to call early in the morning, or late at night, or at mealtimes. Try to avoid these times unless it's a real emergency, or you know that the person really doesn't mind. If you do have to phone at an awkward time, apologise and also ask 'is this a convenient time to talk?' You can offer to call back at a mutually convenient time if possible.

Today, many people have answerphones or voicemail services. Don't be intimidated by these. Some of us dry up as soon as we hear the beep, after which we are supposed to leave a message. Remember that the message will be recorded. If you are unsure of what to say, simply leave your name and your telephone number. Do speak clearly and loudly enough to be heard; there's nothing worse than a garbled message where the number to call is inaudible. If you're worried, you can always call back again later, or call back and record a message once you have it written down.

A golden rule of good manners on the phone is: don't forget

that you are talking to another human being, and treat them with the respect you'd want from them. Sometimes it can be easy to feel that the call you are making, perhaps to a customer service centre miles away, is completely anonymous, but it isn't. Don't take out your frustrations with some company's insanely aggravating automated system on the first poor human being you happen to get put through to. If it helps, swear at the 'hold music', and save your good manners for the person who comes on the line.

Mobile phones

Most of us have a real love-hate relationship with mobile phones. For some people they are as important and ordinary as the bunch of keys in their pocket, or the credit cards in their wallet. Mobile phones have revolutionised the way we communicate – now we can phone just about anywhere from just about anywhere. The trouble is that many of us do that!

It sometimes seems as if mobile phones bring out the rudeness in people, but really it's just a lack of consideration. Once you're on the phone, it's easy to forget about everyone else around you, and who is listening in – not by choice – to you telling your friend all about what you did last night. Although some people would love to ban mobile phones from all public areas, that's pretty unrealistic – but it is possible to use a mobile phone in a way that doesn't disrupt everyone else's life. Keep your voice down, and remember the people around you.

Always turn your phone off in places where the ringing could disturb others. In most cinemas, theatres and concert halls you are warned that mobiles are to be turned off. And you usually aren't allowed to use mobiles in hospitals, or during takeoff and landing in a plane, when the mobile could interfere with equipment on the aircraft. But show good 'mobile manners' and think about turning your phone off at other times – if you're in a place where it would be difficult to take a call quietly, for instance. Also, if you have the option, set your mobile to ring on 'vibrate' – far less intrusive than a loud ringtone, however much you, personally, like it.

Thumbs up

Mobile phones can also be used to send text messages – even if you don't use your phone for that, you've probably seen people using a thumb to tap out messages, which they then send to friends. Texting has its own shorthand, with thumb-efficient abbreviations like: 'Hi m8! How U? Me OK. Meet 4 cuppa T l8r? C'ya'

If you're an expert text messager, don't forget that the person you're sending to might not be. Make sure they'll understand what you're talking about! Granny may have been given a mobile phone, but she may not know that 'l8r' translates as 'later', and be very confused.

A final word on how to show good manners to 'cold callers', those people who call out of the blue – usually on a Saturday morning, or just when you're sitting down to tea – to try to sell us double-glazing or a new insurance policy. They are the ones who are being rude here, and you have absolutely no obligation to listen to them. They'll usually have a 'script' that is designed to keep you on the phone as long as possible. If you're not interested, say so right away: 'Thank you. I'm not interested', and then hang up. There's no need to talk further at all, but do remember that they are mostly underpaid folk who are trying to make a living – so be firm but polite.

The letter

When was the last time you wrote a personal, handwritten letter? Communicating by letter is almost a lost art and many people hardly ever write by hand, preferring to use email, texting or the phone. It's probably ridiculous to bemoan this fact, but there are a few occasions when nothing can beat a handwritten note or letter.

Thank-you letters, for instance, can be emailed, but do look more personal and thoughtful if handwritten, perhaps on some nice paper or a card. Messages of congratulation or condolence are best sent by handwritten note, especially the latter. In general, if the message is a delicate or personal one, or one to commemorate an occasion (the birth of a child, or a wedding, or a first job), a handwritten card or letter can seem more special – and it's also something recipient can hang on to and treasure.

Business letters are another matter. They still thrive, mainly because a 'hard copy' letter provides clear evidence that something has been notified or agreed and that evidence can be kept on file. Even so, many businesses increasingly use email today – print out and keep any very important notifications if you are concerned to have copies on file. How you write a business letter is less a case of good manners than a case of the correct 'protocol'. This is because there must be no opportunity for misunderstanding. So, a formal business letter should state clearly which company it is from, what job position the writer has in that company, and the date. The address provided should be sufficient for you to contact the business if you need to, and will usually have the phone and email details too.

A business letter starts with a salutation (Dear...) and then continues with a line describing the subject of the letter, and a reference to any previous correspondence related to the subject.

Most business letters will look something like this:

Mr James Snodgrass
Sales Director
Widgets International plc
Busy Industrial Estate
Anyroad
Anytown
AN3 WH6
Tel 01222 000000
Email: jsnodgrass@widgetint.co.uk

Your ref DBH/WJP/2376

25 February 2020

Mr D. B. Hardcase
Grummets Consolidated
Otherstreet
Othertown
TH6 TH7

Re: Giant widgets

A good business letter explains the matter concerned simply, and in plain English. If you're the one writing a business letter, don't feel that you have to use strange 'business language' or old-fashioned phrases. Just write in simple language, as you would if you were talking to someone and concentrate on keeping to the subject and explaining it clearly. There's no need to try and impress someone with 'posh' talk, and very few businesspeople would try to nowadays (with the exception of some extremely pompous lawyers, who are probably just showing off).

The important thing is to express the matter clearly and correctly. Make sure that all your sentences make sense and check the spelling and grammar, making sure that all the capital letters and full stops are in the right places. The usual kind of thing. If the letter is an important one, especially if you are in some kind of dispute with a customer, it can help to have someone else read the letter over, to make sure it does the job – a friend or colleague. If it's a legal matter, consult a solicitor, who will usually write the letter for a fee, in a way that fits any legal requirements.

Always be courteous in letters, even if you are in dispute with someone. A good business letter can be firm, and make demands, but should never be rude. Remember, if you end up getting your 'day in court', your letter may do so too – and be read out in front of everyone present.

Addressing people

While we're talking about going to court, we'll point out that this is one of the few places where there are still formal 'manners', or etiquette, defining how you should address someone – what 'form of address' you should use to speak to them.

There was a time when the top brass had to be addressed in specific ways – the folks with titles, honours and letters after their name. As already mentioned, this is really a hangover from the days of formal etiquette, when 'deference' to the higher classes was expected. That's all changed now, and many people with titles, earnt through good works or by inheritance, prefer to keep quiet about them in any case. No sensible, polite person would object if you didn't address them by their title, and used Mr or Ms instead – or even their first name, depending on the circumstances. That being said, few of us would rush over to the Queen and say 'Hi, Liz, how are you doing?'

More seriously, members of the legal profession are still referred to by their official forms of address, when they are in court. So are some senior officers in the armed forces, when they are on official business. And of course some people still prefer to be called by their title in all circumstances. If you're not sure, it's probably best to be as formal as possible first, and see how things go.

And, before you say, 'well, I'm not going to be bumping into Royalty down at the shops now, am I!', never say never. Because you never know. So, just in case you end up sitting next to someone very grand at dinner, here is a list of forms of address, showing the correct formal way to speak to people holding different positions. But don't despair, today it is highly unlikely that someone will take any offence at all if you don't refer to them by their full title, or properly. We're all human under our decorations and crowns.

The tables on pages 137–139 show how to address various notables, such as members of the peerage, clergy and judiciary, both verbally and in writing.

The Royals

A few last words about the Royal lot – if you get to meet a member of the Royal family, or want to write to them, the rules are simple, and not much more than ordinary good manners, actually.

If you want to write to the Queen, you begin 'Madam' and you are supposed to close with 'I have the honour to be, Madam, Your Majesty's humble and obedient servant'. Letters to other members of the royal family should begin with 'Sir' or 'Madam,' but it is also acceptable to start with 'Your Highness' and you can close with a simple 'Yours sincerely'.

If you actually meet members of the royal family in the flesh, men are supposed to bow from the neck and women should curtsy. But you really don't have to bother with all that – you can simply shake hands (whether you are a man or woman). Don't give a bone-crushing handshake, as the Queen has to shake hands hundreds of times and is probably fairly bruised by now! When you first address the Queen you should call her 'Your Majesty' and after that you address her as 'Ma'am' (to rhyme with 'van', not 'harm'). Male members of the royal family are initially addressed as 'Your Royal Highness' on being introduced, and as 'Sir' thereafter; female members are 'Your Royal Highness' and then 'Ma'am'. See, it's so easy you almost want to go off immediately to find a stray Princess to meet and greet!

General advice

If you are going to meet or write to people with titles and honours, one easy way to check exactly what titles and degrees they have is to go to your library, and look them up in *Who's Who* or *Debrett's Peerage and Baronetage.* These two rather dry and fearsome books will tell you everything you need to know about titles, decorations and degrees. If you are prepared to pay, you can consult these publications online. Failing that, you can phone the person's secretary, who will normally be only too pleased to give you the details you need and will no doubt think it very good manners of you to have taken the trouble to ask.

The Peerage

On an envelope:	Begin a letter:	Introduced as:	Addressed as:
The Duke of Hearts	Dear Duke of Hearts or Dear Duke	The Duke of Hearts	Your Grace or Duke
The Duchess of Hearts	Dear Duchess of Hearts or Dear Duchess	The Duchess of Hearts	Your Grace or Duchess
The Marquess of Diamonds	Dear Lord Diamonds	Lord Diamonds	Lord Diamonds
The Marchioness of Diamonds	Dear Lady Diamonds	Lady Diamonds	Lady Diamonds
The Earl of Clubs	Dear Lord Clubs	Lord Clubs	Lord Clubs
The Countess of Clubs	Dear Lady Clubs	Lady Clubs	Lady Clubs
The Viscount Spades	Dear Lord Spades	Lord Spades	Lord Spades
The Viscountess Spades	Dear Lady Spades	Lady Spades	Lady Spades
Baron & wife:			
The Lord Hearts	Dear Lord Hearts	Lord Hearts	Lord Hearts
The Lady Hearts	Dear Lady Hearts	Lady Hearts	Lady Hearts
Baronet & wife:			
Sir James Diamonds Bt	Dear Sir James	Sir James Diamonds	Sir James
Lady Diamonds	Dear Lady Diamonds	Lady Diamonds	Lady Diamonds
Life peer & wife:			
The Lord Clubs	Dear Lord Clubs	Lord Clubs	Lord Clubs
The Lady Clubs	Dear Lady Clubs	Lady Clubs	Lady Clubs
Knight & wife:			
Sir David Spades	Dear Sir David	Sir David Spades	Sir David
Lady Spades	Dear Lady Spades	Lady Spades	Lady Spades

Church of England clergy

Archbishop:

The Most Reverend and Rt Hon The Archbishop

of Canterbury/York

My Lord Archbishop

The Archbishop of Canterbury/York

Your Grace

The Most Reverend the Lord Archbishop of Wherever

Dear Lord Archbishop or Dear Archbishop

The Archbishop of Wherever

Archbishop

Bishop of London:

The Rt Rev and Rt Hon the Lord Bishop of London

Dear Bishop

The Bishop of London

Bishop

All other Bishops::

The Rt Rev the Lord Bishop of Wherever

Dear Bishop

The Bishop of Wherever

Bishop

Deans:

The Very Reverend, the Dean of Wherever

Dear Dean

The Dean of Wherever

Dean

Vicars and Rectors:

Dear Mr Whatever or Dear Father Whatever

Mr Whatever or Father Whatever

Mr Whatever or Farther Whatever

Also you can say Vicar or Rector

Lawyers, politicians and the medical profession

High Court Judge:

The Hon Mr Justice Jailem

Dear Judge

Mr Justice Jailem or Sir James Jailem

Sir James

Circuit Court Judge:

His Honour Judge Justice

Dear Sir

Judge Justice

Judge Justice

MP:

Mr James Slippery MP

Dear Mr Slippery

Mr James Slippery

Mr Slippery

Privy Councillor:

The Rt Hon James Evasive

Dear Mr Evasive

Mr James Evasive

Mr Evasive

Lord Mayors:

The Rt Hon the Lord Mayor of Wherever

Dear Lord Mayor

The Lord Mayor of Wherever

My Lord Mayor

Mayor of a city:

The Right Worshipful the Mayor of Wherever

Dear Mr Mayor or Dear Madam Mayor

The Mayor of Wherever

Mr Mayor or Madam Mayor

Mayor of a town:

The Worshipful Mayor of Wherever

Dear Mr Mayor or Dear Madam Mayor

The Mayor of Wherever

Mr Mayor or Madam Mayor

Medical doctor:

Dr Mark Quack MD

Dear Dr Quack

Dr or Mr (or Ms or Mrs) Quack

Dr, Mr, Ms, Mrs Quack

Surgeon (Fellow of Royal College of Surgeons)

Mr (or Mrs of Ms) William Blade

Dear Mr, Mrs, Ms Blade

Mr, Mrs, Ms Blade

Mr, Mrs, Ms Blade

A good day at the office

At root, we all go to work to earn money to live on. Some people love their jobs, some people don't really think about them much once they get home, and some people would rather do anything else. However you feel about work, if you do go to the office each day, you'll know that there are certain 'rules' of behaviour and office-specific good manners, that help us get along with each other at work. After all, an office is quite an artificial social situation, where nobody has actually chosen the companions they spend so much time with.

The etiquette of work conversation is quite a tricky situation at times, especially when you're the new person in the office. In general, people at work tend to keep conversation light and friendly, not too personal – mostly to do with what was on TV last night, the football, general topics. Chatting is fine, but chatting about very personal matters is, in a way, not good manners, with people you only know through work. Of course, as we get to know people at work better, that can change and people from work can become close friends whom we see outside work. But, in general, it's good manners to keep away from personal matters when having work conversations, and it's certainly not good manners to spread malicious gossip about colleagues, however tempting it may seem when they're getting on your nerves.

What to wear for work? In some situations that difficult decisions is done for you, if a uniform or 'required dress' is stipulated. Some offices do have a dress code, unwritten or not, that men wear a suit and tie, and in general everyone should be smart. It is good manners to fit in, as you are representing the company's 'public face', and never know when you may be asked to meet with a client or potential customer.

Offices have other rules, both formal and informal, that it's good manners to observe. Of course some of these rules – such as when to start and end work, or when to take a coffee break – may well be fixed, and you are required to observe them as part of your job. In some offices, rules on coffee breaks etc are more relaxed, and people can choose when to get up from their work for a break. Don't abuse this flexibility – it's easy to do so inadvertently, but make sure that you put in as much work as your colleagues, and are willing to perform your job duties. People may not say anything, but they do notice the person who is 'always disappearing for a coffee' – don't let it be you!

When it comes to working hours – it's a fact of the working day that, in many jobs, people do work a little longer than their 'official' hours. Perhaps they work through lunch to get an important job done, or stay a little later to finish up something that's needed for tomorrow. Everyone chips in and, providing the employers don't abuse this willingness, it's part and parcel of the job. Take this on board, and don't be a stickler for exact time-keeping, who always rushes off home as the clock strikes 5pm.

Doing a deal

When a deal is struck, a contract is drawn up and the official procedures go into motion. But, especially in the UK and much of Europe, there is still an old custom of 'sealing the deal on a handshake' – this is technically a good-mannered way of saying 'right, we're agreed!', before doing the paperwork. There was, however, a time when a handshake really was all that was needed to strike a deal, and even though a written contract is most normal today, a handshake or verbal agreement can be considered binding in court.

But if you do 'shake hands on it', you should always send an email, fax or letter that confirms the deal and what has been agreed on. And in the case of big deals, a legal contract is vital. You may have the good manners to stand by your handshake, others may not.

Friends and lovers

For many of us the office becomes integral to our social life. Friends from work are people we also socialise with outside the office and become close pals. Usually office socialising is just that – everyone in the office, or everyone in a team or group. Every situation is different, but do think twice before striking up close friendships (platonic or otherwise) with just one or two other colleagues – it can be seen as rather cliquey and exclusive behaviour and other colleagues may feel a bit left out (or that you're a bit stuck up). Use your common sense, and be sensitive to the situation in your particular environment.

On the whole, if you're having a sexual relationship with another member of staff, the situation is likely to be problematic, especially if they are your boss (or vice versa). But many people start relationships with people they have met at work and in most offices there is no strict rule against this. Some firms, however, do frown on it, mainly because it can cause problems in the workplace, and is seen as damaging to the company's efficiency. If a couple break up, it can – as you can imagine – make for a bit of tension in the air. If possible, it's probably best for one of you to find a job at a different company, or in a different department, though of course you may not have that opportunity. It's good manners not to 'canoodle' all over the place in front of work colleagues: behave in a normal and professional manner to all office colleagues, including your partner.

But, on the whole, general office socialising isn't problematic for most companies – in fact it can be a great bonding exercise to have a regular Friday night out at the pub, or a party when some big work project is completed on time.

Hierarchy

Once you settle into a new job you get a much clearer idea of the hierarchy. Obvious information, like someone's job title or description, their office size and, if you know it, their salary, will give you a safe indication of where that person fits in, in relation to you.

Office politics can require good manners in situations when we'd, to be honest, rather be a bit rude! For instance, it's in our own interest to show respect and good manners to our boss or supervisor. After all, to put it bluntly, they may be the person deciding our next promotion or pay rise. If you happen to find your boss a bit aggravating, try not to show it – show them how competent and willing you are, instead.

Remember, even though you may well be on first-name terms with everyone in your office, there is still an unwritten hierarchy, based on job position. That's not to say that bosses are in any way allowed to bully, threaten or otherwise harass other people in the office, but they do – to be realistic – have a bit more power.

If you're looking to move up the ladder at work, get to know where everyone sits in the hierarchy. An easy way to do this is to pay attention at meetings, and be sure you know who does what, and who's 'in' with who. Many offices have a great many meetings – some people say that they have so many meetings at work they don't have time to get any work done! To be cynical, you can get a lot of work done in a meeting, just learning about the office hierarchy.

Passing the buck

Quite often, people are worried about their job security, or anxious to be seen as good at their job. A lot of 'buck passing' can go on in business, done by people who don't want to get the blame when things go wrong and are quite happy to blame it on someone else – or at least imply someone else was the cause of the problem. Don't be a buck-passer: it's one of the most ill-mannered office behaviours going. Nobody will respect you, and even if you think nobody knows, your colleagues are probably onto your *modus operandi* already.

If someone 'passes the buck' to you, there's sadly little you can do about it without appearing to be whining. But there are ways that you can firmly and calmly assert 'actually Jim, Eric was in charge of the Burton's account, and he prepared that report' if there is a factual actuality that you can point to. Otherwise, be assured that most bosses are well aware of who the habitual buck-passers are, and try to shake it off.

Customers and clients: the outside world

Do you work in a situation where you have to meet people from 'outside'? Most people have to be in contact with people from outside the company at some point in their work, even if it's just someone passing through to have a look at the workshop, or visit the factory. And, in an office or a business that provides a service, it may well be part of your job to deal with the general public.

Put yourself in the customer's position for a moment. They are hoping to be met by someone who's clean, tidy, and interested to help them. If you are still wearing that filthy shirt from Monday, haven't shaved, and just grunt at them when they ring the bell on the counter, you're not really going to win the 'employee of the month badge'! But worst of all is being rude, offhand, or simply bored – even if you are very busy, the customer always comes first. That very old adage still stands. And most of all, be informed – the customer needs information from you. If you don't know the answer to a question, find out who does.

But that doesn't mean you have to grovel, and no customer has the right to treat anyone like some kind of servant or slave. So, if you're on the customer side of this equation, remember that you're approaching an equal, and be polite – even if you have come in to complain about something.

If you are introduced to a visiting client at work, simply smile, stand if appropriate, and offer your hand to shake.

If you are introduced to a visiting client at work, simply smile, stand if appropriate, and offer your hand to shake. You don't have to be a conversational genius; you can just say something friendly and polite like 'hello, how are you today?' or 'nice to meet you, how was your journey?'. Most importantly, if a visitor appears in your office and is hanging around looking lost, don't ignore them. There's nothing more embarrassing than being left to wait, without knowing who to approach. If there is nobody to greet them, then you should be on your feet and walking towards them, with a smile and a 'hello, you look a bit lost – can I help you?' or something similarly friendly. If you really have to finish some work first, smile and say 'I'll be with you in just a moment, do sit down' or something like that. Or, if you just can't leave your work, ask a colleague to do the honours.

Do remember that older visitors just may not be used to informality. They may not sit down until offered a chair. Always try to imagine how the other person is thinking.

If a supplier visits your office, the situation is rather different. They are there to sell you something and will be trying to make a good impression. If you are a supplier's rep, you'll know that a polite, friendly and presentable manner will get you a long way.

There's just no point in turning up looking scruffy and dirty, or being late. People won't take you seriously, however good the product you're selling. So, even if you spend most of your time oiling motorcycle gaskets, when you go out on the road to sell those gaskets, put on a clean outfit, smarten up a bit, and practice a few smiles and firm handshakes.

If you're expecting a supplier, be courteous and don't keep them waiting. They may have several offices or businesses to visit that day. It pays to treat everyone courteously, because, for a start, you never know when the tables might be turned and it's you that's waiting for an appointment to sell your wares!

Cross words and confrontations

Perhaps it just can't be helped: it's inevitable that sometimes complaints are necessary and sometimes arguments break out. If you can't avoid an argument, at least play by these simple rules of good manners:

- If it really isn't the person's fault, don't stand there shouting at them. A shop assistant probably has no say in the shop's 'returns' policy, for instance, so you shouldn't take it out on him or her. Shouting won't get you anywhere. Asking for the address of head office and writing a letter of complaint about the policy may, especially if you explain just why you are so cross about it – in firm, but courteous language.

- Even if you have got the 'right' person, what's the point of shouting? There's no excuse for abuse and besides, it just won't help the situation. Of course, we've all given into our anger now and then, but we shouldn't. For a start, you'll upset everyone in the vicinity – not just the person you're aiming at. Stick to the facts, be firm and by all means cross, but in a civil and measured way. Present the facts, be calm and polite, but refuse to be fobbed off. Keep going as long as you have the power to do so in the hope that you will eventually persuade them to help you.
- If you're going to write a letter of complaint, do it with care. Anything you write will leave a permanent record and it can be read by anyone – even presented in court. So bear this in mind and think about how your words will sound to the person reading it. If you sound too angry and aggressive, tone it down – this doesn't mean you have to leave out any facts, or that you have to 'give in'. Simply be firm and demand action. A successful letter of complaint is one directed to the right person (if in doubt, call the company or shop and ask), and one that not only complains but asks for a practical solution. Writing to the head of a company can help too: the chairman of Marks and Spencer may not personally read the letter of complaint you wrote him about the overly small sandwiches, but he'll probably pass it on to someone who will – because your custom is needed.

- Finally, be magnanimous in victory and stoical in defeat. This means that if you get what you wanted from the situation, don't rub your opponent's nose in it. Simply accept graciously. And if you don't succeed, just accept it on the chin and face the fact that you did your best. No point in going on further.

Index

National Trust Membership

Whether you're interested in gardens, castles, wildlife, places linked to famous events and people, looking for a new coastal path to walk or just somewhere peaceful to relax and enjoy a nice cup of tea, National Trust membership gives you a wide variety of things to do, as often as you like, for free.

Join today and you can start to explore some of Britain's most beautiful places, while helping to protect them for future generations.

As a member you'll receive a comprehensive membership pack featuring places cared for by the National Trust.

What's more, National Trust membership gives you free entry to more than 300 historic houses and gardens and information about 700 miles of coastline and almost 250,000 hectares of stunning countryside, so visiting couldn't be easier.

Visit www.nationaltrust.org.uk or phone 0870 458 4000 for more details.